P9-CDE-698

whatever gets you through the night

whatever gets you through the night

a story of sheherezade and the arabian entertainments

ANDREI CODRESCU

Princeton University Press   Princeton and Oxford

Published by Princeton University Press, 41 William Street, Princeton, New Jersey 08540
In the United Kingdom: Princeton University Press, 6 Oxford Street, Woodstock, Oxfordshire
OX20 1TW
press.princeton.edu

Jacket art: Wilhelm Vita, *Sheherazade*, 1891. Courtesy of Sandy Dijkstra. Photo by Rodney
    Nakamoto

Library of Congress Cataloging-in-Publication Data

Codrescu, Andrei, 1946–
    Whatever gets you through the night ; a story of Sheherezade and the Arabian
entertainments / Andrei Codrescu.
        p. cm.
        Includes bibliographical references.
        ISBN 978-0-691-14337-8 (acid-free paper) 1. Arabian nights—Adaptations. 2. Storytelling—
Fiction. I. Title.

    PS3553.O3W37 2011
    813'.54—dc22

                            2010039073

British Library Cataloging-in-Publication Data is available

This book has been composed in Dante MT
Printed on acid-free paper. ∞
Printed in the United States of America

10 9 8 7 6 5 4 3 2 1

framed

One Thousand and One Nights (Arabic: كتاب ألف ليلة وليلة‎ *Kitāb ʿalf layla wa-layla*; Persian: هزار و یک شب‎ *Hezār-o yek šab*; Turkish: *Binbir Gece Masalları*) is a collection of stories collected over many centuries by various authors, translators and scholars across the Middle East, North Africa and Indian subcontinent. These collections of tales trace their roots back to ancient and medieval Arabic, Persian, Indian, Egyptian and Mesopotamian literature. In particular, many tales were originally folk stories from the Caliphate era and the Sassanid-era Pahlavi work *Hazār Afsān* (Persian: هزار افسان‎, lit. *Thousand Tales*). Though the oldest Arabic manuscript dates from the 14th century, scholarship generally dates the collection's genesis to around the 9th century. The collection, or at least certain stories drawn from it (or purporting to be drawn from it), became widely known in the West from the 18th century, after it was translated—first into French and then English and other European languages. Sometime in the 19th century it acquired an English name, *The Arabian Nights' Entertainment* or simply *Arabian Nights*. What is common throughout all the editions of the *Nights* is the initial frame story of the ruler Shahryar (from Persian: شهریار‎ generally meaning king or sovereign) and his wife Scheherazade (from Persian: شهرزاده‎ generally meaning townswoman) and the framing device incorporated throughout the tales themselves. The stories proceed from this original tale; some are framed within other tales, while others begin and end of their own accord. Some editions contain only a few hundred nights, while others include 1001 or more "nights."

—Wikipedia, 2009

We learn from the *Nights* that Shahriyar, a mythical king in ancient times, on discovering his wife's infidelity with a kitchen servant, had the wife put to death and, from that time on, fearing further sexual betrayals, he took virgins to his bed for one night only, invariably having them beheaded on the following morning. After this deflowering and slaughtering had gone on for some time, the vizier's daughter, who was called Sheherazade, volunteered herself, much against her father's will, as the next candidate for the king's bed. Brought before the king, she asked that her sister, Dunyazade, might attend her. She had already put Dunyazade up to asking for a story. Dunyazade, inconspicuously installed in Shahriyar's bedchamber, waited until he had deflowered her sister. Then, when she judged the moment was right, she asked her sister for a story. Sheherazade obliged her with 'The Story of the Merchant and the Demon': but, since she did not relate all of it that night, Shahriyar was impelled to postpone her execution, so that he might hear the end of it the following night. The following night, the story continued, but it did not conclude. Instead, Sheherazade began another story, inset within the first one, and broke off with this story also unfinished as dawn was breaking. And so things continued for several years (for two years and 271 days, if we are to take the 1001 of the title literally), with Sheherazade, night by night, talking for her life. In the end, by the time her vast repertoire of stories was concluded, she had become mother to several of Shahriyar's children, and he had repented from his original determination to execute her.

—Robert Irwin,
The Arabian Nights: A Companion

Then King Shahryar . . . also sware himself by a binding oath that whatever wife he married he would abate her maidenhead at night and slay her next morning to make sure of his honour; "For," said he, "there never was nor is there one chaste woman upon the face of the earth." . . . On this wise he continued for the space of three years; marrying a maiden every night and killing her the next morning, till folk raised an outcry against him and cursed him, praying Allah utterly to destroy him and his rule; and women made an uproar and mothers wept till there remained not in the city a young person fit for carnal copulation . . . His Chief Wazir, the same who was charged with the executions, . . . had two daughters, Sharazad and Dunyazad hight, of whom the elder had perused the books, annals, and legends . . . and the stories . . . perused the works of the poets and knew them by heart . . . Thereupon said she, "By Allah, O my father, how long shall this slaughter of women endure? . . . I wish thou wouldst give me in marriage to this King Shahryar; either I shall live or I shall be a ransom for the virgin daughters of Moslems and the cause of their deliverance from his hands and thine."

—*The Book of the Thousand Nights and a Night*,
translated by Richard F. Burton

At last some storyteller thought of writing down the tales, and fixing them into a kind of framework, as if they had been narrated to a cruel Sultan by his wife.

—*The Arabian Nights Entertainments*,
edited by Andrew Lang

Shahrayar . . . then swore to marry for one night only and kill
the woman the next morning, in order to save himself from the
wickedness and cunning of women, saying, "There is not a single
chaste woman anywhere on the entire face of the earth." . . . the Vizier,
who put the girls to death, had an older daughter called Shahrazad
and a younger one called Dinarzad . . . Shahrazad . . . knew poetry
by heart, had studied historical reports, and was acquainted with the
sayings of men and the maxims of sages and kings. She was intelligent,
knowledgeable, wise, and refined. She had read and learned . . .
She said to her father, . . . "I would like you to marry me to King
Shahrayar, so that I may either succeed in saving the people or perish
and die like the rest."

> —*The Arabian Nights*, translated by Husain Haddawy, based on the
> text of the 14th-century Syrian manuscript edited by Muhsin Madhi

When King Sharyar set himself to the grim task of deflowering
Sheherezade in the presence of her younger sister Dinarzad, he
cursed Narrative. He cursed the history that had imprisoned him in
this story, he cursed his weakness, the cowardice of his subjects, the
flaws inherent to being human, and the gods who may or may not
have been in control of Narrative. Then he entered Sheherezade and
it was like entering another story. No, Sharyar corrected himself, it
was another story. Sheherezade opened to him the first of a thousand
and one nights, she was the crossroads at which it was possible to take
another path. It was possible to live again. The crossroads in his bed
invited him to take the less traveled road, nay, the untraveled road.
Sharyar took it, and Sheherezade remained a virgin (the first night).

> —Alva Gardener, *Stockholm Syndrome or the
> Persistence of Humanity: Sheherezade, the First
> Feminist Prisoner*

Sheherezade saved 1001 girls. We know the stories that saved these girls, but we know nothing of their history; they got away, winning their right to anonymity thanks to Sheherezade's nightly performances, her exhibitionism. If one could imagine the lives of the 1001 girls who weren't murdered by Sharyar, one could write a true history of the Islamic Middle Ages.

—Ali H. Madhouf, *Books I Will Never Write*

The work has an ambivalent attitude toward curiosity; this stems from its ambivalence toward the main object of this curiosity: the "world," as we have termed it, of romance. This world is mysterious, alluring, and attractive, but also full of danger.

—Peter Heath, "Romance and Genre in *The Thousand and One Nights*," in *The Arabian Nights Reader*, edited by Ulrich Marzolph

One mad Queen / One thousand voyeurs.

—Paul Mariah, poem in MS

If you can save one life by telling a story, what story will it be? Start thinking about it now, you never know when you'll be called to tell it.

—L. R. Lied, *Advice to Young Women Based on Literary Themes*

Mysterious strangers. Beautiful women. Enchanted swords. Talking camels. You play members of the Sultan's Court, whiling away the sultry nights by telling pointed stories to advance your own ambitions. Navigate the social maze and you could win your heart's desire; offend the wrong person and you suffer the Sultan's wrath. Is it a wonder those here turn to tales of mystery and magic, beauty and bold adventure, to fly away in thought, if only for a time? And, if one's tale is well told, and brings one favor of one kind or another, so much the better, is it not so? Gather three or more players; more than six becomes unwieldy. Give each a pencil and a character sheet or a small piece of paper. In the middle of the table, put a bowl, pleasing to look at, and filled with dice of many colors, shapes and sizes. These are the gems of the Sultan.

—Meguey Baker, *A Thousand and One Nights: A Game of Enticing Stories* [Night Sky Games]

Recreate the mysterious atmosphere of Marrakech with exotic Arabian Nights themed party entertainment from authentic Middle Eastern bands and drummers; the coolest Chillout DJs to gorgeous BELLY dancers; exciting fire artists and mysterious encounters with a sand reader and hypnotic snake charmer—call us on 020 7401 9745 for more information on how we can bring the mystery, colour and spice of the East to life at your corporate event.

—http://www.calmerkarma.org.uk/Arabian-nights-entertainments.html

Welcome to the Arabian Nights, the Award-Winning, Number One Attraction in Orlando! The Arabian Nights is a dinner show that brings a fairy tale to life on horseback.

—www.arabian-nights.com

The meeting was held at the Waikiki Sheraton the last week of February 2012. The main participants were 1001 young women, most of whom were clones, with a minority of them born through ICSI (Intracytoplasmic Sperm Injection), and the scientists who created them. The conference was called for observation purposes, eighteen years after the first successful cloning of a human being.

—Associated Press, February 25, 2012

I interviewed some of the girls. I asked all of them if they had read the stories of the 1001 Nights that had inspired the number of participants at the meeting. Only one of them said that she had tried, but being a Christian, she found it hard to read "lies." I said that these "lies" were called "fiction," and that they were stories that most people on earth enjoyed even if they were made up. "When did lies become respectable?" she bristled. "When people wanted to escape from boredom and maybe from themselves," I said, rather pedantically. "Well, sooner will a camel go through the eye of a needle than a liar into the kingdom of heaven," she misquoted from her religion, and I felt it futile to insist that her religion was itself a myth made up by the writers of the Bible. I didn't want to be mean and, besides, she was cute.

—Ron May, *Rolling Stone,* March 2012

The automaton, a creature who is neither living nor dead, features frequently in the *Nights* . . . The brass oarsman who bears a tablet of lead inscribed with talismanic characters on his breast and who rows the Third Dervish to the Island of Safety; the little manikin which a dervish fashions out of beeswax and which plunges into the river to retrieve the sultan's lost signet ring; the air-driven statues which seem to speak . . . and the Ebony Horse, which is powered by wind and, when the right lever is pulled, carries a man through the air: they all simulate life, but there is no life in them.

—Robert Irwin, *The Arabian Nights: A Companion*

Dr. Nicole Betrain, developer of the Sheherezade Test, told *Paris-Match*: "We tested 1001 subjects over an eleven-year period between 1999 and 2010, and found a narrowing of human attention span at a rate equivalent to miniaturisation of semiconductors."

—"A Controversial Remark," "Daily Sheherezade, Waikiki Sheraton,"
Paris-Match, February 26, 2009

The borderline between the oral and the written is the subject of the *1001 Nights*. The stories that Sheherezade told Sharyar and Dinarzad in the royal bed were collected and written by the calligrapher who bound them in a book and who reflected on what he was doing while he wrote, which is why all of the *1001 Nights* are pierced by the anxiety of leaving traces and nostalgia for the act of pure fancy that the calligrapher was destroying as he wrote.

—Mary Alther, "Lipstick on the Mirror: Narrative
& Self-Reflection," *Psychoanalytic Quarterly*,
November 13, 1987

If writing is initially a form of scratching or engraving, the cutting of a line, penetration of some hard substance with a marking tool, it may also, after the invention of pencils and pens, be thought of as the pouring out on a flat surface of a long line or filament, lead or ink making a cursive line of characters stamping, cutting, contaminating, or deflowering the virgin paper, according to a not very "submerged" sexual metaphor.

—J. Hillis Miller, *Ariadne's Thread: Story Lines*

Sheherezade dismembered narrative: every story she told ended on the cliffhanger of dawn and resumed on the edge of night, but the two pieces, the starting and the continuation, didn't fit exactly, and in that gap there was something not yet explained, something that historians tried to fill with bits of history, psychologists with sex, and theorists with theory. Perhaps these gaps that advanced the story cycles and kept them going were places where Sharyar and Dinarzad's interventions took place, they were the collaborative interpellations of the other two members of the threesome.

—Regis Cambray, "The Spiralling Sheherezade: Notes on the *1001 Nights*," in *The Infinite Story: Essays*, edited by Loren Donaughy, Interfiction Press, 1996

To conceive the frame story as a genre makes it an entity, a product, a kind of story (Irwin); to conceive "framing" as a device or skill makes it a strategy, one element of the story-teller's range of techniques, which he or she can invoke in multiple ways (Mills . . .). "Frame" is one metaphor; the banyan tree and the umbrella are others[1] (Naithani . . .).

—Lee Haring, "Framing in Narrative," in *The Arabian Nights in Transnational Perspective*, edited by Ulrich Marzolph

Narrative equals life; absence of narrative, death . . . Absence of narrative is not the only counterpart of narrative-as-life; to want to hear a narrative is also to run mortal risks. If loquacity saves from death, curiosity leads to it.

—Tzvetan Todorov, "Narrative-Men," in *The Arabian Nights Reader*, edited by Ulrich Marzolph

Sharyar is the spectator par excellence, the first TV addict, a royal Archie Bunker who controls his aggressivity through the palliative effects of Shezz the Telly (who has the advantage over present-day telly of having a Body).

—Myron Bernstein in conversation with the author, Trieste Cafe, San Francisco, 2008

---

[1] Each technical device wants to be a frame, like the "frame" said to surround the *Nights*, but the *Nights* have no frame: they arise like hatchlings from one egg; they are Russian egg-dolls that always keep the first egg in whatever comes next. A frame dissolves, it is just a pre-text, a technology to get the story-universe started, but the *Nights* are not "framed"—they are generative; they are life.

whatever gets you through the night

no telling without retelling

Even bound in a book, or especially bound in a book, the tales of the *1001 Nights* violate every narrative convention. We know that the stories Sheherezade tells don't have either beginnings or endings: only her first story of the first night has a beginning, but it's a faux-beginning because it's already been rehearsed and set up, so that it is a beginning told and foretold, a recitation rather than a beginning. After the first night, her stories neither begin nor end, they simply continue. Even Sheherezade, the Storyteller, who, seemingly, begins telling stories in Sharyar's bed at the urging of her sister, Dinarzad, does not begin when she first appears. She has been present behind the scenes while the frame that makes possible her appearance is being built by a Storyteller who turns out to be none other than Sheherezade herself, as we discover when on the 456th night she tells the story of the brothers Sharyar and Shahzaman, their betrayal by their wives, their killing of the traitors, their wanderings in the desert, their adventures with the Genius and his wife, their parting of ways, Sharyar's return to Baghdad, Sharyar's vow to take a new bride every night and have her killed in the morning, and his marriage to the Storyteller Sheherezade. If Sheherezade herself is not bound by any narrative convention, we would like to do likewise, but we can't. We are bound to tell her story no matter what our postmodern wishes or rebellious inclinations might tell us: simply pronouncing her name invokes her. When she appears, like the Genie in the bottle of literature that she is, we must obey the order of her stories; this is the exact opposite of the Genii and Genies who are freed or imprisoned in the bottles of her characters, who must obey their liberators. Sheherezade is a peculiar literary Genius who inverts that relationship just as she inverts the conventional order of narrative, the power relations between the sexes, sexuality itself, and memory. Thus:

nostalgia

I n the time before the beginning[2] King Shahanshah, the King of Kings,[3] left his vast kingdom to his eldest son, Sharyar. After the death of the King of Kings, Sharyar, who loved his brother, Shahzaman, made him a gift of the kingdom of Samarkand. Ten years after the death of their father, Sharyar, well established in his authority as ruler of his realms, longed to see his brother, Shahzaman. His immediate impulse[4] was to mount his mare and to take off at a gallop with a party of attendants and a herd of gift-laden camels to visit his brother, but his Vizir[5] advised against it, because it was unbecoming of a greater King to visit a smaller one; he proposed sending a delegation to Shahzaman instead,[6] inviting him to visit Sharyar. Sharyar bowed to protocol, recognizing that it was precisely the observance of every rule, big and small, by his Vizir, that was responsible for the orderliness of his people. Sharyar wrote a letter to his brother (most certainly dictated by the Vizir), beseeching him, in Burton's translation, to ". . . condescend to bestir himself and turn his face us-wards. Furthermore . . . our one and only desire is to see thee ere we die; but if thou delay or disappoint us we shall not survive the blow. Wherewith peace be upon thee!"

A royal party laden with gifts from Sharyar voyaged a great distance to Shahzaman's palace in Samarkand, and the Vizir delivered in person his sovereign's invitation, after making three precise bows to the

[2] There was no beginning, as noted. On orders from Sheherezade, narration is suspended; there is no "before" or "after": yet all that happens is *not* simultaneous; the activity of a body in time is the exploration of an awareness that there are forces that surround and constitute one's body in a seemingly chaotic state. The state of suspended "total study" is not narrative, which makes it imperative to note before each story that its roots are in another story; otherwise suspension of disbelief will be impossible. Of course, we take comfort in the fact that one word follows another, one step another step, so simultaneity and chronology contradict each other only apparently.

[3] Burton: "a King of Kings of the Banu Sasan in the Islands of India and China, a Lord of armies and guards and servants and dependents." Note Burton's blasphemous tinge here: he knows only too well who the "King of Kings" is in English, yet here is another, from a faraway land, who, as becomes amply clear, was not Christ. This King of Kings is the father of the two brothers who divide his kingdom: the elder, who is "a doughtier horseman," inherits the larger kingdom of India and China, while the younger is ruler of "Samarkand in Barbarian-Land."

[4] The bureaucracy of Empire, with the Vizir at its pinnacle, was a calculator whose job was to determine the cost of each royal impulse. The desires, urges, whims, wishes, itches, yens, and fancies of the King produced all the jobs in the kingdom.

[5] Called by Burton "Wazir," with the following footnote that takes issue with all previous translators of the *Nights*: "Galland writes 'Vizier,' a wretched frenchification of a mincing Turkish mispronunciation; Torrens, 'Wuzeer' (Anglo-Indian and Gilchristian); Lane, "Wezeer" (Egyptian or rather Cairene); Payne, 'Vizier,' according to his system; Burckhardt (*Proverbs*) 'Vizir.' The root is popularly supposed to be a 'wizr' (burden) and the meaning 'Minister'; Wazir al-Wuzara being 'Premier.' In the Koran Moses says: 'Give me a Wazir of my family, Harun (Aaron), my brother.' Sale, followed by the excellent version of the Rev. J. M. Rodwell, translates a 'Counsellor,' and explains by 'One who has the chief administration of affairs under a prince.' But both Koranists learnt

ground in the exact middle between King Shahzaman's legs, a space delineated by tradition and known in the Samar language as *teola*.

The splendid gifts were distributed by Shahzaman to his intimates, above all to his beautiful young wife, who received with proper modesty and gracious gratitude the well-proportioned white Mameluke slaves, who were among the many gifts. The horses with gem-encrusted saddles went to his generals, and the high-breasted virgins were distributed among his sons, most of them still under the age of ten, who looked with open mouths on the teen beauties.

Shahzaman had also been missing his brother, so he began immediately to make preparations to journey to his elder sibling's court. The preparations involved finding magnificent gifts for Sharyar and his wives and ministers, which in itself was not a problem for the ruler of Samarkand who possessed rooms full of treasure offered him by traveling merchants in gratitude for free passage along the Silk Route from

their orientalism in London and, like students generally, fail only upon their easiest points, familiar to all old dwellers in the East." Burton sees himself as such an old dweller and a speaker, besides, of the only "pure" Arabic, the Bedouin variety, uncontaminated by Turkish and Egyptian "mincing." It is quite amusing and awesome to see how many shots Burton fires in the preceding paragraph: he demolishes all previous translators in French and English, makes fun of earnest academics, mocks "students" who, obviously, never left the library, and shows off lightly profound erudition in matters of the Koran; one can imagine him atop his purebred Arabian horse with a pistol in one hand, firing with uncanny accuracy at the translators, while wielding a swift epée to wound a few "orientalists" and "students" in his path. Burton's marvelous swashbuckling is evident throughout his decades-long struggle with the *Nights*. Burton lavishes a great deal of attention on roots and spellings in order to invent his own, which makes for delightful reading after initial difficulty, but the language did not, alas, stay on his side. Despite this betrayal by his beloved language, which he tormented often to poetic heights nearly unreachable by the 21st-century ear, Burton has put a definitive stamp on the *Nights*. Haddawy aspires to a "plain narrative as well as a conversational style" and aims for "neutrality," qualities that, given the extravagance of the *Nights*, have all the appeal of dishwater to a man expecting brandy. Haddawy takes violent exception to Burton's translation, a tradition begun by none other than Burton himself, and reveals in the process something less egregious, but just as unwholesome in its own way, namely, the political "corrections" of the late 20th century. There is no end to the quarrels between the *Arabian Nights'* translators; they don't agree on anything; they copy each other but they claim to work from "original" manuscripts; the number of stories varies as well; bowdlerized and popularized editions make their claims even murkier. It is astounding that the three Fates stayed so civil to one another during Sheherezade's Fating, after all the mud they'd slung at each other across time.

[6] Sheherezade's father, the Vizir, is the servant of Protocol and Law; commentators have noted his inhuman lack of paternal feeling for his daughter when he allows her to marry Sharyar, despite knowing that he is delivering her to certain death. True, he makes a feeble (fable) attempt to prevent her, but once the deed is done, he waits every morning at the door of the King's bedroom for the emergence of the royal couple. For 1001 mornings, the Vizir waits to kill his daughter. This is an immensity of mornings that will bring him no human closure but will fortify within him the belief in the Law, which is greater than paternity, above the King even, certainly above all human consideration. The Vizir guarantees the legitimacy of the empire on the basis of the Law, which is inscribed in writing in the Law Library. It is a wretched fate indeed that this servant of Writing has given birth to the Spinner of Tales. Writing and Orality confront each other in this Father and Daughter, in the guises of Law and Fancy, Fact and Imagination, Order and Uncertainty. The unyielding Father embodies the inscribed Letter that foreshadows centuries of textual application, while his wild Daughter keeps the blood of her nomad mother burning with the desire to wander.

China to Persia, but which had to be slightly less splendid than those of the greater King. Shahzaman was less protocolar than his brother, but even he knew that he ought not to match him Mameluke for Mameluke, ruby-encrusted blade for ruby-encrusted blade. And by no means should he compete in the area of high-breasted virgins, though his city teemed with them. King Sharyar might recognize some of Shahzaman's gifts as being identical to his own dearly bought treasures, which, as all merchants knew, had once been a pair, the twain of which had been paid in tribute to Shahzaman. Shahzaman thus chose simplicity over opulence, loading his camels with tiger, bear, and lion furs hunted by his own furriers, and a small number of petite Mongol virgins with long braids down their backs that he had personally captured in a border skirmish, whose breasts were neither too high nor too full.

Suitably equipped, Shahzaman's party and Sharyar's envoys left the royal palace at dawn, seen on their way by his wife and his harem's mournful beseeching heavenward to the wailing of stringed instruments. They rode the whole day, then set up camp on a windy plateau under a starry sky. Unable to sleep, Shahzaman looked through the opening at the top of his tent at the sparkling show above, and remembered! He had forgotten the pearls! The string of pearls! How could he have forgotten them, the pearls that had been surrendered by his wife as a special gift from her to his brother's wife! How often he had listened for their sound, clinking softly as she came to him in the night, a panther dressed only in pearls! Thinking of his wife under the sparkling stars that had reminded him of the pearls, Shahzaman sprang up out of his tent, mounted his steed, and took off for his palace, intending to retrieve the pearls, kiss his sleeping wife, and return to the encampment before dawn, no one the wiser. He entered by a secret door and made directly for his wife's chamber, where the clinking of pearls and peals of laughter stopped him dead in his tracks.

Lying on the marital carpet, spread shamelessly beneath a "black cook of loathsome aspect and foul with kitchen grease and grime," was his beautiful young wife, the only visible thing about her a white thigh arched high over the beastly back, and a strand of the string of pearls snaking away from the sweaty bodies. Before drawing his scimitar, overcome by fury, King Shahzaman had an utterly inappropriate thought: the string of pearls began someplace near the lovers' straining middles and it was being used for pleasure! Without another thought to fuel his already burning fury, Shahzaman struck blindly and killed the lovers, after which he cut each one into four pieces on his own marital carpet-bed. When he pulled the string of pearls from the still-bleeding flesh, he noticed that, indeed, the sinuous ornament had been more than half-buried inside his wife's most cherished place that he'd thought of as his and his only.

King Shahzaman abandoned the dismembered traitors on the marital carpet[7] and rode dejectedly to the camp,[8] the string of pearls flying behind him like the milky tail of a burning comet. The journey began at dawn next day and each day increased his torment, weakening him and giving him no rest. He slouched in the saddle, his growing weakness diminishing his once-proud figure. Time passed[9] and Sharyar's splendid city came into view, its minarets polished and gilded in Shahzaman's honor, its gold cannons firing from freshly tiled towers.

When they embraced, Shahzaman's dejection was immediately apparent to Sharyar, who inquired about the reason. Shahzaman assured him that his condition was due to the rigors of the journey, a halfhearted lie that Sharyar accepted, having no other explanation. He ordered the feast of viands and rare fruits to be brought in by handsome slaves, and bade the musicians and the dancers to begin what he hoped would be a week-long festival of

[7] The dismay of the women who entered the chamber in the morning to prepare their lieges for their baths and dress must have been great: four large, greasy, and muscled pieces of "loathsome Moor" and four pink-edged jagged petals of fair wife lie on the marital carpet-bed; there is no sign of King Shahzaman, no signs of struggle. The entire palace is alerted to the scene of slaughter, and a great din ensues among the chanting of priests, the babbling of slaves, and the ululating of women. Has the end of the world come? Had the nomads snuck into the palace at night and killed the King's treasure, the love of his life? And where is the King? And what is the cook doing there? Questions to which no witness has the answer, but to which we, future chroniclers, must pay close attention because we are detectives. Surely, all figured it out, eventually, after a party was sent to catch up with Shahzaman on his way to Sharyar's kingdom. They listened humbly as Shahzaman, still livid with fury, recounted the night's events, and they agreed with him that he could not have acted in any other way, given such betrayal. Back at the palace, the slaves also figured it all out, and not a few among them thought secretly that the King was a fool, and that his wife's affair had been the most reasonable thing since she had doubtlessly required the cook who pleased her by his food to please her with his cock. Now the palace was both without mistress and without cook, a truly sad state of affairs; at least the King was out of town, praise Allah.

[8] It is raining.

[9] "Time is a man" (Exene Cervenka).

reunion and beatitude. The entire palace had been heated to a pitch of excitement all month as the best of the King's artists had been brought in from all corners of the empire to cook, sing, dance, and otherwise stimulate the nine known senses.[10] Flowers were strewn on every carpet to be crushed by the revelers' bodies, and long pipes of opium and hashish were held to their mouths by muscled youths impressed with jasmine and coconut oil.[11]

Sharyar enjoyed an organized harem that mirrored the administration of his empire: at the head of it was the Queen, his wife, who was tended by twenty concubines who ruled over hundreds of women of various ages, all of them guarded by Mameluke eunuchs who were themselves guarded (in outside towers) by armed and bearded manly Mamelukes.[12] Sharyar attributed his brother's wan state to the exigent journey, but he was disappointed because he had hoped that they might indulge once more in the roughhousing of their childhood and youth when the cares of government were not yet heavy upon them. He had hoped that Shahzaman's good spirits, as he remembered them, would lift his own, and stop or at least slow the passing of time. Days did pass but Shahzaman still did not touch his food or even smile at the choice amusements provided by his brother. Even worse, it appeared that the young King was wasting away from a dreadful disease the cause of which no physician could ascertain. His color was bad, there was a tinge of yellow to him, he stumbled often, and he fell asleep at inappropriate times.[13] Hoping to shock him back to life, Sharyar organized a tiger and monkey hunt and invited Shahzaman to come along, recalling Shahzaman's prowess with the bow. He still had a Bengal tiger skin on his wall, the first tiger either one of them had killed. Shahzaman had brought the

[10] Sight, Hearing, Taste, Touch, Smell, Telepathy, Remembrance, Foresight, Proprioception.

[11] For details of the party, the reader might look up the garden-feasts in honor of the Ismaili hashisheen (assassins) who embarked on a suicidal journey in order to go to a heaven that partied eternally in the exact same manner. The party protocols of the hashisheen martyrs were inscribed on a scroll that Agha Khan allowed R. Burton to read in Afghanistan, where he was in exile at the time.

[12] Ibn al-Rahat, "Sharyar's Side," *Saudi Literary Studies*, May 2001 (my translation).

beast down with a single arrow in the neck. Shahzaman had shortly thereafter forsaken killing most beasts, especially monkeys because their pitiful cries were much too human, but he was almost willing this one time to overlook his own distaste for Sharyar's sake . . . almost. His dejection held him in check. He told his older brother that now he had many monkeys in his household, dressed in fine cloth, who sat at his table and were served gold plates heaped with fruit by Mamelukes, and he cared for them. Sharyar was surprised by the disappearance of Shahzaman's once-legendary youthful fierceness, but as for himself, he killed and captured more animals than ever. Caged tigers guarded his treasure; elephants worked alongside his purveyors and builders, and he had decreed an annual holiday in their honor, but he took them for ivory whenever he pleased. When he went hunting, he did so in a fashion intended to remind his people that he was agile enough to kill many beasts. The clouds enveloping Shahzaman did not lift at the prospect of the hunt, but his excuse was feeble. "You may have become merciful, Brother," Sharyar said scornfully, "but a good kill is a royal duty." Still he refused to leave, saying that he preferred instead to remain alone in his rooms, to fully savor his sleeplessness, the lack of his appetite, and his near immobility. The manner of his refusal intrigued his brother, who glimpsed a certain voluptuousness in his brother's suffering. He left him to the enjoyment of his sorrows and took his party to the hunt.

Shahzaman lay on his carpet stiff as a corpse for one whole night, but at the break of dawn he betook himself to a window that overlooked an inner courtyard with a splashing fountain and a pool of sparkling blue water. A seemingly solid wooden column in the garden wall across from his window slid open, and out of it came tumbling ten comely maidens led by his brother's breathtakingly beautiful youngest wife.[14] That side

[13] We assign to Shahzaman more symptoms than Burton does, because our knowledge of the postrevenge effects on a jealous murderer's body are better known now, though they are by no means uniform. Pure psychopaths show no ill effects at all. Sharyar, the elder, is, it will turn out, a much less affected individual, because he is an out-and-out psychopath.

[14] Burton: "A model of beauty and comeliness and symmetry and perfect loveliness and who paced with the grace of a gazelle which panteth for the cooling stream."

was the women's quarters, and Shahzaman felt briefly ashamed to look on his brother's concubines and was about to draw back to lie again on his bed of pain, when a most astonishing sight met his eyes. The ten maidens disrobed and Shahzaman saw that five of them were men. The women dove into the pool and their five lovers dove after them, beginning a gymnastic display of aquatic love-motions that continued on land, as they could not get enough of one another. King Sharyar's young wife called cheerfully to the lush tree in the garden, and a naked Moor of great physical dimensions leapt down from it and embraced her like a tall black exclamation point around which the milky white Queen wrapped herself like parentheses. The orgiastic frolic continued at a greater pace as the sun rose in the sky heating up the sweat-slicked bodies of the lovers, who swam deftly in their own sweat before leaping into the crystal waters of the cool pool, only to continue their games there, and then in the garden again, for what seemed a very long time to the amazed Shahzaman. Hidden behind the fold of the curtain and seeing all without being seen, Shahzaman felt his melancholy vanish, and a wave of well-being washed over him, pushing away all the suffering within. At sunset, when the exhausted lovers vanished behind their secret door, and the Moor climbed back up into the lush tree, Shahzaman left his chamber and ordered food to be brought to him. He ate ravenously large portions and drank thirstily ten jugs of wine. If his brother, Sharyar, the greatest King in the world, could have such dreadful betrayal visited on him, there was little reason for him, a considerably smaller and less powerful King, to mourn any longer. What had happened to him was by no means unique; therefore he need no longer feel inadequate and reduced. After the meal he took three veiled dancers and four musicians to his chamber and toyed with them while smoking hashish, and he could not restrain himself during his rapture from sneaking a look at the window through which he had seen the scene that had restored his health.

When the hunting party returned, carrying a rich bounty of birds and gazelles, Shahzaman was fully restored to his senses and to his prowess. Sharyar noticed right away his little brother's changed disposition. He marveled at his returning color, his appetite, and his good spirits, and inquired as to their cause. Shahzaman told him that there were two parts to the story of his miraculous recovery, and that he was reluctant to tell either one, for fear of lowering his brother's spirits. Sharyar's curiosity, properly aroused now, drove him to press his brother, until Shahzaman, still gleeful and unable to contain himself, told his brother the reason for his formerly wan state: his wife's betrayal, his rage, his murder of the wife and the slave, and his growing despondency. Upon hearing each detail of Shahzaman's wife's unfaithfulness and his subsequent killing of the lovers, Sharyar clapped his brother on the back and exclaimed in horror and sympathy that, by Allah, if such misfortune were to overtake him, he would kill not only the guilty lovers, but all the women in his kingdom. King Sharyar now insisted, with more curiosity than ever, that his brother tell him the reason for his recovery from his justified melancholy. Shahzaman refused. Sharyar cajoled, then threatened. Pressed in this manner and desiring for reasons beyond his control to tell all, the younger King described in excruciating detail what he had seen from the window overlooking the secret garden.

Astounded, then horrified, Sharyar absorbed each word like a poison and exclaimed that he did not believe him. His wife, he said, had been personally chosen by him from the daughters of all the Kings who paid him tribute; she was the youngest of three of the greatest beauties of the Mongol steppes; if he hadn't married her, she might have succeeded her father, the Mongol Khan, to the throne, and waged war against all, including himself; she was a warrior-princess whom he had patiently taught to love, instructing her in Hindu pleasure arts beyond the reach of most mortals. Such betrayal was inconceivable for one as great as he, who knew the virtue of his young wife to be above that of any other woman, just as her horse-riding and warrior skills made her the equal of any man.

Seeing his brother distraught enough to kill him, a mere messenger, Shahzaman proposed a ruse: let us announce a hunt, he offered, and leave on the instant; we will set up camp a day's distance from the palace; then we will stake our tents in the desert and steal back unobserved in the middle of the night; we will hide behind the curtain of the window above the garden and watch to see what dawn brings. If I am lying, you must kill me for your honor, but you will be at ease and free to trust your wife again.

No sooner said than done. The Kings called a hunt to celebrate Shahzaman's recovery. They rode to the great forest at the edge of the desert and set up camp a day's distance from the city. They then returned in the middle of the night, making sure that their horses' hooves, wrapped in rabbit skin, made no noise as they passed through the wall. They both hid at the window, using the folds of the curtain to hide them, and waited for dawn. As the sun burst over the horizon and daylight streamed over the garden, Sharyar's ten concubines led by his young wife tumbled merrily out the secret door and began their orgy. Sharyar's wife called to the tree and her lover leapt down from a tall branch, to enfold her. It was as Shahzaman had described it, a feast of flesh heated by sun and cooled by desert springs, a circle-dance of bodies at the center of which his tall Mongol wife, milky white and unburned by the desert, wrapped herself and was folded in turn again and again by a body black as a fire-burnished iron.

Sharyar leapt from his hiding place and killed his wife and her lover himself with swift strokes of his scimitar. He, too, like his brother, cut the bodies into pieces—not just four each, but eight pieces each, because, as he was the greater King, his fury was so much the greater. He then seized the ten white Mamelukes, five of whom were men, and personally tied them to the tails of horses he whipped until they took off in all directions, rending the guilty flesh. He then danced like a madman among the hunks of bleeding meat, slashing at it with dagger and scimitar. He ordered a hundred virgins slaughtered secretly that night. But even these bursts of revenge did not ease his soul, and Sharyar felt, as his brother had, that he must possess some unspeakable flaw to be thus insulted, he the son of the King of Kings, and currently the greatest King on earth, ruler of India, China, Afghanistan, Persia, and Egypt.

II

Such as had befallen him was unthinkable, and could be avenged only by the destruction of all womankind within his kingdom's confines. His Vizir, the father of two daughters, pointed out that such a course of action was unadvisable. Without women there would be no new people in his lands, and without people he would be the ruler of no one and nothing. King Sharyar knew with his reason that the Vizir was right, but his feelings told him otherwise. He nearly struck down his Chief Minister, but stayed his hand and shouted instead, "Women be cursed! There are wizards who can make people in jars and pots, without the bother of women! I shall find them, Vizir, and show you then!"

The two Kings retreated then to a small council chamber to consider their next action. The revived and energetic Shahzaman, who had witnessed his brother's revenge and his subsequent oath, approved of the idea of finding wizards who make people in jars, without the aid of women,[15] and he said: "Indeed, Brother, let us wander into the world beyond our kingdoms and find the wizards of which you speak, the ones who can make people in jars and pots without the aid of women, and then kill all the women in the kingdom."

"Yes," replied Sharyar warming up to the idea, "but let us discover first if we can find anyone greater than us to whom such wickedness has happened. If we do find someone more powerful and richer than we, whose wife betrayed him in a like manner, we will indeed conclude that all women are wicked, and we can punish them accordingly."

Shahzaman thought about this, and said: "Perhaps we needn't kill them *all*; we can keep some to please us" (he remembered with a shiver of pleasure the night following the recovery of his health), "and some to give birth to people,

[15] He would indeed find these wizards, in the 21st century. I met Shahzaman in 1999 at the penthouse apartment of Carl Djerassi, "the father of the birth-control pill," who had just perfected a means of technological (nonsexual) reproduction and was hosting a party to celebrate his success. There were a lot of people there, most of them friends and colleagues of Carl's, but some of them alchemists and dervishes who had traveled (with difficulty) through time. I met Shahzaman in the anteroom by the elevator, a rotunda with a painted ceiling depicting the Creation, after Michelangelo, in which the hand of God was reaching not to Adam but to a chemical formula. The obviously bewildered one-eyed time-traveler asked me if this was the place of "the wizard who makes people in clay pots," and I said yes. The party-attenders then engaged one another in a conversation I didn't hear, but it involved a Mephistophelian deal that the dervish offered the chemist, a deal that Dr. Djerassi refused. He later told me that the dervish Shahzaman had offered to take him back in time to his brother's carpet-bed where he could watch their sexual anguish and storytelling and conduct scientific researches on the body of the Storyteller. It was tempting, Dr. Djerassi said, but I knew that the exhausting journey into the past would be unnecessary because Sheherezade would always escape from any test tube to renew our appetite for the unpredictable. Reasoned reproduction is neither productive nor beneficial to the universe, which does not like our attempts to imitate its profound generosity. The ersatz economy of reason is deeply displeasing to creation. In endowing Sheherezade with an inventive means of escaping from the prison of King Sharyar's bed, creation issued its first creative license and declared the creative human season to be exactly 1001 nights long. Sheherezade's heirs subdivided and sold her license to all kinds of pretenders to demiurgy, including to us, scientists. Small bits of it, micro-micro-microns of it, are still for sale, but the wonderful truth is that anyone can have her full license for free, provided that they use it without embarrassment for the full 1001 nights. And so I can have my nights right here: why travel with cumbersome machinery to the Middle Ages? I didn't agree, but then I was there only to lend an ear.

since I doubt that we can find enough people-making wizards to populate our large kingdoms."[16]

"You speak wisely, Brother," the bereft Sharyar moaned. And thus, taking nothing with them, the two Kings, disguised as monks, took to the dusty roads leading beyond the civilized world, in search of greater men betrayed.

search

It was now one year since King Sharyar and his younger brother King Shahzaman had left their kingdoms, their palaces, their slaves, and the hacked-up bodies of their wives behind. Now the former Kings were penniless monks wandering through the desert in search of someone greater than them who had been betrayed by women as they had been.

"What we are searching for is impossible," said Sharyar, the older brother and the more powerful King, "There is no one greater than me."

A crow perched on a tree branch over his head would have laughed, had there been a tree in the desert, and a crow. As it is, *something* laughed, but it wasn't a crow in a tree, or anything capable of scorn. The *something* was Shahzaman, his brother.

Shahzaman, who was younger and had ruled only from the splendor of Bukhara in the kingdom of Samarkand that oversaw the Silk Route from China to Europe, agreed that his brother was indeed great, but reminded him of Allah. It was in the name of Allah that he laughed. Allah the All-Knowing, All-Powerful, and Not-Too-Easily-Amused, to

---

[16] In this he was mistaken, as he found out in the time we met, a time when misogyny was considered wrong, so nobody could kill women with impunity, though such murders were still committed.

whom Shahzaman had pledged his faith just before leaving to visit his brother, laughed through Shahzaman. Sharyar had himself performed ablutions and learned Islamic prayers, but he had paid equal attention to other religions at the court, mindful of the strength of religious sentiments. He knew that Allah was in a hurry, a deity on horse and camel, who had been gathering converts for fewer than one hundred years since the Prophet Mohammed had revealed him, and in those years he had received thousands of worshipful interjections from his devotees, but the world was still too shaky, unformed, quick to switch allegiances. A King had to be careful. Just before he had been stricken by his misfortune, Sharyar's tutor had told him: "This world is yours, but everyone in it is subject to dreams they are apt to mistake for reality. These dreams whisper in the mind with a melodic voice, and all that now seems pleasurable and unchangeable can give way to a desire to be elsewhere. Until you learn how to make your nightly dreams obey, you will be flotsam on the waves of time, just like everyone else, King or slave, and you must not give yourself too rashly to the service of any one god, O young King!" His teacher was evidently Greek, a Platonist.

"Is my job to crush dreams?" Sharyar asked, and his tutor sighed, "I'm afraid so." Sharyar had forgotten all about it, but now, burning and freezing in the desert alongside his brother, he remembered and wasn't sure that he wanted such a job. Dream crushing is for clerks, he thought angrily. Besides, who was to say that what was happening to him and to his brother, Shahzaman, right now was not some kind of bad dream?

At this time spiritual revelations and upheaval were taking place in the deserts of Arabia and the mountains of the East. Between them, the two Kings had ruled over Hindi, Sumerian, Babylonian, Egyptian, and Persian lands, as well as numerous tribes of Mongols, thousands of Chinese clans, and innumerable Turkic, Afghani, and Tajik people. Most of these had been subdued by their father, the King of Kings, Shahanshah. Some of these subjects obeyed deities that could not be described in words or drawn in ink, and some deities forbade such attempts; some gods were loud, others silent, but all of them demanded sacrifices, and, if they were not properly tended, the people whose gods they were exited the chronicles of Shahanshah's history as mysteriously and as violently as they had entered them. Some of them fell with their cities burning to the ground, but this was no guarantee that they were truly gone, because when it was least expected, wild men appeared in the streets of Baghdad holding the glowing shards of a burned god, the broken statuette of a horned bull, a torn page of goatskin inscribed with letters of blood, or humming a dreamlike song, and these nameless remnants were not harmless. Like his father, Sharyar had issued standing orders to have such prophets killed, but now that he was absent, it was possible that these grotesque cultists were gathered around the Persian throne using their pitiful magic to influence his Vizir. Sharyar shuddered. Having been taught since early childhood that the only way to shield the throne from the poisons of defeated gods was with rivers of blood, he felt very much out of place wandering through the desert with his brother, like a child who had run away from home.

"How did we come to such a dream?" Sharyar mused out loud, and his brother, the smaller King, said, "We were born to dream it." And after a long pause, he added, "Our cities were built with camels, horses, scimitars, maps, stars, strategy, and engineering by our father, the King of Kings Shahanshah, but I fear the descriptions of his scribes."[17]

"Sure, I know all that, but we haven't done much to better our father's work. What are we doing?" Sharyar put his royal head between his hands and pulled his hair.

[17] The King of Kings, Shahanshah, the father of Sharyar and Shahzaman, on the verge of retirement, realized, like most great men on the verge of retirement, that his great power and holdings meant little if he did not take measures to have his deeds recounted in splendid language, and his holdings accounted for and attested to with accuracy, which is why he kept a Ministry of Scribes under the command of a faithful Chief Scribe; the scripting and scrolling of his reign went on day and night, catching up at some point with deeds and words at the very moment that they were committed and spoken, and sometimes *before*. Prophetic scribing, or avant-reporting, was widely practiced in times of peace, though anyone caught describing catastrophic events before they happened was beheaded. Only poets were permitted to write about things that hadn't happened, provided they did this mellifluously and for entertainment only. Oracles and priests were also accorded poetic privileges, but they inhabited special quarters and were consulted only privately during Shahanshah's reign. The King of Kings' administration was more fact-based than any previous empire, and for this reason we have few accounts of it; subsequent rulers eliminated or substituted accounts, corrupted scribes, and elevated oracles, priests, poets, and even handsome eunuchs to positions of "official descriptors." This hasn't changed much down to our day, when everything we call "history" is a revision by those who weren't there and didn't like it. The only relative and approximate accuracy we might trust is the scarce cuneiform clay tablets of Ur because writing was still new and difficult. When scribes became fluent, reality disappeared. Shahzaman was right to suspect the scribes of monkey business.

The two young Kings had left the opulent chambers of the palace dressed in coarse robes and sandals that were already shredded. They had traveled as beggars for one whole year. They had met many holy men, who resembled them, a half-conscious humanity fighting god-wars that raged all about. The desert teemed with leathery monks in rags or naked, seeking visions of new gods, or at least some signs that the old ones were still in business.

One dusk they met the Circumnavigator, a man who rolled rather than walked, having made himself round by some trick. This seeker cared not a fig about God, the object of his search being proof for the theory that the world was round. He was launched upon the road away from Damascus believing that he would eventually arrive back in Damascus at the end of his life. He called himself "the Circumnavigator," a mission he described as "the attempt to prove a thing before a language for it existed."[18] He saw his mission as needing physical proof beyond his eventual arrival in Damascus, so he intended to circumcise all the men he encountered in order to introduce belief in roundness everywhere on earth. As one might imagine, he did not have many willing acolytes, so his knife was far from dull, but he had circumcised enough men to leave a trail, by burying the foreskins in places he named "The Mount of Circumcision," or "The Desert of Circumcision," or "The Isle of Circumcision," for instance. Upon his arrival back in Damascus he was going to rename the city itself "The City of Circumcision," and then he was going to die happy, knowing that he had rounded the world.

Needless to say, neither Sharyar nor Shahzaman submitted to the procedure, though they listened with great interest to the round man. Shahzaman asked why it was so important to him that the world be round. The man replied that all the holy teachings involved sacrifices

---

[18] Of course, the 7th century was an ideal time for such exploration. It is also an ideal time for a writer in the 21st century to look back at a time before many phenomena had a language of their own; psychology, for instance, whose practice is recurrent in the *Nights*, had neither language nor theory—it was just brute practice.

of one sort or another, the most common being circumcisions. These circumcisions removed a ring of flesh that, much like a wedding ring, signified a bind to God. However, just like wedding bands, these symbolic bits of flesh were only beginnings, rehearsals, or dry runs for the final circumcision that was the spiral-cutting of one's whole body away from the soul. His own project, that of circumnavigating the earth, was a grand geographical circumcision, an act of imperial divestiture that would remove the world to allow God an unimpeded view to Himself. He believed that God was prevented from seeing His own grandeur by the opacity of His creation. Remove the creation and, lo and behold, God could revel in Himself.

"Such insanity!" Sharyar laughed. "You are a lamentable kebob, explorer, and yet you have such ambitions! You're not content to remove yourself from the sight of God; you'd cause the whole world to perish! I should dismember you now into a number of uneven parts, before you put your mad harmony to the test!" He picked up a rock and readied himself to smash the round man.

"Wait," Shahzaman said gently, "Why smash this pitiful roll of flesh? You'll only use your strength on a trifle. It's better to let him go on until his flesh falls off. His roundness is only a magic trick; he is made only of long white bones like everyone else. The earth is not round."

Sharyar dropped the rock and shook his head. "Why aren't these seekers satisfied with what scholars of arts, not to speak of Abraham, Moses, Mohammed, and Jesus, revealed about the world? Why do they keep looking?"

"They are vain people," said Shahzaman. "Each one hopes to have a revelation of his own, hopefully of a new god he can bring news of, and so become a new Mohammed or Jesus. It's like a treasure hunt, as if the vaults of heaven are still open and anyone can find riches if they suffer enough. These people understand something even Kings can't comprehend: you don't need armies to conquer the world. All you need is a religion that promises a rich afterlife. The desert is full of such promises now."

Still, Sharyar shook his head in disbelief. It made sense to him that some of the body should be surrendered for infractions, but fully reduced by devotion? No. Becoming lighter for losing a hand used in theft, or an eye for looking on a forbidden face, or a leg for stepping on the robe of a superior, yes, this made sense. Suicide didn't.

Future ages would prove Shahzaman right: the quick way to victory is to hijack a utopia. For some reason, the deserts of Arabia held such promises for three centuries. At the end of the 9th century the heavens closed and nothing divine has been heard from there since. Yet self-sacrifice as a quick means of reaching god remained in use well past the second millennium CE.

The royal brothers, who knew only what they themselves were seeking, namely, *"someone greater than themselves who had suffered the betrayal of women,"*[19] had many conversations with these god-crazed anchorites, but were never able to get past half of the explanation for their quest, namely, the effort to find *"someone greater than themselves . . ."* before the possessed tramps interrupted, and, eyes closed in ecstatic delirium, proffered numerous examples of people or spirits greater than all of them. Their chief theme seemed to be their insignificance, a quality by which they hoped to lure a vision. Among the many ambulant ascetics, there were some stationary ones perched atop tall poles in the bright sun, some of them barely alive, some of them mummified and impaled, and some of them just a circle of scattered bones at the foot of their poles, picked clean by beasts. These dismembered and shredded

[19] Not an exact quote from any translation, but a general sentiment culled from all of them, a synthetic quote as it were, to which we have inexact mnemonic recourse, but feel nonetheless that some sort of diffuse probity requires the use of quotation marks. If we were entirely upright we'd use quotation marks around every single word, like poet Alice Notley in her splendid poem "The Descent of Alette," in which all words are channeled, as words indeed are, and placed between quotation marks.

remains were tended to by swarms of devotees picking through bone and ash, long after vultures and hyenas had made off with the edible parts. Sharyar and Shahzaman were quite amazed at the fervor with which these seekers divested themselves of their flesh, and how many people found this desirable. It seemed that their fervor was increased by each ounce of flesh lost, flesh that quite possibly fed the spirits inhabiting what looked to the brothers like empty space.

Sharyar and Shahzaman had themselves lost a great deal of flesh after leaving home, but they were in no way hoping to be rewarded for this; so their amazement was even greater when one monk, with barely a stitch of cloth on his dark sinewy body, told them one starry night that, *"just in the human world, there are two Kings greater than all others, King Sharyar and King Shahzaman, who, not content to rule the world, had forsaken their earthly riches, and taken the roads of sacred pilgrimage and ascetic wanderings and are, possibly right now, drinking from the fountain of wisdom all others search for in vain."*

If only it were so. It was all Sharyar and Shahzaman could do to keep themselves from bursting out laughing, or weeping. The next day, they met a mystic who told them that everyone had two bodies, a day-body and a night-body, and that the two bodies were so busy looking for one another in the mirror of time, they never noticed anyone else. Next night, a vagabond shared a salted dried fish and told them that the fish they were eating was a god who in his goodness shared himself with all. On yet another desert eve, another creature, wrapped in its own matted hair, so that it was impossible to tell whether it was male or female, said that each soul had ten bodies, corresponding to ten elements, ten qualities, ten letters, ten emanations, and ten flesh creatures; it started to draw these ten bodies in the sand with a stone, but night was falling fast and the two brothers left the hairy decimal at its art, to look for a cave in which to spend the night.

When they found a stone ledge to huddle under, they could not sleep. An indeterminate number of days and nights had passed, and they had found no one to offer directions to where the one they were seeking might be nursing his wounds.

"Such talk of bodies! Every one of these wretches, without an ounce of spare flesh on them, talks about doubles and spirit-bodies, and they seem to have never heard of women! Does it not seem to you, Brother, that these men are on a course of extinction? They appear to seek wisdom at the expense of their flesh; they are begging the sand-winds to file away all that is sinew and bone in them," said Sharyar.

Shahzaman thought it strange indeed that the two of them, who had had their choice of women, and could dispose of the bodies of their subjects in any way they pleased, were embarked on a journey involving a malady of the soul. "Perhaps we are all of us, Kings and monks, seeking the same thing, an answer to the question, Why me?"

This angered Sharyar. "I am not seeking an answer!" he said proudly, "but a being more powerful than I betrayed as I was. Wisdom is depressing, a form of inaction. You're an old man, Brother." He rolled himself in the one holey blanket they both still had, leaving Shahzaman to shiver until dawn.

The roads also teemed with bandits, who were often no better dressed than the others, unless fresh from a caravan raid, but they usually left the god-seekers alone, because they were hardly worth wasting a twist of the knife blade on. The two brothers had divested themselves by now of nearly everything, except for their royal rings that they were careful to hide under bits of twisted burlap. They also had the blanket that they (sometimes) shared when night fell. When all their cloth wore away, they carried their rings in their mouths when someone approached, putting them back on their fingers only when they were alone. Sharyar passed his tongue through the middle of his heavy ring and made himself unable to speak. This made him a good listener, and many of the hermits they encountered took his silence for self-discipline. In truth, if the ring hadn't held his tongue, he'd have let loose a string of imprecations that would have greatly offended those gentle souls. Shahzaman kept his ring in his cheek, which gave him a slightly deformed countenance, but he was able to answer positively whenever someone asked whether his brother was mute or wise. But whether their royal rings were on their fingers or in their mouths, the two young Kings soon concluded that there were vastly more seekers than sought objects, and that perhaps (we say perhaps because they were nowhere near ready to give up!) the desired treasure did not exist.

So far, their original purpose *to find someone greater than themselves who had been equally betrayed by women* hadn't gotten very far, certainly not as far as they had, because they understood by "greater" someone more powerful in *this* world. This is what the god-crazy didn't understand, and, for his part, Sharyar cared nothing for another world. This is why he had insisted, against his brother's feeble objection, that they take their signet rings with them, should they be called to show their sire. The being they were seeking had to be like them, not necessarily richer, because they knew that they were the richest men in the world, but more powerful, because the betrayal of their women had made them doubt the magnitude of their power. Until their wives had betrayed them, they had been quite certain that the power of life and death, which had always been theirs since they had been born, sufficed to establish their absolute rule. Their power over life was twofold: their wives ensured the constant perpetuation of their seed, while their power over death consisted in the knowledge that the spawn of their seed would extend the royal bloodlines through time. The betrayal of the women had opened gates for the serpents of doubt: their seed may have been supplanted by that of others. Not just any others, but kitchen cooks, inferior grimy beings. Before hacking the betrayers to death, neither Sharyar nor Shahzaman had entertained seriously the thought of the existence of beings greater than themselves. For Shahzaman, the All-Knowing Allah whom he had formally but expediently adopted, took on greater weight. And weight, he thought, whether of this or another world, was what, in the end, power was all about. He must have lost fifty pounds.

"Surely you are not greater than Allah!" exclaimed Shahzaman, apropos of his brother's remark from the night before.

This time Sharyar decided to be more humble. You never know.

"No," he hastened to confirm, "not even as great as his Prophet, Mohammed. Surely no one could imagine that Allah's or Mohammed's wives would betray them as ours did. We don't even know if Allah has wives. Allah, they say, is in everything everywhere, so it is inconceivable that any of his wives, in whom he lives, as he does in all other living things, would dare to be unfaithful." Sharyar knew that Allah's Prophet had wives and children, a fact that impressed him less than if he'd been told that Mohammed had a body of incense that poured forth thick cinnabar smoke: prophets were a piastre a dozen—they had just run off several. Being human did nothing to enhance anyone's credibility, but Allah was another matter, and his Prophet might indeed have access to divine wrath, even if his own wives weren't exactly faithful. Thinking such a thing would, centuries hence, become so heretical that an automatic death sentence would be pronounced against anyone daring to question the fidelity of Mohammed's wives, but we are still in those tender beginning-times when a god, no matter how popular, had to pass certain tests before being pledged to. "Yes, Mohammed was a man," Sharyar answered his own question, "the most powerful man because his power came from Allah, just as I am the most powerful man because my power comes from being the firstborn of the King of Kings, our father."

"There are two possibilities, then, for our failure," Shahzaman said. "Either we have inherited less than our father's power because there are two of us, or womankind is evil. It is only right that I should inherit less power than you, because I am secondborn, which leaves only you to fully consider the two possibilities."

Sharyar did not like being charged with the full weight of such stark possibilities, any more than he had liked his younger brother's glee when he'd discovered Sharyar's wives doing what his own had. Until Shahzaman had discovered Sharyar's wives shamelessly frolicking, Shahzaman had been suffering dreadfully, showing a face morose, taciturn, withdrawn, and listless; but as soon as he found that his more powerful older brother's wives were capable of acts of even greater disgrace than his own, his mood lightened considerably. After confessing to Sharyar all that he had seen through the folds in the curtain from the window of his room, he'd tried hard to keep on the gloomy mask he'd worn since arriving at his brother's palace. It was only after Sharyar had taken his revenge by killing all his wives with his own scimitar that Shahzaman reverted briefly, but not with whole sincerity, to his earlier despondency. And it was only after witnessing his brother's fresh distress that he subscribed to Sharyar's desperate proposal that they leave all their worldly goods behind and go as beggars into the desert *to search for one greater so woefully betrayed.* It made Sharyar suspicious from the very beginning that his younger brother appeared so ready to undertake this quest; after all, if Shahzaman had truly wondered *if there was anyone greater than himself so woefully betrayed,* his question had already been answered: *yes, Sharyar, my older brother.* So it was only Sharyar's quest after all, and this made him even more bitter, as Shahzaman seemed more and more at ease.

And it was now, after the passage of a year and many months, after trudging through sand dunes and barren rocks and fruitless conversations with circular and angular hermits, after they had exhausted all their provisions and lived solely on the flesh of scorpions and lizards, that Sharyar began to suspect that there was *no one greater,* and that he had been singularly unfortunate and cursed for eternity with this shame. And so it was only now at the end of his wits that he sat down with his brother, Shahzaman, on two worn rocks at the bottom of a dry wadi to discuss what might be done next. And it was precisely now that an answer came, in the form of a demon.

The sky darkened. A tall leafy date tree stood above them. The shimmering desert horizon came into view like the waves of a sea, and it was a sea.[20] The mud beneath their feet became soft sand. They looked up into the tree and saw it full of ripe dates. They did not wait another second before climbing to the first branch and stuffing two or three ripe dates into their mouths at the same time. How they had gotten there they knew not, but as the dates melted in their mouths, they were overcome by sleep. They barely made it down to lie in the shade under the tree before they fell asleep.

They didn't rest long. They were awakened by the roar of thunder. The mirror-calm of the waves rippled and a funnel-shape drew itself angrily from the water, becoming larger and larger until it grew into a giant monster who blotted out the sun. The terrified brothers climbed back up the tree and hid in its branches. The sea-monster came ashore dragging a glass coffin wrapped in thick iron chains and locked with shiny brass locks. He set the glass trunk down in the sand, and then he seated himself before it, shaking the tree as his huge body thudded down. Sharyar and Shahzaman hung on for dear life like two ripe gourds about to fall. From where they trembled, they saw a shape twisting inside the glass coffin, but they could not make it out. The Genius,[21] because that's what the monster was, took a good look around and saw no one. He pulled off the lengths of chain and unlocked and opened the trunk. From within sprang a beautiful naked woman the sight of whom again nearly toppled the brothers from the tree. She was in every aspect as perfect as their wives, and each brother recited silently and involuntarily to himself several verses of sublime pornographic poetry. For a moment of wonder, terror, and desire, they forgot that they had destroyed such beauty with their very own hands.

The giant contemplated his splendid prisoner and roared, "My beauty, I have kidnapped you on your wedding night and made you mine for

[20] The sea that appears suddenly is a magical event in the *Nights*, and it appears often, inhabited by multicolored fish who are enchanted princes or hiding splendid cities bewitched for capricious reasons. The *Nights* are themselves a sea of stories that drowns the poor writer who, driven by hubris or fascination, lowers herm's innocent pirogue on its waves; suddenly, there is no land in sight. J. L. Borges has compared the *Nights* to a vast "cathedral"; B. Odagescu compared their attraction to that of "a moth to the flame." Both of them ground their metaphors in important motifs: Borges in the Alhambra, Odagescu in the magic lamp of Aladdin. But to us, just out for a foolish cruise, the *Nights* became an angry sea we trust to navigate to safety by following closely the sound of Sheherezade's voice weaving the salty vastness from the lighthouse of Sharyar's bed.

[21] Genius: this creature, a regular in the *Nights*, is called by Burton an "iffrit," by Haddawy a "jinn" (*fem.* jinnie), by others a "djinn" or "djinnie," and by Lang, a "genius." We prefer "genius" because these beings are very smart, which makes those humans who outwit them even greater.

love, and I have been much pleased to see that every time we alight on land, your love for me grows stronger. Barely one year has passed, but you are already returning my affections with greater ardor."

With these words, he stretched out and drew himself in as much as a monster of his size could, his feet barely visible in the distance, his ginormous head as big as a cloud resting on the sand. The lovely princess clambered deftly to his lips, using his beard as a rope-ladder, and as she reached his lower lip she began to dance until she described many sinuous circles on the lips quaking like sea-serpents, and then, spinning and shimmying faster and faster, she traveled up and down his body like a whip of light, eliciting a range of monster noises we'd be foolish to try to describe. Suffice it to say that when the sea Genius reached the peak of his pleasure, his effluvia geysered with the princess atop it for such a great distance, she found herself in the middle of the sea and would have drowned if the contented giant had not thrown his long arm over the waves to retrieve her between his fingers. He sat her down on the beach right under the two brothers, who had somehow clung to their branch when the thunder of the monster's joy roiled the seas. No sooner had the thunder died down and the princess been safely brought to land than the Genius fell into a deep sleep, with a huge finger still curled about the waist of the beauty.

Gently, the girl disentangled herself and looked up. She had noticed the men while dancing on the giant's lips. Her eyes filled with delight and she motioned the brothers to come down from the date tree. When they shook their heads in fear, she pointed to the sleeping giant, signaling with an unmistakable gesture that should they refuse she would deliver them straight into the blasting furnace of his snoring mouth. Trembling, the brothers climbed down. When they reached the ground, the princess walked to them, circled their waists with her soft arms, and kissed now one, now the other. She then leaned into their ear, one at a time, and whispered something so obscene that even Sir Richard

Burton was too shy to translate it. In short, she ordered them to make love to her. Visibly aroused and unable to hide their arousal, for they had long before worn away their clothes, they followed the princess down as she lay in the sand. She laughed as she offered both of them the pleasures of her body, and, unwilling as they thought that they ought to be, they nonetheless seized upon it at once and commenced to love her in tandem with exquisite simultaneity choreographed expertly by the great beauty from the sea.

When they were spent and lying on either side of her like the peels of an orange, she eyed the kingly rings on their fingers and demanded to have them. In their haste to eat dates and to hide they had forgotten they had them on. When they protested, remembering that they were great Kings and that these rings symbolized their power, she pointed to the Genius whose snores were shaking the ground to the center of the earth. These snores, incidentally, had greatly contributed to their mutual pleasures, because the sound had moved the sand beneath them like waves. They removed their rings and handed them to the princess, who, though naked, reached within her mane of long hair and pulled out a gold string from which hung many rings. "I had ninety-nine rings,"[22] she laughingly said, "and now I have one hundred and one. Each ring is from a man I loved while the giant slept." She set their own rings with the rest, hid the string back in her hair, and curled herself to

---

[22] The string of rings, the keepsakes of the Genius's clever sex slave, are symbols of her triumph over captivity, and their great number suggests not only the insatiable sexuality of women, but also the foolishness of trying to obtain love by force and the limits of power. The rings are the stars in the sky of the outer shell of the story that contains all the *Nights*. Robert Irwin, in *The Arabian Nights: A Companion*, writes that "the frame story of the *Nights* seems to have been known in medieval Italy. The *Novelle* by Giovanni Sercambi (1347–1424) comprises 155 tales told by characters . . . fleeing the plague of 1374 . . . a few of his tales are . . . taken from Boccaccio," and in one of them, ". . . the king recovers from a melancholy, brought on by his being cuckolded, when he succeeds in making love to a woman kept in a casket by a Siennese merchant. After making love to her, the king gives her his ring." There are many stories of European origin in the *Nights*, but here we can see the difference between Europe and Asia: one ring in Europe becomes 101 in the Arabian desert; passion is multiplied by something no longer extant in Europe. Or we can say that after she fled her Siennese captor, this European nymphomaniac and liberty lover felt such fury when the Genius captured her and took her far from Sienna, she increased her sedition 100-fold.

[23] We imagine that they didn't speak for a while. Let's take advantage of their silence to consider for a moment what just happened. Uncomfortable as the subject is, we might ask how the lovemaking was choreographed. We know that simultaneity occurred, but was the greater King put to use by the Genius's wife in front and the lesser King in the back? We are not naive enough to make this a simple matter of double penetration by the two Kings, but *beginning* with such a chesslike figure we wonder whether the greater King was indeed more potent and the smaller King smaller, or vice versa. R. Burton's footnote (p. 26, p. 6, line 19, in Heritage Press edition) makes a claim for the Moors' larger sex organs and seems to imply that the more oppressed the species (or closer to nature), the bigger its penis. "Debauched women prefer negroes on account of the size of their parts. I measured one man in Somali-land who, when quiescent, numbered nearly six inches . . . whereas the pure Arab, man and beast, is below the average of Europe . . . moreover, these imposing parts do not increase proportionally during erection; consequently, 'the deed of kind' takes a much longer time and adds greatly to the woman's enjoyment." Leaving aside the hilarious spectacle of Burton measuring the Somali man, we can see that even in its abbreviated form (we've cut the more obviously colonial racist essay that Burton set where now there are ellipses), this note synthesizes centuries of male sexual insecurity. We are not inquiring into either adaptive traits or the prejudices of Victorians, nor are we concerned with pornography, though commentators have dealt with this matter at some length, so to speak, because foregrounding or foreshadowing it was of concern to the literary fate of the *Nights*. Sir Richard Burton, adventurer and libertine, foregrounded it; Antoine Galland, the first translator from the Arabic into French, shaded it à la française, and Hussein Haddawy, the 20th-century translator, treated it as does Hugh Hefner, with oversize spotlights. The choreography set in motion by the desire of the Genius's prisoner-wife was a ballet challenge for Michel Fokine and the Kirov dancers (less so for Rimsky-Korsakov, who composed the music), and continues to be one for every choreographer who stages it. The challenge is to make three human bodies demonstrate with maximum economy

sleep in the monster's hand. The two brothers stole away as quickly as they could into the night.[23]

"That was the test. *We found someone greater . . .*" said Shahzaman, ". . . *than us, who was betrayed by a woman,*" concluded Sharyar. Indeed, the Genius had been greater in every respect, invalidating in this way at least one of their suspicions as to the motives of their wives' unfaithfulness, namely, the large sizes of the manhoods of their black lovers.[24] The sea-beauty had loved them, mere men, despite the paucity of their phalluses.

"We can go home now," Sharyar said, thinking of the pleasures of his palace, the sumptuous carpets, the colored glass windows, the rich foods, the thick pipe smoke, the high-breasted virgins, the cup-bearing boy-slaves, the unguent-appliers, masseurs, brocade cutters, perfumers, well-combed horses, Egyptian dogs, midget clowns, wounded enemies torn apart by tigers, captured Mongol women who fought for many nights before they were tamed, the thrill of public executions, and the myriad other pleasures that he had enjoyed since his earliest years. He knew that his servants had by now cleaned up the chunks of the twelve lovers that he'd left in the flower beds of the perfumed harem garden, and that some explanation by his Vizir had satisfied the curious. His Vizir, whom he had secretly appointed to rule in his absence, was a clever fellow, clever enough to explain away such horror, but not clever enough to usurp power, he hoped.

Shahzaman thought differently, though he, too, dwelt for a moment on the pleasures of his palace in Bukhara. But even as he envisioned the splendor of its interiors, long cleansed of his own revenge, and teeming with fountains and slaves, he could not suppress two half-thoughts: (1) was the interior of his lush palace worth reinhabiting, or was the nomad life of an anonymous beggar preferable? and (2) was there something about his own self that he did not yet know? He had so enjoyed making love together with his brother to the beautiful naked princess while gripped by fear and enveloped by the monster's snores! Was there something within him that craved more than the mere fidelity of a wife? This last was not a question likely to be answered in the plush confines of his womblike palace with its round walls and layers of silk carpet and Persian lamb's wool. The more Shahzaman thought of the pleasures of his palace, the more anxious he became. He looked at his brother, hunkered low to the ground against the cloying hot wind. Everything that had befallen him was the result of living within the opulent rooms of the kingdom he had been given by his generous older brother. After expecting no more than the life of a soldier on horseback, he had been made a King and had become as soft as a belly dancer's haunches. The wind full of sand felt suddenly like the caress of the skilled prisoner of the monster Genius. He felt his rugged naked body and truly he missed only his horse. The memory of sweaty horseflesh between his thighs, as he rode at great speed into a cluster of turbans he made fly up in the air with his scimitar, gave him a shiver of delight akin to being inside the sea-monster's wife. Shahzaman knew then that he preferred the

the power dynamics among gods, Kings, brothers, women, and storytelling. This writer would like to choreograph this quickly but firmly as well, because these first bodies that give birth to 1001 nights of bodies and stories contain the seeds of the mystery of the word becoming flesh, and the crucial junctions of the word's flesh-making in the *Sheherezade Folds*. So if we allow either that the smaller King was bigger and that the greater King was smaller, or vice versa, we are still left with the mystery of the decision by the Genius's wife as to what to do with either of them, since she had no idea who they were and what their worldly positions were. The entire question may even be a feint by another male translator who does not understand the fluid nature of a woman's body and its ability to model itself on its lover(s) while dictating the flows of desire. The geometrical model may serve for nothing here, but we introduce its cumbersome figure anyway because, as we shall see, the brothers gained an understanding from their lovemaking that they had hitherto lacked, and it was not entirely mechanical. They have now broken their silence, so let's listen.

[24] Burton, note on p. 26.

cold, hunger, and rain to the flattery of courtiers, the practiced caresses of courtesans, the dutiful loyalty of slaves. He had been made so weak by the duties of kingship that he had barely had the strength to quarter his wife and her Moor lover on the marital carpet: the exertions had nearly toppled him. He had admired his brother's skill and strength when his time had come to slaughter the twelve: after the frenzy of slaughter Sharyar wasn't even breathing hard. Reflecting on his brother's greater strength, his more powerful rule, the greater area of his lands, and the superior number of lovers he had effortlessly butchered, Shahzaman realized that he could never compete with Sharyar in the human world. There was another path left open for him: striking at God. It had been Fate, after all, and the God who saw all and set everything in motion, that had caused their tragedy. One could either look down on the present world and tighten his grip on it, as Sharyar was clearly meant to do by virtue of his greater physical strength, or one could aim at the source and strike up at God. And if God turned out to be a soft and untouchable target, there was still the fact and pleasure of living hard with a taut body of corded purpose. He would travel on, meeting god-seekers, learning ecstatic dances, running into the unexpected magic of a demon with a beautiful wife, carrying tales and magic spells gleaned from vagabonds along the road. Shahzaman felt suddenly strong in his tramp's body. His heart wept and his mind recoiled when he recalled Samarkand's reliance on his whims. Tyranny repelled him, it was exhausting, and he must forsake it. He would take the hermit's road, live the life of a seeker, an adventurer, a rogue, a vagabond; he would abandon the human world the better to understand it. He would be spat at, reviled, and perhaps martyred for his freedom, but he would never tell anyone, fellow tramp or assassin, his origin. A vulture settled on the jaiyan stone that sat at the crossroads, and looked at him. Shahzaman looked back. The jaiyan stone was the only visible sign of the crossroads. A sandstorm had erased the tracks made by caravans. The only thing a crossroads requires is that you recognize it. There are obvious crossroads and there are hidden ones, but signs always mark the ones that do not announce themselves. The vulture was there to confirm the stone.

During their long journey in search of *somebody greater than themselves who had been more grievously humbled*, Sharyar had been restless, angry, and fearful. There were times when he saw his brother sleeping contentedly under the stars, and he'd had difficulty controlling the impulse to bash his skull in with a stone. He hated Shahzaman's contentment, and he attributed it to the fact that Shahzaman had only a small appetite for life, while he, the greater King, had yet to slake his many thirsts, including his thirst for revenge on womankind, the open wound in his chest. He wanted to kill Shahzaman for agreeing to this journey, instead of opposing his momentary weakness. He could have stayed in Baghdad instead, to unleash the reign of terror it was his duty to unleash. He missed the comely wife he had killed, the ruler of his consorts and concubines, but he regretted killing her so mercifully. He should have caused her to die slowly, and he imagined strangling her over and over, but allowing her to live at the last moment so that he could strangle her again. He imagined also her black lover Saoud[25] whom he ordered to strangle her even as Saoud was being simultaneously strangled by his Vizir. His mind roamed over all the great rooms of his palace where fires burned in copper braziers and heavy curtains hid prying eyes; he imagined running the curtains through with a straight sword he'd captured from a Crusader, and heard heavy bodies fall clutching the velvet folds. His imagination was all that kept him on this nightmarish road he traveled with his brother. When rain drenched them and they waded waist-deep in mud, Sharyar thought about caressing his jewel-encrusted scepters and saddles, running his hands over crystal globes, and slowly draining the life of a slave girl with his hands on her throat as his seed gushed inside her. Over and over he watched Saoud strangle his wife while being strangled by the Vizir, even as he, Sharyar, strangled another girl. He missed the great gathering of men ready to make

---

[25] We know his name because Sharyar's beautiful wife called to him twice, "Saoud, Saoud," before he leapt out of the tree to embrace her. "Saoud," according to Burton, derives from the root "auspiciousness, prosperity," and by extension "fertility," a suggestion even more offensive to a King than the size of his penis, namely, that he, the royal, wasn't fertile (enough). Did Saoud bear any relation to the House of Saud, the originator of Wahabbism, a strict form of Islam that forbade all but utilitarian contact with women? The Arab poets, particularly the seditious ones, that is to say most of them, say yes, definitely. The well-endowed lover of Sharyar's wife was reborn repentant to such a degree that he introduced fierce misogyny where confusion had reigned before.

war at his shout, and he saw the sparking of scimitars and his bloodied army dragging slaves and treasure back to the city. His mind dwelt lovingly and at length over the battle itself, the clash of human and horseflesh and steel and leather, and he was seized by indignant righteousness. I am a King, a lawgiver, the ruler of an empire. My place is on the throne in my palace, dispensing and disposing, or on horseback killing and leading. I love palace life, the rhythms of my city, my aroused warriors, their fast horses and sturdy camels. What am I doing wandering naked through this desert, bereft of my signet ring, the symbol of my true standing? Thinking further, Sharyar realized that his present misfortune had begun with an uncharacteristic impulse, nostalgia. He had given in to his longing for his brother and he had sent for him, and that action had brought misfortune and unpredictability to his life. Sharyar despised disorder and felt that his wives' betrayal was, above all, an unauthorized entry of disorder into his world. That this was so was made even more grievous because he had found them out through the agency of his brother, who, although similarly betrayed, was clearly a lesser King.

What neither the smaller nor the greater King understood is why their wives, who had everything their hearts might desire, including Kings for husbands, would give themselves to grotesque and unclean slaves with nothing to their name. Sharyar saw in this an original imperfection installed in women since Creation. Shahzaman agreed, but he said that perfection was itself a flaw specific to all humans, because only God was perfect. For humans, the meaning of perfection was the same as the desire for happiness, which shifted with the sort of people who sought it. There was no intrinsic need for perfection within human beings; the desire for it was a habit of worldly standing; the higher a man ranked and the greater his power, the more perfection he required. Having everything, and wanting for nothing, left one with an inexplicable longing for imperfection.

"Yes, I am at odds with myself in expressing this," Shahzaman said, begging his brother's indulgence, "but I am simply saying that in this world eating is the very goal of perfection for the poor, while for the powerful, who are perfect, the only perfection to be had lies in imperfection." He explained that the poor, who were flawed, dirty, and asymmetrical, needed to serve those more powerful in order to keep their bellies filled, which for them was all the perfection they required. On the other hand, the beautiful wives of the powerful longed for a different kind of perfection. Their own lives were easy compared to those of the poor, but they were in thrall to a desire to be folded within the imperfect and cruel darkness of debasing forces that were the opposite of the great power of their King-husbands. Something like perfection opened in them when they surrendered to the grease-covered cooks, something that was like a fountain covered by a heavy gold lid. When this lid lifted, as their hips did, under the heavy burden of monsters, they were filled with hopelessness and they were powerless. Why they desired this Shahzaman could not tell, because neither the language nor theories of psychology had yet been invented, and he knew that such insights had only limited practical use.

Sharyar objected violently to Shahzaman's interpretation of women's need for the grotesque. Some flaw had occurred in them in the beginning, and there was nothing anyone could do about it.

"Maybe," said Sharyar, "it happened when they realized that they are smaller creatures. Smaller creatures despise larger ones, and they take revenge by making allies of coarser and larger forms, human or not. In any case, it is a mistake for us to seek answers to such questions in the desert, where man is the tallest creature, except for horses and camels. We stand so tall here we have no rival. All those God-seeking beggars, did you see any humility in them? No, because they are men of the desert. Where there are mountains and trees, man doesn't spend life in search of gods. In the mountains the clouds and trees are taller than men, and in the city, women and children are smaller." Sharyar longed for the tree-covered mountains of his kingdoms, and for the cities where towers dwarfed men, and where proportions checked each other's growth, keeping fancy within reason and hierarchy supported at its base by reasonably sized classes of servants to the King.

The two brothers now sitting at a crossroads knew of an instant that they would part ways. Sharyar would return to his palace to take back his rightful place as the great King of India, Persia, China, Egypt, and lands beyond. Shahzaman would keep traveling on the road that led to unexpected places, suffering the vicissitudes of weather, the whims of men, and the intrusions of spirits.

"Brother, you will take the kingdom of Samarkand from me, pray, and treat my subjects as you would treat yours?" Shahzaman beseeched him.

"I will," promised Sharyar.

Shahzaman then planted a date pit below the jaiyan stone at the cross-roads. They embraced and made a vow to return to that place in ten years. If the date pit in the ground had grown into a tree when one of them returned, it meant that the other was dead.

"Brother, mourn me if you find the tree," Shahzaman said.

"I will," Sharyar replied, knowing that he would never return to this place.

And with that, the brothers went their separate ways, Shahzaman into the unknown, and Sharyar back to his palace to set in place a new and greater order. In their heart of hearts they both knew that they would never see each other again because at that very moment the paths of the mystic and of the earthly King diverged. Their parting of ways took place at a mythic and historic crossroads, but its momentousness was not yet in evidence. Not even the shadow of the great story-universe that would unfold was yet visible; they had no way of knowing that looming over their parting was the Storyteller's fast-spinning spindle that would shortly fold time and generate more creatures than were now living. Theirs was but a binary division, a fork in the road, not as primary as Cain and Abel's, since a great many brotherly forks had forked out from that first fork, but close enough to those forking beginnings to still be visible to our eyes from the future, which have seen such efflorescence of divisions and arborescent plenitude, it is a wonder they stay open.

Sharyar's journey back was long and solitary. He was still burning with the fiery desire to kill all women, but he had time to reflect that killing all women might be unwise, so he resolved to kill only one thousand, preferably ones who had known his treacherous wives. He would then marry a virgin[26] every night and have her strangled in the morning by the Vizir. This way he would not be deprived of company, but there would be no time for his brides to be unfaithful. Then another idea occurred to him, an idea that made even the killing of one thousand women unnecessary, yet would slake nonetheless his thirst for revenge. He had never enforced female circumcision in his kingdom. This practice, widely observed among the Bedouin Arabs,[27] had been frowned upon by his teachers, and he had never, until his wife's betrayal, found any reason to curtail a woman's pleasure. He would now reverse himself and claim that, inspired by his devotion to the Prophet, he had seen the light. He would uproot the source of all evil from all women. As his land came in sight, he wondered how long he had been gone.

---

[26] Virgin—for most of human history this word stood for "unmarried woman," or "maiden," but the need for some kind of physical proof of maidenhood led to the discovery of the hymen in the 16th century. In 1544 "the internationally famous Flemish anatomist Andreas Vesalius finally found the hymen in dissection . . . although . . . he failed to sketch what he saw. The second woman in whom Vesalius . . . located a hymen was a seventeen-year-old hunchbacked girl." Hanne Blank, *Virgin: The Untouched History.* There are many hunchbacks in the *Nights* too; they fascinated the researchers of the Middle Ages because they were useful to the study of beauty and ugliness, the tension of goodness to badness as reflected in the physical form, and, as in the case of the girl, the certainty (of the physician) that she was "untouched" because she was ugly. For Sharyar, there would have been no physical proof of a girl's purity, except the word of her family, her social class, the precepts of her religion, and her young age. Sharyar's penis was going to be very sore because of his nightly exertions over his ever-new brides, and he took it for granted that his labor would be in unexplored regions.

[27] Circumcision of both sexes is a very ancient custom among the Arabs. Commentators explained the cause of this practice in man as cleanliness and health, and in a young woman as preventive against unchastity. Burton claims that "Asiatic peoples . . . all consider sexual desire in a woman to be ten times greater than in man," which may be the reason why the delicate operation of removing the hood of the clitoris reverted in time to the barbaric excision of the entire organ. Burton quotes the religious authority, Shaykh al-Nazawi: "Female circumcision is the universal custom in Egyptian Kahira and El Hejaz. The Bedouin tribes do not wish to marry a whole wife." God's fury at being disobeyed yet again can be seen in various subsequent events in "history." All this happened in Ur, not far from the Tree of the Knowledge of Good and Evil in Eden.

sharyar's return

That day, the city rang with the music of heralds, and the populace put on its festive clothes and its happiest faces. The prayers of the people had been answered. Although pleased with the rule of the Vizir, they felt shame for being without their true ruler. Merchants traveling to faraway lands nearly sank below the ground with shame when asked about their King. They stammered that their King was on an important journey to heaven in order to bring back wondrous information and gifts to his people. Every other multitude in the world had a King, but the subjects of the vast Persian Empire did not. It was enough to make you want to behead yourself for embarrassment.

His small bent figure, easily mistaken for that of a beggar, had been spotted a night's distance from the city. Measures were taken immediately to provide him with a horse and a retinue, and to make every step of his approach memorable. In addition to putting on festive clothes and happy faces, Sharyar's subjects rehearsed arts they hadn't practiced in a while by calling on performers from all corners of the empire to play solemn and exalting music, dance triumphal dances, and recite the most elevating sutras. This wasn't easy because in the King's absence, solemnity, praise, and elevated sentiments had fallen into disuse. Rough and prurient humor, rude chants, lewd dances, and ironic or downright parodic recitations were the preferred entertainments in the Vizir's easygoing empire. Reverting, even wholeheartedly, to the solemnities due a true King was no easy work for subjects apt to giggle at the slightest provocation. As soon as the King was spotted, every known instrument was reconfigured for seriousness, and the friendly elephants, snakes, tigers, lions, and horses that had been running unsupervised all over the city, being fed from the dinner table and allowed to sleep in children's beds, were herded together and outfitted with magnificent leathers and harnesses pulled down from attics and dusted off in a hurry. The gates were festooned with flowers. With musicians, dancers, and actors more or less sobered up and in some kind of formation, all creation, it seems, was ready to welcome back its King.

Only the Vizir was a little wary, though he did his best to hide it. He had had to pick up dozens of still twitching pieces of Sharyar's wives and their lovers, clean up the place so that nothing incriminating could be seen, and then slowly release bits of stories as to what had happened to the royal harem, and why the King left. These bits of stories congealed over the years into a legend that held that Sharyar had taken his harem with him to a magic world in order to bring back to his people many blessings and wonders. There was nothing in the Koran or the Hindu sutras or in any other book about anyone ever visiting heaven with a harem, but this was a point only the scholars argued and disbelieved. This was the legend that traveling merchants hinted at in more or less credible ways when they were questioned abroad, and eventually, when people looked up into the night sky, they discerned there the figure of their King and his concubines holding council in heaven with the stars. The Vizir did not begrudge his subjects their penchant for poetry, so he was happy to see them so ecstatically welcoming back their ruler. He donned his blue robe and took up his sapphire scepter, and ordered his daughters, Sheherezade and Dinarzad, to be clad in rich but modest dress and to wait veiled in the women's rows.

Sharyar noticed none of it. He passed through the flower-festooned gates without acknowledging the musical salutes, the welcoming shouts of the crowd, or the bows of his captains. He looked neither right nor left and rode straight to his quarters. He dismounted like one needing nothing and no one, and walked up the flower-strewn path to his throne room as if it were only a forest path. He passed his ruby-encrusted throne without a glance at it, opened his bedchamber door, collapsed on his two-hundred-carpets-thick bed, and looked up at the black marble dome through which the evening star pierced him with a cold ray of starlight.

After a few hours, the Vizir rang the bronze bell at the door of the King's chamber; upon Sharyar's listless assent, he entered, bowing, and performed the required prostrations before his sovereign. The precise space between the royal legs designated by tradition for the reception of tribute looked immense and bottomless to the Vizir, who had fallen out of the habit of complete submission. This was the equivalent, the Vizir realized to his horror, of forgetting his signature. The King himself, having walked the earth and spent time among the hungry and the humble, had lost considerable weight and was unsure where to place his royal legs. They would both have to relearn, one to obey, the other to rule.

"We have concluded our journey of discovery and feel no ease," Sharyar said, "though my brother took another path that he believes will cause his heart to embrace wisdom instead of passion. As for me, I intend to marry a new virgin every night, and when morning comes you must strangle her. I am going to start this very night, so you must find me a suitable girl who must be graceful in addition to being pure."

"S-s-sire," stammered the astonished Vizir, "this could lead to discontent among the subjects you just now saw at the peak of happiness at your return. In your absence, your people have flourished and excelled, in order to make themselves worthy of you when you decided to return. If you kill their children, they will be most confounded."

"I will deflower their daughters!" Sharyar spoke sharply, "You are going to kill them. Womankind cannot be trusted. My intention before leaving was to kill every woman in the kingdom, if you recall, but I have decided instead to be measured in my dislike. I won't even kill the one thousand I confined myself to in deference to your reproductive philosophy, which, incidentally, I don't believe any more. Killing after loving is, you must admit, a wiser course. I am also promulgating universal female circumcision, in the name of Allah and his Prophet, and I wish our physicians to begin this very day with girls as young as three days and women as old as sixty."

What could the Vizir say? He thought of his own daughters and his heart sank. He was a Persian, not bound to Allah's laws, and he would never allow surgeons near Sheherezade and Dinarzad. Hoping to change the King's grim outlook on life, he told the King all that had happened in his absence. Trade with neighboring kingdoms was flourishing. There were new mosques and temples in the city, and the borders were secure. The people led peaceful lives and crime was unheard of, with the exception of petty thievery, which the regime punished by cutting off the thieves' hands, a collection of which he kept in a cold dungeon ready for viewing by the King whenever he felt up to it. There had also been two murders, and he had kept the heads of the decapitated culprits to show the King. But Sharyar wasn't going to be placated with that bit of gore. There were but ten surgeons in the city, so the vast butchery of women's private parts would be left to the hundreds of itinerant barbers and tooth-pullers who plied their trade in the poor quarters. The Vizir could already hear the deep moan of his wounded kingdom.

"How fare your daughters?" asked the King, seeming not to have heard a word of his Chief Minister's report. "I am sure," he said, without waiting for an answer, "that they are lovely young women now, but I swear on my heavy heart, Vizir, that I shall not harm them even when all the maidens in the kingdom are gone."

If until this point the Vizir had been racking his feverish brain for the best way to dispose of the King without incurring his suspicion (or even *if*, he thought contemptuously of his own caution), now he wasn't so sure. Other people's daughters were, after all, a different matter. He owed complete allegiance to his King, and he could not, by law and tradition, question his motives. If Sharyar had to have a new wife every night and see her killed in the morning, there was a profound reason for it, though a mere mortal like himself couldn't see it. He mourned in his heart for all the dead girls to come, the daughters of the better people of his city. He would begin finding wives for Sharyar among the poorest citizens so that there would be no outcry among the nobles, but he knew that, eventually, he'd have to start drawing from the palace. The other business, the Night of the Circumcision, as he already called it to himself, would have to be sudden and swift and, to the extent of his influence, inefficient. For a moment, the Vizir felt grateful for the widespread corruption among his subjects, the practice of which might spare quite a few wealthy widows and pampered children from mutilation.

"King," the Vizir said, following each word with three prostrations between his sovereign's legs, each one more precise. "How. Increase. People. Of. The. Kingdom. Without. Women.?. Have. You. Found. People-making. Wizards.?."

"Quit doing that," said Sharyar. "It's hard to make sense of even one word when you prostrate so many times. The people will be born as they always were, from words."

"How could that be?" cried the Vizir.

"You may have noticed," Sharyar replied sarcastically, "that babies are made after talking, following Allah's command to be fruitful and multiply. Only the Mongol barbarians produce babies wordlessly. The rest of us have some conversation before going through the procedure."

It was difficult for the Vizir to think of the act of union between man and woman as a "procedure." "What is woman then?" he exclaimed.

"A human delivery device," Sharyar said.

The Vizir thought of his Mongol wife and felt the pain of her absence and how wordlessly they had loved. His entire being revolted against his sovereign's callousness. He had loved the Mongol who, furthermore, had told him that she had been taken by force in the Spartan way, and that Sheherezade was a child of wordlessness, that not one word passed between her rapist and herself during the "procedure." Whatever that meant. Sharyar was talking centuries ahead of himself. The Vizir could see that philosophizing with the King was useless because love between humans could not be explained; the language for it hadn't even been invented, though the gods were often enmeshed in it. He should at least propose some kind of compensation to the bereaved families, and to this Sharyar agreed reluctantly: he would pay ten piastres for each wife. This made him more generous, he would have pointed out if he'd known, than Persia's huge neighbor and subject, China, where the killing of baby girls would be a common practice all the way into the 21st century. Happily, he didn't know this, or his hardened stone heart would have turned to steel.

That very night he had a pleasing girl of thirteen brought to him. She had been oiled with essence of roses, depilated, and combed until her skin was smooth, her hair silky, and she smelled fresh. She was also taught to step high so that she might be thought of as "high-breasted," and she was instructed briefly in the arts of sighing softly and offering complimentary interjections. Her name was Fatima, like the Prophet's wife, but this remained a secret because Sharyar requested that his brides be numbered rather than named: Fatima was One. He would also have liked her not to talk, but this was impossible because as soon as the girl was led into his bedroom clad in a transparent silk sari, she began a rehearsed lament. Sharyar ordered her to cease, but she switched to the rehearsed interjections when he penetrated, with some difficulty, her tiny opening. Her still-raw circumcision didn't help the matter. Sharyar's seed rose quickly and spent itself because he had not had a woman since he'd shared the Genius's wife with his brother. He pretended to sleep after that but couldn't help hearing her soft weeping, which reminded him of better days when his wife had been faithful and the weeping of a virgin brought to bed for the delectation of them both was a joyful occasion. He ordered One removed and spent the rest of the night thinking about restoring order to the empire the Vizir had evidently allowed to lapse into complacency. In the morning the Vizir was waiting in front of his door, flanked by two muscular Mamelukes with arms crossed over their broad chests. They led the King to a newly minted dungeon where One was affixed to a wooden platform with her arms tied behind her and her legs fastened with brass rings to the sides.

The Vizir grasped her thin neck with all ten fingers and squeezed with all his might. He kept his eyes closed and shut off his mind, but try as he might, he did not have the strength to squeeze out her life because he was old, and a writer, besides. One of the Mamelukes finished the job quickly and without any effort. Sharyar felt no satisfaction but was annoyed with his Vizir for his lack of strength.

"You must write less and fight more," he told him. He also said that he would no longer be present at the morning's strangulation, but that it must be carried out without fail, because if he ever heard of any of his wives being spared, he would make sure that the Vizir would lose his head. The memory of disobeyed Kings whose subjects released children of the Moses type in Egypt, and elsewhere, was still fresh, though he thought it most unlikely that any of his brides were holy. You never know, though, so he appointed a magician to verify his brides in order to make sure that none of them were either supernatural or learned in magic.

The next night he possessed Two, whom he enjoyed a great deal more than One, because he took his time taking her and he found her screams credible. He even kept her to enjoy again in the morning, just before he handed her to the Vizir and his Mamelukes. Three was a challenge because of a thick hymen that gave way only after a great deal of resistance, and exhausted him. Four turned out not to be properly circumcised, and it was evident from her twisting motions that she was trying to cause his royal club to rub against the remnant for her own pleasure, a tactic that displeased Sharyar because he spent his seed owing to the extra excitement. He almost ordered Four kept for observation because he wondered whether another night might not elicit some unknown excitement, but he was loath to go back on his word. Five begged him to fill her with child, so he had her removed less than one hour after she'd been brought in. Six he deflowered with an ebony flute and took his pleasure in her behind. Seven he did not look at or touch, but slept next to, nearly dead from exhaustion. He ordered her to deflower herself with the ebony flute, so that she might meet her death properly wifed. Eight, Nine, Ten, Eleven, Twelve, Thirteen, Fourteen, Fifteen, Sixteen came and went, forgettable, though occasionally delightful. His nightly labors were beginning to seem more and more like a chore, and Sharyar thought with envy about the Genius's wife and her hundred rings, each of which represented a triumph of pleasure over fear.[28]

During the day, Sharyar ruled. He was informed by the kingdom's managers of the progress of crops, crafts, trade, treasure, diplomacy, intelligence, the state of roads, the weather, and the condition of buildings. The Vizir beamed at these meetings, his ledgers up-to-date in every way, always ready to add mostly approving notes to his ministers' reports. He now tallied carefully the number of female circumcisions carried out every night since the King's return, until he could report, in a loud and affirmative manner, that all females in the kingdom had been subdued according to the King's command, and that the bits of removed flesh had been combusted on the pyre that was still burning outside the city and could be seen from the window if the King cared to look. The King didn't. He could smell the acrid smoke in the air. After the morning's state-of-empire meetings, Sharyar received his mullahs, gurus, astrologers, and oracles. He received forecasts, auspicious dates, portents, dreams, and signs from the future. When the foreseers were finished, chemists and leechers studied his color and teeth, and tended him with potions of powdered gold and lizard gall and drained him of a cup of blood. To all of these faithful servants he issued instructions to be more vigilant, extract more taxes, and frighten the people more. He suspected that his Vizir had drained away some of his people's respect for authority. He ordered the number of spectacles reduced and doubled the ranks of his spies in the streets and in the marketplaces. Pleasantly exhausted after his exercises of attention and tyranny, he was brought lunch. After his days and nights in deserts and forests, he

---

[28] In an era when the Dionysian orgies of the Greeks were still remembered and practiced under the tutelage and administration of Bacchantes, Sharyar's attempt at serial monogamy seems pathetic, besides being clearly unsuccessful.

ate voraciously. He devoured whole chicken-stuffed lambs, steaming pots full of smothered birds, mountains of saffron-scented pilaf, sweet fig balls rolled in sesame seeds, and he drank prodigious pots of honeyed tea. After the sumptuous lunches he deeply inhaled the smoke of hookahs filled with rosewater and hashish, and had his small gold cups refilled often with hot coffee from tall ibrics. Musicians behind curtains and dancers in front of them sharpened his enjoyment of tastes. Dozing after lunch, with eyes shut in hashish reverie, he then listened to storytellers who never finished a whole tale before Sharyar began snoring peacefully while black slaves fanned him.

The eyes of his wives started to make an impression on Sharyar. He avoided the dark depths of their troubled gazes. Some of them changed like deep pools when clouds pass over them, looking into the narrow opening of his own dark eyes that, he hoped, allowed nothing of his soul to be known. In some of them he saw generous wonder, as if the imminence of his possession of their bodies took precedence over the proximity of their deaths, while others were capable of communicating both fears with childlike expectation. Sharyar ordered the veiling of all his brides. In the interest of what the girls' preparers thought to be comeliness, these veils were gauzy at first, often transparent, so that instead of being invisible, their eyes became magnified and more troubling. He called for darker veils. The girls were now sent to his chambers heavily veiled, but their dress, nothing but flimsy Indian silk, was still revealing enough to excite, it was hoped, the King's desire if not his mercy. When the eyes were obscured, Sharyar felt briefly relieved, but the girls' bodies grew more pronounced in the absence of the eyes and began to acquire a kind of gaze, as if the breasts and hips had taken over the eyes' function and were now watching him. Most of his wives had the tiny pale breast-buds of girls barely beginning to develop, but some of them had already grown women's nipples, and these watched him with intently dark eyes. Sharyar started to discern eyes elsewhere in the girls' bodies, even at the tips of their slender fingers under the nails lacquered carmine or violet in his honor. He ordered that his wives be henceforth clad in an impenetrable cloak of coarse dark cloth that allowed no hint of their womanly pronouncements. This, too, eased his nights for a time. Still, it wasn't long before the chore of dispensing with their maidenhood presented him with the dilemma of their sex. Their light, but sometimes reliefed pubic mound, though closely depilated and incised, allowed for the glimpse of the thin fissure continuing underneath, and this fissure, barely visible as it was, looked at him with the insistence of an eye; if Sharyar looked away, as he often did, that eye looked directly into the opening of his glans, which also acquired the qualities of an eye. The once-pleasurable act became a contest of gazes as the two bodies locked eye to eye in the ritual act. There was no problem once he succeeded in entering, but the initial contest of gazes by the ocularized organs unnerved him, and he demanded that the mons veneris be covered as well, with some kind of mesh that permitted only the opening strictly necessary for his entry. Sharyar foresaw with dread a time when he could no longer hope to make more mysterious what he already knew.

The King's nightly struggle began to strain the empire. He went incognito among his people and noted with displeasure how easily they reverted to bad manners and laxity of dress. Women, after a month of terror had passed, did their utmost to immodestly display themselves in the marketplaces and even in places of worship, attracting the gazes of men of all ages and girths, who did not bother to hide their states of arousal. Though places of merriment had been officially closed, every corner of the city sported a coffee shop featuring lewd dances, behind some shingle advertising an innocuous business such as "Knife Sharpening." Behind curtains at the back of these shops, narrow stairways led to carpeted balconies where pleasure was casually bought and sold. Intricate rings for every part of the body, male and female, were crafted and affixed by jewelers whose businesses thrived, as did those of body painters who wielded sharp glass knives to inscribe finely detailed likenesses on skin. His people were adorned and colored like vain fowl, and Sharyar was outraged on behalf of virtue. The circumcisions he had ordered seemed to have had no effect, if they had been carried out at all; it appeared that women of a lewd disposition had transferred the functions of their pleasure organ to other parts of their bodies, so that their fingertips, their toes, their lips, their ears, their eyelashes, and even their hair, had been suffused and soaked in clitoral essence. Was the operation being performed properly? It wasn't long before his decrees regarding decency were nailed on every door in Baghdad. Henceforth, anyone deemed immodest would be flogged and possibly stoned. The veil and the formless covering were made mandatory in public. Women were forbidden access to coffeehouses, and their appearance in public was limited to three forays per week to purchase foodstuffs. Sharyar would have liked his dress code to be enforced within households as well, but the Vizir pointed out that the number of spies needed to peek through gates and windows would exceed the royal budget. When he proposed a network of volunteer spies, the Vizir objected by reasoning that these spies would encourage lewdness in themselves through watching and, possibly, increase hidden lewdness that often takes pleasure in being watched.

For the moment Sharyar abandoned his idea of a voyeur army, but he was not pleased. His own program of attrition was not visibly reducing the numbers of womankind, though it did cause a deficit of marriageable maidens. Just as the Vizir had predicted, there were soon fewer poor maidens because, in addition to Sharyar's purchases, many young women began to shed their maidenhoods as soon as they could, sometimes in their eighth year. The Vizir proceeded to draft the daughters of wealthy merchants, soon to be followed by the children of nobility. The outcry grew louder, and many important citizens sent their daughters to the countryside or disguised them as boys at birth. The King's nightmare of his ten unfaithful Mameluke concubines, half of whom had been men, started to haunt him again as it became impossible to identify on sight who was male or female, a situation made worse by his dress decrees. No veils or coarse formless dresses were to be seen anywhere, the city having changed overnight into a multitude of men among whom no women were to be glimpsed, though Sharyar strongly suspected widespread disguise. He regarded his subjects' loose, flapping wide shalwars and their wide-sleeved jackets, and could feel without being able to prove it that virgins hid within. The random searches undertaken by his private guards uncovered a few girls, but a quick check revealed them not to be maidens. The streets of the kingdom lost their ease and a furtive atmosphere prevailed. Much commerce ceased and the trade missions conducted so successfully by contented and generous delegations became less profitable as the ambassadors carried their worries abroad. The barbarians at the borders, envious as always of Persia's wealth, but unable until now to overrun it because of the sincere devotion of her armies, began to conduct small incursions to test the Persians' will. A rebel band attacked a unit of dress-enforcers at night and, after extinguishing their torches, knifed them to death and removed their masks.

One hundred and twenty virgins later Sharyar sought to correct a flaw he had discovered in his last dozen wives. Of noble provenance, these girls had been taught to read, write, solve algebraic problems, and understand basic geometry. Eager to impress him, they demonstrated their skills in bed in ways Sharyar found less than amusing. Number One-Hundred-and-Eleven attempted to draw a diagram in his chest hair as a gesture of affection, but incurred his wrath to such an extent that he demanded that her head be shaved before she was strangled. Other playful attempts that included reading the bottom of his coffee cup, or trying to change his frown into a smile with childish fingers pushing at the corners of his lips, were punished likewise in a manner befitting his irritation. Such pranks, he decided, were the result of education. He forbade teaching girls reading, writing, algebra, geometry, dancing, dream-interpretation, and any subject that was not of demonstrable use to their faithful discharge of wifely duties. He knew that bans on dancing and oneirism could not be enforced because they were either self-taught or developed within households, but he made sure the law was written this way and supported by the words of the Prophet.

The Koran was carefully studied for any of the Prophet's pronouncements or gestures that supported the King's growing suspicion of the source of his women's flaws.

sheherezade daughter of the vizir

It did not take long after King Sharyar's return from the desert for all to know that a great evil had returned with him. The deep cry that shook the city of Baghdad could be heard throughout the empire. Fifteen-year-old Sheherezade saw and heard the women of the city shake their fists to the sky and curse after they had been visited by surgeons. In anticipation of surgeons' coming to them in the night, Sheherezade ringed the bed where she and her younger sister Dinarzad slept, with small bells and made a place at the foot of the carpet for her two pet tigers. She slept lightly with a curved knife under the pillow, her right hand wrapped around it. No one came through the locked door of their room, and she began to hear stories of noble women spared in exchange for bribes paid, but she did not lower her guard. When Sheherezade also began cobbling together bits and pieces of the rumor that King Sharyar, whose melancholy visage she had now watched lit by flames near the great braziers of the reception hall, was a troubled man who took a wife for only one night, then had her killed in the morning, she decided to be even more wary. She noted her father's distress and exhaustion. She saw very little of him, something she attributed to his need to be by the side of the King. The few times she sought him out, he was joyless. Her father had been ecstatic at first at the return of his sovereign, but now he looked physically smaller, the kindness in his eyes extinguished. Once she surprised him throwing a pair of fine doeskin gloves into a fireplace, but when she asked why he was burning perfectly good gloves, he said that they were bewitched; anyone who put them on was compelled to commit murder. Sheherezade laughed and said that she could wear any gloves without feeling such an urge, and she dared her father to find another pair. The Vizir said that many such pairs could be found; the point was not to test oneself with them, but to find the bewitching spell and break it. If that was done, no gloves would ever have such power.

Sheherezade rarely had any opportunity to be alone with her father, who went everywhere now accompanied by unsmiling Mamelukes. The Mamelukes who watched her were sometimes the same ones she saw in the company of her father, but they had had their tongues removed and did not speak. Sheherezade and Dinarzad discussed endlessly the darkness that had fallen over the city and over their father. They were puzzled by the Vizir's lifelessness, after he had ruled so wisely and vigorously in Sharyar's absence. His strength was ebbing as news of Sharyar's cruelty spread. They even entertained the idea that their father had been enchanted by a Genius that the King had inadvertently brought with him from the desert, a Genius who had replaced their father in all but form. Soon, Sheherezade knew that the rumors of the King's nightly weddings and morning murders were true. They were confirmed by the weavers who whispered details of the crimes under the clacking of looms. Whenever Sheherezade ran into her father now, he went out of his way to avoid her, and did not speak.

Others began acting strangely as well. Her Master-Teacher, who was famous for expansive digressions and, sometimes, childish gestures that made him endearing, ceased abruptly to deviate from the strict rhymes and meter of the sutras and suras, and rarely took his eyes off the text. Sheherezade did not know that he was lucky to be alive, after having gone before the King to argue against the circumcision of females. He cited the Koran as proof: women guilty of lewdness should be committed to the house until four witnesses testified against them and then, only then, put to death; the King's slaughter of his wife and concubines on the strength of only two witnesses, himself and his brother, Shahzaman, was a breach of the Law; furthermore, he was duty-bound to take unto himself at least four wives and see to the welfare of the kingdom by giving them heirs; and, most importantly, there was no mention of Makromah, or female circumcision, in the Koran. In his defense, Sharyar quoted a hadith to the effect that "circumcision is a commendable act for men (Sunnah) and an honorable thing for women (Makromah)," to which the Master-Teacher replied with another hadith that told how the Prophet Mohammed passed by a woman performing circumcision on a young girl, and instructed her by saying: "Cut off only the foreskin, the outer fold of skin over the clitoris, but do not cut off deeply for this is brighter for the face of the girl and more favorable with the husband." This instruction was directly pursuant on Allah's anger at the first act of genital mutilation committed by Abraham on Hagar at the urging of his jealous wife, Sarah. Abraham, assisted by Sarah, tore Hagar's clitoris from its root while the girl slept, arousing Allah's ire, who commanded thereby that all men would hence be circumcised and that both men and women have part of their genitals removed, but only the foreskin covering both. Sharyar countered that the foreskin of the clitoris was an ineffable and nearly invisible quantity, that no surgeon could be trusted to have a hand steady enough to remove only that part, and that, therefore, Allah allowed for what was humanly possible. They argued thus back and forth, until Sharyar ended the debate by pointing out to the Master-Teacher that he was a Qadiri Sufi and thus not a true authority in Islam, it being well known that the Sufi poets were worshipped by women. The Master-Teacher bowed and left seething with anger, determined to enter *taquia* and conceal himself until the time he could take revenge.

Sheherezade's other teachers also lowered their eyes and mumbled only the strictly necessary, as if a hardened thumb had extinguished the wick of their inner flame. The city itself became utterly quiet, and the dancers, acrobats, and storytellers began to vanish. The marketplaces displayed their wares listlessly with posted prices; there was no bargaining, no talk, no shouting, no singing, not even fighting. The silence of the city was pierced only by the shrill muezzins who called the faithful to clockwork prayers. King Sharyar's complete conversion to Allah was broadcast in mosques and distributed by messengers to all the provinces of the empire. Women disappeared behind veils and cloth or within men's robes with hardly a hint of flesh or a scent of perfume. Sheherezade saw the bewildering changes take place rapidly, almost overnight, and she decided to ride out of the city to the mulberry forests to think. She mounted Abd al-Hakim, her horse, and took off at a gallop for the gate of the city, but found it barred by giant guards unknown to her. She explained in vain that she was the Vizir's daughter and that she often left the city this way, but they did not allow her to pass. When she demanded an explanation, the largest of them spoke morosely: "No one is allowed to leave; maidens are forbidden more than all others."

Sheherezade and Abd al-Hakim turned back and made for the stables.

"What can this mean? The King's weddings of a night and killings of a morning must be true, and women have been robbed of joy," Abd al-Hakim said to Sheherezade when she dismounted. "'Tis true, my steed," she answered. "This is no longer the city we knew. It is as if a plague or an alien invader has come, not our King and protector."

"I fear so. The King must be forbidding all to leave the city for fear that the virgins might flee." Abd al-Hakim knew from other horses that virgins had indeed been fleeing Baghdad, sometimes disguised as men. "Commerce has even come to a standstill. We have all become hostages of a madman's nightmare. Even my own kind are no longer being trusted with long-distance journeys or races. We are trained only for war and whipped without mercy."

"You speak freely, horse," Sheherezade praised him, "but if this is indeed the case, I must act. You were bred for racing and for carrying our merchants to the farthest corners of the earth to spread the news of our laws and harmony,[29] and I have been bred to give birth to fearless children."

"Whatever you do," her horse said, raising lightly his right hoof, which in horses stood for

[29] Just when and where domestication of horses first occurred is a mystery. Most researchers believe that it took place on the steppes of Ukraine, Russia, and Kazakhstan, where wild horses were abundant, and burials included the skeletons of prized stallions and early chariots. In his authoritative book *The Horse, the Wheel, and Language*, David W. Anthony writes that some of the evidence puts the beginning of horse domestication around 2500 BC, but more recent research suggests an earlier time, 3500 BC, for the beginning of the horse-human relationship—a relationship that, according to Dr. Alan Outram, who excavated horse remains in Kazakhstan in 2009, has "immense social and economic significance, advancing communications, transport, food production and warfare" (PlanetEarth online, http://planetearth.nerc.ac.uk/news/story.aspx?id=309). He did not mention the highly developed use of language by some breeds, like the one Sheherezade's horse belonged to, but horse-to-human communication is attested by history. Talking and flying horses are found in myths and folktales, and their diction is impeccable.

a hand over the heart, "I will aid you, my mistress Sheherezade."

It was not long before Sheherezade knew every rumor to be true. Three of her friends from the weaving circle were buried secretly at night. The weeping of mothers and fathers could be heard behind shuttered windows and doors. The narrow streets of Baghdad rang with the cries of mourners as they followed small bodies wrapped tightly in fresh cotton. Families buried Sharyar's brides of a night and called to Allah for mercy. While the nights rang with anguish, the mosques and temples were filled all day with mourners. Mute guards in leather armor and bright scimitars stood at intersections and asked everyone: "Who are you?" The intimidated citizens spoke their names, and when their names were not enough, they produced proof of their citizenship, and recited the names of their fathers and mothers and children, and produced all sorts of documents newly minted by priests. Checkpoints were established on nearly every street, and the need for documents caused most people to hide in their homes. Families with young daughters offered them willingly to King Sharyar's guards in the hope that they might take them as wives and save them from the King's bloodthirst. Soon, most guards, but also merchants and cooks, had more wives than they could remember, and they started passing their days drinking wine and eating hashish in coffeehouses, listening (secretly) to storytellers and dancing in male brothels.

Sheherezade watched as her playmates and friends, the daughters of her father's friends and advisers, vanished one by one into the King's chamber, and were never seen again. She heard the cries of bereaved mothers and saw the ashen faces of their fathers. She thought of her sister, Dinarzad, and she could not bear the thought that Sharyar might take her one night for a wife and send her to the land of the dead in the morning. For herself, Sheherezade had no fear. In her mind she had fought creatures a thousand times crueler and stronger than dagger-faced Sharyar. After a hundred nights passed and neither she nor Dinarzad had yet been called to the awful duty, she started to suspect that they were being spared because they were the Vizir's daughters.

One day, she was approached by a weaver who asked her to meet a group of women that called itself Al-Adl. The group had been formed not long before, when Sharyar's madness was confirmed. They discussed the situation and agreed that Sheherezade, the Vizir's daughter, was the only maiden in the kingdom capable of deflecting Sharyar from his vow, not only because of her position but also because she believed strongly in justice. She must offer herself to the King on her fifteenth birthday and stay his hand. If she failed, Al-Adl was determined to aid her in assassinating him. They were going to avenge the deaths of their daughters and sisters, and put a stop once and for all to this madness. They were prepared to die with Sheherezade if her attempt failed, and they discussed a plan of attack. Sheherezade agreed.

The morning after this meeting Sheherezade announced to her father that she intended to marry the King. She could not tell her father about Al-Adl, but she claimed that her extensive studies and brilliance would overcome the King, who would be unable to kill her, thus putting an end to the kingdom's sorrows. She wasn't a particularly gifted student, though she was a great liar, and the Vizir knew it. He had strangled to death with his own hands girls more beautiful and better educated than his daughter. In fact, the Vizir had agreed to become the King's executioner only on the condition that he never marry his daughters. The King had promised. So when Sheherezade presented herself before him, without knowing of his deal with the tyrant, the Vizir clutched his trembling hands behind his back as he listened, preventing himself in this way from strangling her.

"If you marry the King, you will die the very next day," he said.

"I must marry him. The fate of the daughters of Persia rests on me."

"If you die, womankind will be doomed all the same, but I will be doomed first because it is my duty to strangle you with my own hands." The Vizir unclutched his hands and held them shaking before her, a ges-

ture repeated throughout history, as the first expression of abject pow-
erlessness by humans owing blind obedience to their superiors, especially Kings.

"And if you don't?"

"Then I'll be tied to four horses and torn apart."

Sheherezade did not like to think about this, but she felt that she had
little choice now. She argued gently that she had learned a number of
magical arts by means of which she would bring Sharyar peace of mind
and quench his bloodthirst. She claimed that she had memorized hundreds of charms and knew many recipes for sleep and forgiveness. In
truth, she did know certain arts, none of them very precise. Even the
plan that Al-Adl had proposed had many flaws and suffered from the
lack of a reasonable chronology.

Sheherezade had not thought much about how her actual first night as
Sharyar's bride would pass. She did dwell briefly on the deflowering, an
action inappropriately named because she knew from books that the
flower inside her would not even bloom until seeded, so that "deflowering" was the wrong word, a better one being "inflowering," since
this is what the King was expected to seek. She had prepared a story
to tell the King after he had inflowered her, and had even contrived
to bring her little sister, Dinarzad, into the nuptial chamber to ask for
a story. She had no idea what she would do next, if the story failed to
interest the King. She told her father that she knew enough magic to
transform everyone in the palace into animals, and that when she had
transformed the King into a mute swan,[30] she would turn herself into
a leopard and tear him apart. (Or open the door to Al-Adl to watch her
plunge a kris into his heart, she told herself.)

[30] The Mute Swan was first described by German naturalist Johann Friedrich Gmelin in 1789. Both *cygnus* and *olor* mean "swan"
in Latin; cygnus is related to the Greek *kyknos*. In the 1930s when the American Ornithologists' Union changed the species name,
it was known as *Sthenelides olor*, or Cygnus, Mute Swan. There are no recognized living subspecies of the Mute Swan. Transform-
ing a man into a swan was among the more common forms of magic in Persia, valued because its victim could not cry out for help.
Zeus took the form of a swan to rape Leda, though he turned himself into a white bull for the more difficult task of raping Europa.

"Aye," moaned her father, "better a mountain goat than a city philosopher!"

It had never occurred to her that she might fail, but if she did, she now knew that her father would be tied to the tails of four wild horses that the King would then personally whip to run in four different directions. Then Sharyar would strangle Sheherezade himself, if not with his hands, then with his swan wings. She had seen executions before, the rending by horses being the most horrific. But what if her father did not refuse to strangle her? It was an unimaginable thought, but Sheherezade was now firmly set on the path of thinking the unimaginable. This was bigger than herself, and Sheherezade told herself that she would marry Sharyar no matter what happened. This was the only way to save Dinarzad and the other girls in the kingdom. This was what she had been born for, and this was the heroic fate that she was destined for. Her future had different ideas, of course, but even those present when the Fates had foretold her life had already forgotten the details. She steeled herself for her father's rebuke: it wasn't long in coming.

the thing called yoke

"Why?" shouted the Vizir.

"By Allah, O my father, how long shall this slaughter of women endure? Shall I tell thee what is in my mind in order to save both sides from destruction . . . either I shall live or I shall be a ransom for the virgin daughters of Muslims and the cause of their deliverance from his hands and thine."

The overwhelmed Vizir said in as stern a voice as he could muster: "There is an order in the universe and you will obey it. I am going to tell you the tale of the Ox, the Ass, the Rooster, the Merchant, and the Wife, and you will draw your lesson from it."

"Sure, Daddy," quoth Sheherezade, lifting her eyes to the ceiling in the manner of teen rebels in all times, and then she sighed deeply, the deepest sigh this Christ and Gandhi of proto-feminism was capable of, considering that she didn't yet know who either Christ or Gandhi was.

"There was a rich merchant called Hassan who understood the language of animals."[31]

"Getting rich!" Sheherezade exclaimed, "what a use for such a gift!"

"Keep sarcasm to a minimum, Daughter. You're kneeling over a precipice. This Hassan understood the language of animals, but he was under oath to never reveal to anyone his gift. He could hear what they said, but he could not share what he heard under penalty of death."

"And did he who bestowed the gift attach the penalty?" wondered she.

"Allah did and that's that, and if you ask any more questions, you will end up like Mohad Hajin's daughter who asked so many questions that she was turned into a shepherd's crook."

Sheherezade wanted very much to hear the story of Mohad Hajin's daughter, but she held her tongue and stuck to languages instead. She thought of her talks with her horse. She spoke his language and he spoke hers, but the thoughts of other living creatures were inaccessible to her. Knowing their languages would have been great indeed, even with the death penalty attached, but then she remembered what they were *really* there to talk about, and she laughed. The penalty of her death had already been pronounced. She was going to marry Sharyar. On this matter of understanding the language of animals, she had her own the-

[31] What is "the language of animals?" It is their shape and behaviors, but in this instance it is also what they have learned about humans, whose much simpler language they speak without difficulty. Every hunter and farmer speaks some of the language of animals, but some special humans, like this merchant, have been vouchsafed the gift of understanding the commentaries of animals, not just their shapes and behaviors; this is a dangerous gift insofar as it is practically a residual organ (or brain volute) that had been expressly circumcised from people by some still-powerful original force. Every animal, with the exception of horses and monkeys, was subjected to the excision of this volute by the same God who ordered universal circumcision as punishment for Sarah's transgression. What caused this second edict of surgery is not known. What *is* known is that as the God of Abraham becomes more irritable, the number of punishments multiplies, as evidenced by many holy texts and present-day humans who are as full of scars as trees chewed by beavers.

ory. Once upon a time, before Babel, humans and animals spoke the same language, and proof of it remained to her own day, imbedded in the names of animals themselves. The Bull, for instance, who was also an Ox, and a Taur, and a Taurus in different tongues, had kept in her own language the sounds of the One Language, before they were all scattered.[32] As to how the memory of the One Language had been removed from all but a few people gifted by Allah with its knowledge, she thought of it as a kind of surgical operation, the physical removal of a bit of brain flesh where the One Language lived.[33] Removing the universal language from the human brain was the First Circumcision. There had been others before the one currently decreed by Sharyar, some of them performed by Allah himself, like this Circumcision of the Universal Tongue, others performed by men interpreting the Prophet's words[34] or the words of other deities. The urge to remove all that was or seemed inimical to the gods was inbuilt in people at Creation, she thought sadly, but there was no reason, she also reflected, why such practices should continue. Was it not possible to restore somehow all the good qualities that people had once possessed before being convinced or convincing themselves of their unworthiness? If that was the case. It was possible that even when gods, people, and animals spoke the same language, people's qualities were not necessarily better, given

---

[32] "The Arab word is 'Taur' (Thaur, Saur); in the old Persian 'Tora' and Lat. 'Taurus,' a venerable remnant of the days before 'Semitic' and 'Aryan' families of speech had split into two distinct growths" (Burton).

[33] Sheherezade is wrong in this: the One Language was not removed; it was diluted by the addition of vowels, which, just like water, dissolve everything, but especially understanding. The consonants, particularly the cognates led by the labials, had resisted the dissolving action of vowels for a long time, but they were eventually riddled with holes like limestone by water, and the One Language is now just a world of caves with a flimsy lace of consonants still linking them. This is a materialist description of the process; to believers in the desert God it's just more surgery.

[34] In other traditions, there is a general deflection of the question. For example, in Islam the Arabic language is the language of the Koran, and so universal for Muslims. The written classical Chinese language was and is still read widely though pronounced somewhat differently by readers in different areas of China, Vietnam, Korea, and Japan, so it is the universal language for those cultures. In India Sanskrit was the literary language for many to whom it was not the mother tongue. Comparably, Medieval Latin was the universal language of the learned in the Middle Ages, and the language of the Bible in the Catholic lands that covered most of Western Europe and parts of Northern and Central Europe also. In the 20th century English is the lingua franca. All of this proves to us that writing writes humans the way writing wants us to know them.

that they were the ones who lived with the knowledge of their certain deaths. The gods didn't care because they were immortal, and the beasts knew nothing of it, if it came swiftly. The dread of suffering was most of what men and horses had in common, and this was doubtlessly the chief subject of conversation, except in special cases. Abd al-Hakim, for instance. But even he, when they ceased speaking, went on to graze without a thought, while she went on thinking of death.

"go on, father," sighed sheherezade

"One day Hassan passed by the stables where his Ass and his Ox dwelt in adjoining stalls. The stall of the Ass was roomy, swept clean, and had a window with a view of the road. The Ox's was filthy and dark, and flies buzzed in his eyes; he didn't even have the strength to flick them off with his tail. 'How I envy you, Awakener Ass,'[35] said the Ox to him. 'All you do is carry our master to town and back, then are brushed and fed the choicest oats, while I labor pulling a heavy plow in muddy fields in the rains and cold and I am cursed by the Farmer for my laziness; then I am fed slops and made to sleep in my own waste. Early in the morning while you are still asleep, the Farmer makes me go back to my labor, and I cannot even lie down in the heat of midday for fear of being whipped. I am wretched and would rather die than continue such a life. Tell me the secret of your easy life, Ass, and I'll die grateful to one creature at least, and go to my roast-pit knowing that a kindness was done unto me.'"

The Vizir had tears in his eyes, so carried away was he with the plight of the Ox, but not quite as carried away as Sir Richard Burton, who, centuries later, made the lament of the Ox sound like the bellow of all the oppressed people in the world. In truth, the Vizir, too, was weeping for the lack of kindness in all the world, and he melted his daughter's heart.

[35] "Arab, 'Abu yakzan = the Awakener, because the Ass brays at dawn" (Burton).

Wiping away the tears that fell into his beard, he went on. "The Ass, moved to tears by the Ox, said to him, 'O you foolish Ox, you ignorant drudge who neither reflects nor plans ahead, it is only your habit and forbearance that keep you chained to such an existence! I will tell you a means to escape from your wretched labor, but you must follow my prescription without deviation.' 'Anything, anything,' cried the Ox, seeing his Liberator suddenly haloed in the dawn light, even as the Farmer's heavy steps could be heard approaching, dragging the Yoke. 'Well, this is what you do,' the Ass told him, and now we quote one of your Fates, Daughter, Sir Richard Burton:

"'When thou goest afield and they lay the thing called Yoke on thy neck, lie down and rise not again though haply they swinge thee; and if thou rise, lie down a second time; and when they bring thee home and offer thee thy beans, fall backwards and only sniff at the meat and withdraw thee and taste it not, and be satisfied with crushed straw and chaff; and on this wise feign thou art sick, and cease not doing thus for a day or two days or even three days, so shalt thou have rest from all toil and moil.'

"And the Ox thanked the Ass, and when the Farmer tried to yoke him, he lay down, and no matter how hard the Farmer whipped him, he made no motion, and when he was given his beans, unaccountably called 'meat' by Fate-Burton, he touched them not. The Farmer went to the Merchant and told him that he feared the Ox was sick. But the Merchant, who had heard all that had been spoken between the two beasts, told him to yoke the Ass to the plow instead and work him as hard as he usually worked the Ox."

"Father!" cried Sheherezade, "you go too fast for me. In the first place, what is the context in which my Fate, Burton, told this tale at my birth? And in the second, what sort of mean use of Allah's gift is it when the words of one beast are used against another? Does a gift not mandate one to charity?" This last she had been taught by her Master-Teacher as an inviolable law: misusing a confidence obtained through grace was a crime.

How could her father repeat all, or any, of what the Fates foretold at her crib, when he hadn't even been there himself? He knew only what his sovereign had reported, which had sounded to him like nonsense even then. For one thing, the disguised King of Kings, Shahanshah, was not a very good reporter; something had come over him, as it had over all those present, except for his sons, who were too tender and spoiled to cease from motion. The King of Kings had told him that after removing the female silks he'd been wrapped in, as his servants rinsed off his kohl and henna with warm water from a gold basin, he remembered only that he'd experienced something beatific and hypnotic as the Fates were speaking, something that made understanding possible in a fraction of an infinity of a second,[36] but faded shortly after. The Fates had apparently told many stories, but the great King of Kings could remember only a few of them. His sons, Sharyar and Shahzaman, remembered none. Sheherezade was now a woman, and the fifteen years since the Fates had spoken had become a river of forgetting, flowing with other barely glimpsed and ungrasped tales into a sea of oblivion called the Sea of the Erasure of the Context. The Vizir, too, had had to forget, or else he could not have kept his mind on his daily duties, but, oddly enough, some of what Shahanshah had told him rose spontaneously in his mind when the occasion demanded. He never questioned the source or speculated on the nature of memory, but he did wonder about these invol-

[36] A Bible-centered discussion of the question would treat the glossolalia (speaking in tongues) of the New Testament Pentecost story: "And when the day of Pentecost was fully come, they were all with one accord in one place. And suddenly there came a sound from heaven as of a rushing mighty wind, and it filled all the house . . . And there appeared unto them cloven tongues like as of fire . . . they were all filled with the Holy Ghost, and began to speak with other tongues . . . devout men, out of every nation under heaven . . . the multitude came together, and were confounded, because that every man heard them speak in his own language. And they were all amazed and marveled, saying one to another, Behold, are not all these which speak Galilaeans? And how hear we every man in our own tongue, wherein we were born? Parthians, and Medes, and Elamites, and the dwellers in Mesopotamia, and in Judaea, and Cappadocia, in Pontus, and Asia, Phrygia, and Pamphylia, in Egypt, and in the parts of Libya about Cyrene, and strangers of Rome, Jews and proselytes, Cretes and Arabians, we do hear them speak in our tongues the wonderful works of God. And they were all amazed, and were in doubt, saying one to another, What meaneth this?" (iPhone *The New Testament*, Acts 2:1–13). What this meaneth is that when God stops being mean, everyone speaks his mind and is by all understood.

untary recollections. Every decision he made was contextual, and he looked only at consequences and results. He left the mysteries of feelings and memory to the priests. Sometimes he thought that it might be wrong to leave the roots of the present in the hands of the altar-keepers: they extracted a heavy tax on them, and they turned them into greater mysteries than they already were. For all he knew, and strongly suspected, the priests were only keepers of fanciful symbols by means of which they guarded an empty vessel, as empty as a drained gourd, from which all true mysteries had fled. It wasn't fair for his daughter Sheherezade to ask such a thing of her father, but it had certainly been foolish of him to bring up her Fates, knowing that such mention would not easily get past his bright daughter. Nor could he answer her other question, as to the fair use of the Merchant's gift for understanding the language of beasts. Such a gift, being rare if not entirely invented for fabulistic purposes, had not manifested often enough in his jurisdiction to merit an opinion of law. If the Koran thought that the language of Allah was Arabic and the Merchant was a devout Muslim, then his beasts spoke Arabic and he should have practiced discretion. But if the Merchant was Persian, Chinese, or Hindu, then his beasts spoke those languages, and there was a profusion of moral commandments as to the disposition of information obtained from beasts, and this was not the time for such a discussion.

this was the time to knock some sense into his daughter

"You will see what happened soon enough and you can think better of whatever it is you're thinking of, Daughter," he said severely, "but I beg you to interrupt me no longer, or I shall be compelled to examine your recollection of what I have just said. What was the advice the Ass gave the Ox?"

"Oh," quoth Sheherezade, fearfully disappointed, "'Tomorrow morning,' the Ass said, 'when the Farmer comes early to harness you to the plow, do not get up. If he whips you, remain on the ground, with your head hanging in your filthy bed. No matter how hard he tries to make you get up, stay put, and if he tries even harder by switching to the iron-belted whip, scratch the ground with your paws in anger, make frightful noises, and start rushing at him with madness in your eyes so that he will be certain that you are going to kill him.' The astonished Ox said, 'But Ass, what if he kills me then and sends me to the roast-pit for disobedience?' 'He won't,' the Ass said firmly. 'He will conclude that you are sick and need care. He has need of you. He will bring you milk and wash you clean to cure you of your illness, he'll have your stall raked and freshened, and he will cut a window for you to look from. But you must refuse to get better. No matter how well they treat you and feed you, you must remain stubborn and threatening. When a month passes, he will beg you to plow the field, but if you do accept, you will do so under much better conditions, I promise.'

"Next day, the Ox did as the Ass advised. He lay still, he pawed, he threatened, and, true to the Ox's words, the Farmer cleaned his stall, combed him, and brought him choice hay to eat and cut a window in his dark cell. When days of such good treatment brought no improvement to the Ox, the Farmer saw the Merchant, who did not, at first, want to reveal what he had heard, despite the loss of money caused by the stubbornness of the Ox, either because he thought that his great gift obligated him to overlook the understandable weaknesses of his farm animals, or because he was afraid that the death sentence pursuant to his revelation of the gift might attach in some measure to any decision obtained from it. Still, after calculating, like any good Persian, the actual amount of the loss incurred by the advice the Ass gave the Ox, he told the Farmer to harness the Ass to the plow and whip him into the mud field and make him work until the night, leaving the Ox alone to his caprice. So the Farmer did as he was told, and when the Ass was brought back to his stall, he could barely stand. The next day he was whipped again before he was harnessed to the Yoke and was given slop to eat while the Ox lazed on clean hay and ate gourmet oats. On the third day, when the Ass was truly too weary to stand, the Farmer beat him with the iron-ball whip and boarded up the window with the view of the fields, and poked him in language so coarse the Ass couldn't believe his asinine ears. He now regretted bitterly having revealed to the Ox the secret for leading an easier existence."

"Wait, wait," cried the distraught Vizir, "I haven't even gotten to that part of the story."

"Sure, Father," Sheherezade said obediently, and waited for him to catch up.

"While the Ox lolled about in fresh hay," continued the Vizir, "and contemplated the world out the window with a view to becoming a poet, the Ass couldn't even manage to find a restful position for his sore bones or his tender skin. His eyes burned from looking straight ahead into the rising sun and into the setting sun on the way back. His irritated ears couldn't stand the blessings and praises the Ox bestowed upon him like a shower of fool's gold or burning straw. Over and over the Ox thanked him for his good advice and described in nauseating detail his leisure and his pleasure and the taste of his unhurried oats, as well as several artistic ideas, including rhymes, that he had forged in his mind in his time of freedom, and each one of these ideas was a spear in the Ass. And so, Daughter, this is what comes of trying to ease the suffering of others by offering your good sense to them. You will take their place and die in their stead, O silly good-hearted one. Do you think that any of them will remember you in gratitude after Sharyar has taken your maidenhead at night and your head in the morning? You will be worse than the Ass in your suffering, while those you saved from the King will gain but a short respite from his cruelty! Their turn will come when you are gone! You will have bought them but a day with your life."

Sheherezade laughed tenderly. Her father had no way of knowing that she prized her life much higher than one day; the price of her life was equal to the price of Sharyar's. She was going to take him with her, but even as she caressed the sharpened stiletto she carried in the folds of her robe, she was curious to know what the Ass had done.

"I mean to marry the King and no silly story is going to prevent it, but I would just like to know to what silly lengths the Ass went to regain his position."

"Very well then, listen well, foolish Daughter; there is more to come. The pained and sleepless Ass pondered late into the night how to take back his formerly privileged status. 'Ox,' he said, 'I fear that terrible things are in store for you. What are you doing?' The Ox had been contemplating the moon now that he had a window. 'Contemplating the moon,' he said, paining the Ass even more because the Ass had a window no more.

"Now, the Merchant, surrounded by his children and friends, sat with his wife on couches of rich carpets contemplating the same moon, which was very golden and ripe in Persia that night. He listened to his beasts in the stall and heard the Ass say: 'Today while you were lazing about composing verses, I overheard the Farmer tell the Merchant that your upkeep was not worth the expense now that you are not doing any work, and they have decided to send you to the roast-pit tomorrow.' 'What should I do?' cried the frightened Ox, now fully awake and inconsolable. 'Do not fret,' said the Ass. 'Tomorrow when they come to bring you your tasty oats, hold out your neck for the Yoke. Go into the field and pull even harder than you did when you were wretched. Do all you can to convince them in the coming days that you are back in your best health and ready to become the beast of burden they know so well.' 'How could that be?' wondered the Ox, startled hard from his delicious moon-absorption, 'when everything is working out precisely as you advised me?' 'This is true,' the weary Ass said, 'but I can understand their language, Allah be praised for this gift, and this is what I heard them say as I went about in the burning sun.'

"The Ox considered his choices and resolved to do as the Ass advised: his few days of freedom had taught him that living was worth the expense, even if the moon was no longer his. He did wonder briefly about the luck of the Ass who had even been granted by Allah the gift of understanding the language of humans, among his countless other blessings. 'Im'shallah, Ass,' he said, 'Allah made some of us sleek and smart and some of us dim and obedient.'

"Upon hearing this, the Merchant burst out laughing, and everyone around him started laughing, too, without knowing why. But his wife asked, 'What are you laughing about?' When the Merchant was able to stop laughing, he wiped away his tears and said, 'Wife, I cannot tell you. I am under a sentence of silence. If I told you what I was laughing about, I would die on the spot. I'm laughing at something I heard but cannot reveal because my death would follow on the instant.' Now his wife was sure that he was fibbing, that he was either laughing at her, or laughing about something he did not want her to know, maybe something another woman had said, something delicious and funny. She began to cry and throw her sadness about until the children began crying too, and all their friends got up and went to their homes. All night she cried and asked why, and all night he told her that he would be killed if he told, and all night she said, 'You must tell me.' 'But wife, I will die if I do. You will be left without a husband, our children will have no father, the business will collapse, and your life will become sad and hard.' 'I don't care,' the wife cried, 'you must tell me why you were laughing or I shall die myself at this very instant.'

"Days passed, but the wife would not forget the matter. Hassan had long since stopped laughing and was thinking only of ways to make her forget all about it. Nothing worked. Day in and day out and every night as well, she bothered him incessantly with her desire to know why he'd been laughing, and the more he tried to put the matter away, the harder she persisted. 'I prayed to Allah,' he confided in vain, 'to give me the

64

gift of understanding the language of beasts, and he granted my wish on condition that I never ever reveal what they say.' But his wife would not be placated. 'You wish me to die then?' he asked at last, weary from the long nights of discord, as the moon paled yet again in the sky. 'If you want me to die, I will tell you.' 'Yes,' she said, 'I want you to tell me, I don't care if you die.' 'Im'shallah,' he said, and told her that he would set his affairs in order and prepare for death. And for the next few days, that's what he did. At the end of the week he asked her one last time: 'Do you want me to die? If you do, you truly do, I will tell you.' 'Yes, I do, I do,' she said as gravely and solemnly as if she were saying her wedding vows. 'I must know why you were laughing; I do not care if you die.' 'Well, in that case,' the Merchant said, 'this is no longer a laughing matter,' and he went about calling together his children, his grandchildren, his brothers and sisters and their children and grandchildren, and his friends in the village. When a sizable crowd numbering hundreds of his kin and associates had gathered, he told them that he must reveal a secret to his wife, the price of which revelation would be his death. He reassured the assembled that his business was sound and that he was sufficiently prosperous to make provisions for all those present, especially his dear wife, so that all might benefit by his death. He paid his debts and he made gifts to the poor. He bequeathed the Ass and the Ox to his wife, along with his best fields. Those gathered in his house were astonished and asked his wife over and over to abandon her quest, but when no amount of persuasion from family and friends proved sufficient to make the wife change her mind, the restless people began eyeing the long table on which a multitude of covered dishes waited to be consumed in his honor after he died. Hassan then went to the bathhouse to take his ritual bath before death.

"He walked across his prosperous yard, full to bursting with busy, fat, happy animals, the result of his wise husbandry over the years. He saw the Dog running in a terrible hurry to the Rooster, who was engaged in mounting one of his hens, while his forty-nine other hens milled about waiting their turn and talking all at once. 'Rooster, Rooster,' cried the

Dog, 'haven't you heard the sad news? Our master is going to die this very day, and you go about shtooping your hen as if there were no other thing that mattered in the world.' 'And why,' asked the Rooster, without ceasing his activity, 'is our master going to die?' Breathlessly, the Dog responded, 'Because, because, Rooster, his wife must know a secret that will cause him to die if he tells her. She won't rest until she hears it, and he has agreed to tell and is right now walking to the bath to cleanse himself for death.' The Rooster, come to a peak of pleasure, nearly fell off his hen laughing. 'Well then,' he said, regaining his equilibrium, 'he fully deserves his death, this silly master of ours. He has but one wife and can't keep her in check, and I have fifty and they are all happy, as you can see. I mount one, I confide in another, I keep others waiting, I praise one's eggs, I ruffle another's feathers, I set one to counting eggs and another to hatching—I have them do a hundred busy things and take my pleasure all the while. If I were the master, this is what I would do: I would go to the mulberry tree, cut down some green switches, go to the wife, and take her to the bedchamber, where I would give her a good thrashing on her bare bottom, and if she still asked, I would keep on going over her legs and back and not stop until she fell to her knees and begged, "Master, I will never ask another question again! I beg you to stop!"'

"Hassan the Merchant, who understood every word that passed between his animals, was struck by the Rooster's good sense. He went to the mulberry tree and cut a good bundle of green switches. He returned to the house where his would-be mourners sat around his sulking wife, gossiping as if he were already gone, eyeing more and more openly the covered dishes. Without a word, he took his wife by the arm, led her to the bedchamber, stripped off her robe, and brought the switches down on her buttocks. After wailing and crying and shouting she saw that the thrashing would not stop, as the switches never broke and never ceased, and she shouted loud enough for the whole house to hear: 'Husband, I will never again ask that question! I beg you to stop!' And she added, for the benefit of the crowd, 'I will be a good wife and I will restrict my curiosity to the things that benefit you, not kill you!' So the Merchant ceased from his violence and his wife put her robe back on, and together they stepped arm in arm into the large room.

"The assembled gathering was astonished by all this, and by the sight of them, and most of them were not in the least disappointed because Hassan, a man with a good heart, decreed that the dishes meant for his death-honors be uncovered and eaten. The crowd fell to them and rejoiced in his survival. All but a few who stood to inherit, of course."

"And what am I to learn from this?" asked Sheherezade. "That mulberry branches make good whipping sticks?"

"You are to learn that if you insist on your foolish request to marry the King, I will do to you what the Merchant did to his wife!" her father burst out with what he hoped was ferocious credibility.

"Well, I must go to the King myself, then, and tell him that I offered myself to be his wife, but that his Chief Minister, the Vizir, my father, forbade me. How do you think that he'd take the news?"

Not well. Sheherezade looked at him silently, and he could not, for the life of him, understand what her gaze meant. It was not an arrogant look; it was not a look of foolish belief that she was somehow better than other women; it was not even a look of defiance. It was a mild gaze filled with tiny question marks with a glint of steel behind them. Indeed, Sheherezade wondered with affection at her father's naive faith in the power of such a simple parable. She wondered at the lovely simplicity of involving farm animals in the fate of the Persian Empire and the future of storytelling. But most of all, she wondered whether her father had any idea what was on his daughter's mind. She wondered also how it could be that such an authority as her father could not impose his will either on his superior or on his child. My father, thought Sheherezade, has only horizontal authority. He can compel the citizens of the empire to pay their taxes and follow the law, a horizontal chain of actions and consequences linked by chronology, custom, tradition, precedent. Her own authority, like that of King Sharyar, was vertical: he ruled from horseback, she from the blade of her knife, poised above his chest. The warrior-king and the assassin-wife had much more in common. Oh, poor Daddy, Sheherezade inwardly lamented, your horizon is endless; you ensure the status quo; you are a good man. Your daughter is a different species, my Mongol mother's daughter.

"And what precisely do you have to offer the King that other girls, some of them more beautiful than a drop of dew on the lip of a rose, could not offer him?" the sad father said.

"A story," replied Sheherezade, "a long story. It will be as it was with the Merchant and the wife, only he will be the wife and I will be the Merchant. I'll make him my bitch. And he'll be the cat, the one curiosity killed."

The Vizir knew not what his daughter had just said, and he felt guilty, as well he should, because he had just told his daughter that she was nothing, just one of many hens in the rooster's harem, and that her sacrifice would come to naught: new hens would take her place, but she, the apple of her father's eye, would be dead. He mixed his metaphors some more, and then went to work, seeing that there was no way to deter Sheherezade from her foolishness. The Vizir froze his heart and capped the fountain of tears. Leaving her to be prepared by women for her fleeting nuptials, he went to King Sharyar and told him that he was offering him his daughter Sheherezade that night.

The astonished King reminded him that he had sworn not to harm his children, but the sad Chief Minister explained that it had been Sheherezade's own idea. "Oh, immeasurably naive and unfortunate girl," lamented the King, "does she not know what the fate of my wives is? And do you, her father, not take measures to protect her? It is your job to see to it that my wife of a night is strangled. If you fail to carry out your duty, I shall take your life instead before her eyes, then take hers myself."

"You do not know Sheherezade, great King! Her mind is filled with dreams and her memory is stuffed with teachings of every sort. She is a splendid rider, an idol to her sister and friends, and she will listen to nothing but her own counsel. If I were to imprison her, she'd find a clever way out. If I tied her to a post, she'd persuade the post to sink into the ground to free her. She is a master of chess and a lover of algebra, geometry, and languages. I had planned for her a future as an ambassador of Your Highness's empire. She prefers your company for one night instead."[37]

Sharyar became quite intrigued by this advertisement, though he had promised himself only wives with minds as clean of letters as a fresh snowfield. As for Sheherezade, he had glimpsed her in the palace and liked her vivaciousness and her languor, two contradictory qualities that she embodied. When he looked at her, she looked back and then vanished, instead of lowering her gaze and falling to the floor as women were required to do. He had seen her also way too often outside the women's quarters, intent on some scroll she carried in her hand, or walking purposefully to some inner chapel. He knew that she had important teachers and was looked upon as some kind of prodigy. After the Vizir left, Sharyar called his Chief of Bodyguards and asked him to charge the kingdom's best investigators with the task of finding out all that could be known about Sheherezade, beginning in her childhood, with special attention to the details of her life during his absence. He demanded that the investigation begin immediately, and that it be truthful, unsparing of anyone, and secret. Not long after, he received

the findings: scroll one

Sheherezade's father, the Vizir, to whom you entrusted your kingdoms while you were seeking Allah's divine guidance in the desert with your brother, Shahzaman, has served your father, the

---

[37] In the 20th century, the daughters of New Orleans gentry were often given a choice: go to college or be Queen of a Carnival krewe for one night. The two cost the same and aimed for the same goal: a husband.

King of Kings, King Shahanshah, with honor. He was by your side in your childhood and youth, Your Majesty, and was charged, among other things, with your education. When the Vizir's first daughter, Sheherezade, was born, your father was overjoyed on behalf of the Vizir, and he ordered a great feast in honor of the Fating. According to custom, only firstborn sons are accorded Fatings, but your father so prized his Vizir he broke with custom. The ceremony of the Fating itself is attended only by women, but the feast that follows blesses all, including the lowest servants.

On the appointed day, the women of the family gathered around the crib of the Vizir's daughter, Sheherezade, and prayed until one of the Fates appeared. And then, to everyone's surprise, another. And after a few moments, another yet. It was a great blessing to have three Fates, because there were more children born than there were Fates, and the Fates were always in a hurry, arriving from different times and places, at times not even speaking the same language; they were woefully overworked. Their job was to apportion a fate to each newborn child, bestow a future on it, as well as watch over it to make sure that the future they had given it unfolded as told. Being wrong could mean the end of their job as Fates, which was akin to erasure, though they were, for all other purposes, immortal. They traveled from place to place, like itinerant actors or musicians, and no one knew who might arrive at the side of a newborn. It has to be said that things are not much improved since the days of the King of Kings, and the quality of the Fates keeps declining, a matter that we, Your Majesty's chief spies, believe should be discussed.

The Fates attending Sheherezade's birth were late creations, appointed long after the fearful Fates of ancient Greece had retreated into myth. Sheherezade's Fates, in addition to numbering three, were also well versed in the history of Fates, bearing on their shoulders not only the duty of apportioning an appropriate destiny, but also the knowledge of past Fates and the awesome powers they had once had. In the Greek world their ancestors had been the sisters Moirae, the daughters of Zeus, feared even by their father; their names were Clotho, the "spinner," who spun the thread of life from her distaff onto her spindle; Lachesis, the "allotter," or drawer of lots, who measured the thread of life allotted to each person with her measuring rod; and Atropos, the "inevitable," or the "unturner," who was the cutter of the thread of life and chose the manner and timing of each person's death. When she cut the thread with her shears, their charge died; her Roman equivalent was Morta, death. Each Moira controlled one-third of a newborn's future life, but human newborns were merely their day job: at night they amused themselves by toying with the gods. The gods quivered at their approach, because their foreknowledge held as much dread for them as it held for humans—perhaps more, because immortality ensured only that the dreadful things that were sure to happen to them might be even more dreadful than they imagined (their immortality did not, alas, confer self-knowledge). The mother of the Fates was Nyx (Night), who was also the mother of the Erinyes, the three Furies, who were neither as wise nor as playful as their sisters, the Moirae. The Pythian priestess at Delphi feared the Erinyes but was only in awe of the Moirae's sagacity. The Erinyes were thrice as fierce as the Moirae precisely because they lacked self-knowledge: they were endowed with boundless energy and a wicked imagination. Their family reunions, presided over by Nyx, were wild affairs, like the meetings of outlaws; the gods knew to clear out on these occasions, preferring the company of humans to Nyx's orgies. Over time these doings receded into myth, like all beginnings. If time was a death sentence for humans, for gods it was a boredom sentence. The descendants of those first Fates engaged in the same trade, though with considerably less anarchy.

The lineage of Sheherezade's Fates was not very clear then, though they were still descendants of the Moirae and Nyx. When they approached the crib, the women cried out in dismay, seeing that the Fates were all men. Happily, the chief Carpet-Weaver in those days, who was a learned woman, remembered that the Fates of the Christian God were called the Three Wise Men, so things had changed and there was precedent. She calmed down the assembly and told them that much water had flowed down Lethe, the river of forgetting, since the Greeks. Generations of Fates had come from all geographical directions, speaking Babylonian, Greek, Norse, Latin, Aramaic, Hebrew, Mongolian, Bedouin Arabic, Chinese, Hindi, sacred Sanskrit, Persian, and bastardized Arabic Egyptian. Eventually, the need for Fates had grown so great, they were even being recruited from the future, she sighed. This was quite unfair and lacking grandeur, because those Fates from the future knew each child's destiny from a much longer perspective; for them it wasn't even a matter of bestowing a fate, but often just a survey of what had already happened, a prior knowledge that was repackaged to look like an original gift. Fates like that, who needs them? Any oracle can do *that* job. But tradition is tradition and, besides, a great feast awaited them all when the ceremony was completed. She sighed and everyone sighed with her.

Sheherezade was lucky. She had drawn a trio of Fates who, even though they were men from the future, had her interests at heart, because, as it turned out, their existence depended on her. In addition to providing her with a unique mission, they were charged with acquainting her with a complicated story that would in time make possible her appearance within her destiny, a story that was unlike any that anyone present had ever heard.

You will shortly see what we mean, but we would like to add a significant detail that may escape Your Majesty's recall. Mixed in the crowd surrounding the cradle were two boys dressed as girls at the request of your father, the King of Kings, Shahanshah, who was himself dressed in women's clothes: the two boys were none other than yourself and your Exalted Brother, Shahzaman. Your father, the King of Kings, made an unusual request of the Vizir: he desired to be present, with his sons, at the ceremony of the Fates for his newborn. The Vizir did wonder at King Shahanshah's odd request, but since custom had already been breached in the Fating of a girl, he assented. He ordered female disguises for yourself and King Shahzaman, and saw to it that the King of King's silk robes were of the finest quality. And so it happened that when the Fates fated Sheherezade, your father heard the future. You were very young, Your Majesty, at that age when there is slight difference between boys and girls, so you did not take in the ceremony very attentively. Being fifteen years of age, you were naturally more preoccupied with the not-unpleasant and strange feelings that the delicate fabrics and jingles of your anklets and bracelets gave you, and you were distracted by the young visiting princesses, as is only fitting, and so it is not a failing in you to have heard nothing of what the Fates told the baby.

Here, the reporter of *the findings: scroll one* stepped inadvertently over the border of facts and allowed himself some philosophical liberty. (Police reports had not yet acquired the dry faux-factuality that would characterize them in the future.)

In those days, O great King, in matters of importance there were always three of everything. There was, for instance, the merchant who stopped to rest in the shade of a date tree by the sea to eat his lunch. The tree was heavy with ripe dates and he gorged himself on them, chasing them down with raki from his flask. He then spit out the date stones on the ground. A frightful Genius rose from the sea, darkening the sky, and told him to make ready to die. The terrified merchant wanted to know why, and the Genius told him that he had killed his son with the date pits he had spit out. There was no arguing, though the merchant tried: how could such pitifully small stones kill a giant's son? The Genius would hear none of it, so the merchant begged for a reprieve of thirty days to go back home to set his affairs in order, after which time he would return to the same spot to be killed. The Genius granted him this; the merchant did as he had said and, after thirty days, returned to meet his death. While he stood at the ready, an old man leading a chained gazelle stopped to ask him what he was waiting for. On hearing that he was waiting for death at the hands of a Genius whose son had been killed by date pits, the traveler asked permission to stay and watch. A second traveler with two black greyhounds came by and asked for the story, and he, too, wanted to stay and watch. A third wayfarer happened by with a she-mule, and he likewise heard the story and stayed. Finally, the waves parted, and the Genius funneled out of the angry water, scimitar in hand, as the date-killer bowed his head for severing. The first traveler stayed the hand of the sea-giant by proposing to tell him a story of such interest that if the Genius found it satisfying, he might want to reward him with one-third of the condemned man's blood. This he did, and the Genius found it satisfying indeed and granted the traveler with the gazelle one-third of his prisoner. The traveling owner of the two black greyhounds promised a similar tale in exchange for another third of the condemned, and he, too, told a tale extraordinary enough to cause the monster to release another third. Finally, the traveler with the she-mule obtained another third by the same means, and the merchant was saved. All the tales that redeemed the merchant's life were extraordinary, so extraordinary in fact that they not only stayed the monster's hand, but they saved Sheherezade's life during the first night of her marriage to you, great King. This brings Your Highness up-to-date, but this reporter does not presume to know what will go on tonight, so he will not get ahead of himself. The sails of the *Nights* will not unfurl until Sheherezade, Dinarzad, and Your Majesty are firmly planted in your bed-ship tonight and voyaging to unknown places.

Sharyar had no idea what this meant, but he supposed it to be a poetic image. He did not envision any circumstance under which the next night would end with anything but a morning strangling. He would

38 With all due respect to Sharyar, the future would prove the spy right, at least in the circulating versions of the *Nights* where the Merchant and the Genius story comes first. In the light of what follows in **the findings: scroll one**, we can safely assume that the spy reporting to Sharyar on the matter of Sheherezade came from the future. We can also safely assume that Sharyar had no idea what he was talking about. We have tried to find out who the authors of **the findings** were, and this difficult undertaking (spies then, as now, operated under covers and pseudonyms) revealed two possible sources: two eunuchs so valued for their prettiness that they were shared for amusement by all the bearded men in the kingdom, and by women as well; while occupied by their service of being penetrated, stroked, or made to tongue, they were told everything there is to tell, partly because their employers tried to delay their orgasms by tattle telling; the names of the eunuchs were Toomusz and Notenouf, according to one poet.

nonetheless remember this part of the report best for many years to follow, not because the expected did not happen, but because Sheherezade told an entirely different story, and he had spared her life to hear *its* ending. This story, he would later reflect, about a merchant redeemed by old men, had no charm. This discrepancy would make Sharyar doubt later findings, to some extent, but he would forgive them their errors: so many things will have happened, by then, that errors were not just possible but inevitable and, perhaps, desirable. It was also conceivable that the merchant story lacked charm because it was reported by a spy, not murmured enchantingly by Sheherezade, just as it was possible that the spy had somehow confused the story of the first night with one that came later.[38]

since no story can proceed without its founding tripod,

the report continued, invoking Allah at the very beginning of all stories establishes the presence of all his dominions: earth, heaven, and the underworld. The Fates and the assembled thus invoked the name of Allah, the All-Seeing, the All-Knowing, and the All-Just.

39 Antoine Galland, French orientalist and numismatist, was born in Picardy in 1646. In 1675, 29-year-old Galland accompanied the marquis de Nointel to Jerusalem, and in 1679 he was charged by the King of France to report on the Levant. He learned modern Greek, Turkish, Persian, and Arabic, and in 1701 he was appointed to the chair of Arabic at the Collège de France. He is chiefly famous for his translation of *The Arabian Nights* (Paris, 1704–8). At his death he left many translations, including "Indian tales and fables of Pidpa and Lokman"; "History of the princes of the line of Tamerlane," translated from the work of the Persian historian Abdel-Rezzac; "Ottoman History," translated from the Turkish of Nam Effendi; "History of Ghengis-Khan," from the Persian history of Nurkhoud. Galland was accused, by Haddawy among others, of fabricating the story of Sinbad the Sailor in the *1001 Nights*, but if he did, we say Amen; we are sure, however, that he didn't, stories of this kind having been currency for centuries in the cauldron of the Levant, and the "near" and "far" East. Antoine Galland can be said to be also Andrew Lang, who adapted his translations into English, and praised his renderings for having "dropped out the poetry and a great deal of what the Arabian authors thought funny, though it seems wearisome to us. In this book [*The Arabian Nights Entertainments,* ed. Andrew Lang] the stories are shortened here and there, and omissions are made of pieces suitable only for Arabs and old gentlemen."

40 Captain Sir Richard Francis Burton (1821–1890), English explorer, translator, writer, soldier, orientalist, ethnologist, linguist, poet, hypnotist, fencer, and diplomat. He was a captain of the East India Company, a spy, a satyr, a master of *taquia* (disguise), a convert to Sufi Islam, and the first white man to visit Mecca (disguised as an Arab). Guided by Omani merchants, he traveled

Sheherezade's three Fates were called Antoine Galland,[39] Richard F. Burton,[40] and Husain Haddawy.[41] They came from the future, from a time when people no longer believed in Fates, so the three of them were known in their time as *translators*.[42] The occupation that gave them their names, *translation*, had become the only fate that people of the 18th, 19th, 20th, and 21st centuries were willing to accept. A person had a destiny in those future centuries only to the extent that one was translated. We must add a footnote here on the process whereby translation became synonymous with fate. Your Highness can skip this footnote without fear of losing the thread of the larger story, but if you don't, you will be rewarded by surprises concerning your own fate, as well as

to the Great Lakes of Africa in search of the source of the Nile. He was engaged by the Royal Geographical Society to explore the east coast of Africa and led an expedition guided by the locals, which discovered Lake Tanganyika. Explorers in the 19th century believed that the source of the Nile was a kind of planetary Rosetta Stone, but it was in fact only a romantic feat, a poetic adventure. In the 21st century, any humble device that incorporates a GPS is more efficient than the great-

est territorial romance. Not so with languages. In his later life, Burton served as British consul in Damascus and Trieste. He spoke 29 European, Asian, and African languages, and translated, in addition to *The Book of the Thousand Nights and a Night*, the *Kama Sutra*. His prolific journals and writings were only partly seen because, after his death, his wife burned most of them for reasons of English propriety. Unlike Galland-Lang, he delighted in precisely those things "only suitable for Arabs and old gentlemen." These are the facts, but this personage, portrayed in many biographies, was more than the sum of his parts. We greatly regret Isabel Burton's act of posthumous vandalism, not because she disposed of reams of writing (in some writers' cases this would be a blessing), but because Burton was a careful observer and compulsive note-taker who wrote down the minutiae of everything he saw, even if he had to use his underwear and improvised ink for his notes. We know that Isabel was no angel herself and that she partied with Sir Richard in more than unconventional ways, but we wish that she'd valued sodomy, pederasty, and Sapphism at least as highly as local cuisine (she left the manuscripts concerning it untouched).

[41] Husain Haddawy was teaching English at the University of Nevada in Reno when his translation of *The Arabian Nights*, based on Muhsin Mahdi's edited manuscript of the 14th-century Syrian text of the *Nights*, was published in 1990. Professor Haddawy was born and grew up in Baghdad, taught English and comparative literature at various American universities, wrote art criticism, and is now living in retirement in Thailand. The vehement introduction to his translation reveals a deep fissure among academic Arabists, some of whom, like Mahdi and Haddawy, attempted to claim the *Nights* for some kind of exclusive Arabic imaginary. Like many overtly or covertly political attempts to give any imaginary a national character, this one has no reality; it has even less reality than Edward Said's nearly successful attempt of lumping all oriental studies together with imperialism in the notion of "orientalism." Neither imprisoning a woman in a nationalist cage nor throwing out the baby with the bathwater works in this case. The *Nights* are a world, a world, moreover, that deconstructs the imperial and theological worlds set up by Islam in various phases of self-consciousness. If anything, attempts to assign the *Nights* to a psychological-theological space underscore the practices of slavery, subjugation of women, sanctioned sodomy, pederasty, and drug addiction that were widely practiced in the "oriental" space for centuries before and after Islam, practices that, I might add, held great fascination and charm for "Westerners" sick of Christianity, and writers such as Richard Burton, Lawrence of Arabia, Isabella Eberhardt, Paul and Jane Bowles, and William Burroughs.

[42] Each of the three translators, Sheherezade's Fates, had had three Fates present at *his* birth; their Fates were drawn by lot from a vast array of past and future translators, commentators, and fictionalizers of the *Arabian Nights*; altogether they would have had nine Fates, among whom we must mention Honoré de Balzac, the blind Argentine writer Jorge Luis Borges, the Italian linguist and novelist Umberto Eco, the American novelist John Barth, and the Anglo-Indian novelist Salman Rushdie. Barth was Richard F. Burton's Clotho, and he wrote a robustly heterosexual history of Sheherezade (whom he called "Sherry") and Dinarzad (called by vari-

ous nicknames, including "Duni"); his manly need to straighten out Burton had the opposite effect: the baby Burton grew to loathe the gingerly concern Clotho Barth showed for the sisters' menstrual cycles, and the clever manner in which he worked his way around the misogynistic violence of Sharyar's world; he did appreciate the class analysis that revealed just how impossible it was for the noble women of the kingdom to mount an armed revolt without the support of their husbands, but he did not buy for a second the idea that the rivers of blood that ran through the warrior-kingdom were less criminal than other mythical crimes; the baby Burton who grew

a partial, very partial, view of the distant future, and we promise that Sheherezade, the subject of the report, will not be lost by it.[43]

the fates speak:

Richard F. Burton, or Clotho, the "spinner," began to spin the story of what happened before Sheherezade assumed her storytelling destiny, with another invocation to Allah. He said,[44] "Praise be to Allah, the Compassionating, Lord of the Three Worlds . . . ," and so on, through all of Allah's ninety-nine official names plus ones he set himself to inventing, such as "Who set up the Firmament without Pillars in its Stead and Who stretched out the Earth even as a Bed . . ." until Husain Haddawy, Lachesis, the allotter, interrupted him angrily, exclaiming, "Why can't you just say, 'God knows and sees best'?" Galland laughed. This was not his duel.

into the horseman who spoke Arabic spent much of his youth washing from his ears the booming verdicts of postmodernity inserted there by John Barth. Balzac, who became the "great Balzac" only after he transposed one of the Nights to Paris in *La peau de chagrin*, was Galland's Clotho. Umberto Eco, who was Burton's Lachesis, confined himself to stretching a paragraph from the *Nights* into the book-length tale *The Name of the Rose*. The more modest Fates of the other translators also contented themselves with squeezing Sheherezade's fancies for drops of inspiration. The same situation pertained in some measure to all the three babies (future Fates/translators) employed here, all of whom received the story of Sheherezade with many footnotes from various future and past meddlers and *penseurs*, including the one currently writing this, who (I confess) was also one of the Fates present at Richard F. Burton's birth; he (I) was Atropos, the job of Antoine Galland in the story you are reading.

[43] *translation*: After Babel, fate became the necessity to translate. To exist for others one needed to translate, an activity that wasn't confined to languages. People's more and more complicated inner lives demanded explication to even one's dearest and nearest, and, more and more often, to one's self, to the extent that the thing called "self" still existed in a future that deconstructed it for the purpose of selling it in small increments. Until the 20th century the telling of history, the chronicles of great events, had the greatest importance as the facts recalled in the language of conquerors sought to erase the more poorly distributed memories of those who'd been there. Toward the end of the 20th century a series of analyses revealed that families, tribes, religions, and nations had been born from a series of translation mistakes that had become the founding stones of empires and reasons for war. Differences could be resolved only by translation, which was a negotiation, often a retranslation coming at the end of conflict after a great loss of life. Each god, herm's cult, the tribe that worshipped herm, and the founding epic that justified claims to a separate identity were founded on cherished translation mistakes renegotiated through heavenly and earthly wars for the purpose of retranslation. The uncovering of these mistakes through deconstruction did not lead to their correction. On the contrary, mistakes started to be celebrated as generators of civilization. If such a gross mistranslation as the golden tablets of the Mormons could lead to the development of a great civilization, such as that of the Mormons in Utah, then, clearly, it was *necessary* to make a great mistake *at*

"Because," Burton Clotho said, "a proper invocation must be spun in such a way as to draw the listener into the story, to suspend time, to ask for the indulgence of one who existed before time, thus reassuring listeners that they are in the hands of a blessed tale-spinner, one who has divinity on her side," and then he gave a brief lecture on invocations at the beginning of tales, a lecture that never left his lips because the impatient Haddawy Lachesis from the late 20th century had the attention span of a gnat, like everyone else at the end of that century. For all that, we cannot let Burton's learned remarks pass in silence, so we'll say only that he spoke in elegant, roundish phrases loaded with the tonic fruit of lifetimes of experience riding fast horses and standing perfectly still in infernally hot tents, sweat streaming down his insect-covered body as he labored over the Hindu prose of the *Kama Sutra* and the Arabic of the *Nights*; he spoke in the ironic tones of an homme-du-monde whose greatest appeal, he let everyone know, was being unafraid to experience wonder. He clearly valued horses and monkeys above scribes and

the beginning. This was understood already in Sheherezade's time when the carpet-weaver left an intentional flaw in the weave, in recognition of the fact that only God's handiwork is perfect. The flaw in the weave might seem small compared with a mistake in translation, but thanks to Sheherezade we now know that it was not. Of this we will have occasion to speak later, but it suffices to say that Sheherezade adored mistakes: she saw them as opportunities to straighten out the narrative whenever it teetered dangerously on the edge of disenchantment because of some sudden reality check, such as a ringing bell, or the untimely call of a muezzin with a cold. She experienced a physical tremor, a flush of delight when she found herself on the edge of a reality cliff; her great ingenuity was called to the fore in such an instant, a call that touched her nerves and tensed her muscles; her nomad senses awoke then, and she felt ready to fight to the death for fiction. Of course, at this moment she is still a baby bound tightly in fine cloth, looking like a butterfly larva, but this is a good place to note that by the time her 1001 nights of stories arrived in Arab space, they were already translations from many languages; by the time they settled into writing, they had Arabic and Turkish veneer hastily added on; by the time Galland arrived to bring them over to lacquer into French, they were already universal, mythic structures that could be read like large buildings, in Hindi, Sumerian, Greek, Chinese, Aramaic, or Arabic, depending on the position from which one contemplated the structures. Different "postcards" of the *Nights* were mailed to Europe from 15th-century Syria, but like "Chinese" porcelain made in China for Europeans, the "views" were only those currently in demand.

[44] For what Richard F. Burton said at length, consult pp. 1–24 of his translation of *The Book of the Thousand Nights and a Night*. I have used here only those things that outline the story before the stories proper of the *1001 Nights*, headed by some of Burton's most striking language. For the full flavor of the rhymed prose and fanciful poetry of the arrogant and erudite Burton, go to the source. You will be rewarded by a kind of languorous paralysis, brought about by Burton's vigorous libertinage and his intimate acquaintance with Arabic and Arabs, an intimacy that made it possible for him to keep his colonial Englishman's prejudices intact, and to mythologize his subjects simultaneously. Orientalism is in full bloom here, and its grotesque flowers are still headily appealing to the senses.

preachers, and made it abundantly clear that a healthy eros is preferable to learning, if a choice has to be made. A choice not only does not have to be made, but the mixture, he let it be understood, is exhilarating and a path to God. There is nothing, he said, more pleasing to God than an uncompromising erection in a library. He gave his audience a description of the library: heavy with rolled papyrus and walls covered with splendid carpets between crystal windows that let in rich autumn light as naked boys[45] brought the hard-as-rock scholar his requested books.

"For Chrissakes,"[46] interrupted Haddawy Lachesis, who spoke American English and would never take Allah's name in vain, "this is a baby girl whose fate we are revealing, and you go on about naked boys . . ."

B. Clotho raised an eyebrow and said, "In the crib before you lies the Library itself, my good man . . . It is to her I speak, to her and all womankind . . ." This stopped H. Lachesis just long enough for Burton Clotho to continue: "My Library of Libraries," he said to the baby in the crib and to everyone else who was listening, "I will now tell the story into which you will walk to begin your destiny." He then proceeded, in the inimitable style that we cannot even begin to paraphrase, to tell the story that Your Highness will come to know in due time.

The fate that B. Clotho, H. Lachesis, and G. Atropos each told in his own words about the future of the baby Sheherezade was true but only insofar as it was the translation the Fates made of the history that Your Highness is going to experience in the flesh. They repeated for those gathered at the Fating that your bride, freshly deflowered, will begin telling stories in your bed for one thousand nights and one. This prophecy you did hear, great

[45] This was one of many misunderstandings between R. Burton and H. Haddawy; it is possible that Burton had said "youths," but Haddawy heard "boys." At issue was more than simple mishearing: a quarter of a century of feminist theory has thrown a great deal of light on the hideous sexism no longer acceptable at the end of the 20th century; Burton's sexism was also aware of itself, and there is an ongoing struggle visible in Burton's writings, an effort to overcome through exaggeration the prejudices of his day, an excessive push into absurdity of "oriental" cruelty. Burton admired violence, both for its own sake and in the service of a "higher" cause, but had no tolerance for injustice; in the absence of "theory" he resorted to the Absurd, a quality that has always stood by good men and was a weapon in the hands of storytellers.

[46] "For Chrissakes," related to "Zounds!," originating in the expression "By God's Wounds!," first used by Shakespeare, then by cartoons. Christ's Five Wounds were a Christian believer's greatest articles of meditation and empathy. This is a good example of just how thinly sliced and fertile the 1st through 6th centuries of the Christian millennium were: the five wounds of Christ generated five religious orders, numerous styles of wound-imitation, and mythologies specific to each wound, from which followed visual and written iconographies of the human body and its earthly and divine purposes. The five wounds were "the four corners" (hands and feet pierced by nails) and the almond-shaped wound in the side. The wound in

King, but being of an age when the words of old men made no impression, you may have forgotten them, so this reporter takes the liberty of recalling them.

sharyar was eager to marry sheherezade that very night,

having heard such strange things about her, but he had to wait because even though the nights were brief and the mornings swift, the ceremony of marriage had to be performed by priests, documents had to be signed, witnesses had to testify as to the purity of the bride, incense had to be burned, choice fowl and meats had to be consumed, and wedding music had to sound. In the old days, such an occasion would have been greeted by popular rejoicing, but knowing what they knew, the people of Baghdad began weeping as soon as they heard the wedding music, and many a gentle soul died in the night by its own hand rather than hear of another death in the morning. The ceremony, even in its abbreviated form, was a funeral rite as well as a wedding, so even the most callous courtiers found it hard to swallow the nuptial viands. The Vizir was more upset than anyone, but his face had turned to stone. He pronounced the wedding legally binding before the clock had struck midnight. The guests disappeared as quickly as the dishes, and musical instruments vanished into their cases like ghosts in their shrouds. None of this mattered to Sharyar, who was so intrigued by the report about his new wife, he could think only of the sound of the bedroom door closing behind the two of them, and this he told his veiled princess.

the side is sometimes depicted so that its meaty edges allow for a view to the interior of Christ's body: the bleeding carnal edges resemble a menstruating vagina or a bleeding mouth that "all mystics long to kiss when they kiss the crucifix, possibly for performing a transfusion, a mystical communion with the Savior." In some representations, Christ himself urges this delirium on the believer by exhibiting his wound, pointing to it with his finger. "St. Thomas' doubt . . . causes the apostle to insert one or maybe several fingers inside the resurrected Christ's chest; the open wound offers itself to the gaze of the astonished saint whose uncertain hand . . . [,] guided by Christ, explores the opening" (Jacques Gélis, in *Histoire du corps*, ed. Alain Corbin, Jean-Jacques Courtine, Georges Vigarello). The repertoire (or choreography) of gestures of the moment of conversion to one wound or another in Christian iconography proceeds from the "iconography of the moment" of conversion by Mary Magdalene, the Christian Sheherezade. The mystics' goal of emptying themselves of the body is also the attempt to eliminate all stories, leaving only one story: that of Christ, whose suffering body they imitate with puppet-bodies, flesh marionettes frozen in prayer, Christ without the Magdalene and her tales (of resurrection).

[47] Each night, in Sharyar's bed, storytelling begins anew in this way, *"When it was night and Sharazad was in bed with the King, Dinarzad said to her sister Sharazad, 'Please, if you are not sleepy, tell us one of your lovely little tales to while away the night.' The King added, 'Yes, let us hear the conclusion.' Sharazad replied, 'As you wish,'"* and each story ends in Sharyar's bed with the formula *"but morning overtook Sharazad, and she lapsed into silence. As the day dawned, and it was light, her sister Dinarzad said, 'What a strange and wonderful story!' Sharazad replied, 'Tomorrow night I shall tell something even stranger and more wonderful than this.'"*
This is Husain Haddawy's 1990 translation into English, a translation based on the decades-long work

"Three," she corrected him.

"Did I hear you right, my Queen? Three?"

"Yes," Sheherezade said, "I beg Your Majesty's permission to allow my sweet little sister, Dinarzad, to join us in our nuptial bed. She is delightful and eager and so fond of me that she cannot stand not to see me for what may be the last time."

"May be . . . ," laughed Sharyar, "It *shall* be the last time. All my brides die in the morn."

"Then I might as well die now," said Sheherezade, with her arm wrapped around the shoulders of Dinarzad, who was weeping. "I am ready to die; call our father now!" Her other arm was draped across her chest and her hand disappeared within her gold-threaded dress as her fingers closed around the stiletto.

Sharyar looked at her hidden hand, as if sensing its intention. "Very well," he said, "Dinarzad may assist."

And thus it came to pass that the three of them went over the threshold of the King's bedchamber and made for the carpet-bed that began to

with the 14th-century Syrian manuscript undertaken by Harvard professor Muhsin Mahdi. Haddawy's late 20th-century translation of the formulaic device for entering and exiting each night dispenses entirely with the chilling framework within which the *Nights* take place: there is no hint that Sheherezade (whom he spells *Sharazad*) will be killed in the morning like all of King Sharyar's wives before her; there is no hint that the King is a serial killer, a dim tyrant ruled by jealousy, with an infantile need to have a bedtime story, and no hint that it is precisely this infantile streak that Sheherezade counts on to keep his murderous rage in check (she understands that in her storytelling capacity she must mother him, while her younger sister, Dinarzad, is there to provoke his lust); there is no hint that we are dealing with a threesome in a tenuous Oedipal balance steadied by the skillful manipulation of Sharyar's libido through questioning and answering in a manner that delays his orgasm night after night; there is no hint that the marvelous stories that he and we are about to hear are the desperate tricks of two young girls trapped in the bed of their killer with only imagination for defense; there is no hint that this King's long story of betrayal by his wife and his subsequent adventures with his equally betrayed brother, Shahzaman, have preceded Sheherezade's first night by many years; there is no hint either that there is cultural realism here, introduced by the 14th-century Syrian anthologist who collected the stories Haddawy based his translation on—this anthologist gave the stories Sheherezade's voice, a place (the court of Haroun al Rasheed), religion (Islam), and the city (Baghdad and/or Cairo). There is no hint of the religious framework that the stories subvert, but Haddawy is actually indignant about the liberties translators such as Galland and Burton took in including (or even inventing, Allah forbid!) stories that are not in the "pure" Arabian/Syrian manuscript toiled over by Professor Muhsin Mahdi. *"The failures of past translations,"* Dr. Haddawy tells us, *"lie in assuming the work to be other than it was intended to be, a collection of tales told to produce aesthetic pleasure in the Arabic reader."* He lambastes one translator, Edward Lane, for *"emasculating"* the text, Richard Burton for reproducing *"Arabic peculiarities"* and *"idiosyncracies of his own,"* and Galland for *"altering it to suit French taste."* Professor Haddawy assumes (1) that the listener or reader was *Arab*; and (2) that distortion up to its apex of *"emasculation"* occurs in the work of Western translators. But the anthologist, who wrote Arabic, collected stories commonly *told* in marketplaces and coffeehouses, most of them originating sway like a boat in a rising wind, and all of them stepped aboard. Long hours passed like stormy waves, and when the sea was becalmed after many a trial, there was but one hour left before dawn and all three of them lay sleeplessly side by side listening to their own thoughts. It was then, one hour before sunrise, that Dinarzad asked in a hushed voice: "Sheherezade, can you tell us one of your stories?"

"If my husband allows it," said Sheherezade.
"You might as well," said the King.[47]

"it is the story of the monkey-scribe,"

Sheherezade said.
"And what of it?" grumbled Sharyar, "you'll still meet your fate in the morn. What of this monkey?"

in India, China, Persia, and Greece before the writing of the Koran. Having gained popularity in medieval Baghdad and Cairo, invoking Allah became a convention, a satirical device to warn listeners that under Allah's omnipotent protection, spicy stories will be told. When the storyteller got down to the business of entertaining his tobacco-and-hashish-smoking, tea-and-coffee-drinking audience, he did so in whatever language or slang was called for. Multiple manuscripts of the *Nights* circulated in the Middle East from the 9th century on, and while only the 14th-century Syrian manuscript is extant, the Galland and Lane translations were also based on Egyptian and Turkish versions that no longer exist, but were published in Calcutta and Cairo at the same time as the Galland edition, from which they also borrowed. Stories are a nomad business, and their listeners or readers are whoever puts a piastre or a shilling in the storyteller's or bookseller's hat; the *Nights* were most certainly not told for the aesthetic pleasure of the Arab reader, which is not even a convention of the stories themselves: they are told for the pleasure of a (possibly Arab) tyrant, orally, in bed, for the unaesthetic desire of living for another night; the aesthetic pleasure born of terror is then recalled for pleasure in the coffeehouses and marketplaces. The circulating manuscripts of the *Nights* were most likely used by itinerant storytellers as scripts for learning them—they were performance scripts, which is why so few survived; they were *used*. And finally, it is in the nature of the *Nights* to invite the listener/reader to participate, to add, to invent, to imagine *more*.

"*And Shahrazad perceived the dawn of the day and ceased her permitted say. Then quoth her sister to her, 'How fair is thy tale, and how grateful, and how sweet and how tasteful!' And Shahrazad answered her, 'What is this to what I could tell thee on the coming night, were I to live and the King would spare me?' Then said the King in himself, 'By Allah, I will not slay her, until I shall have heard the rest of her tale.' So they slept the rest of the night in mutual embrace till day fully brake.*" and, "*When it was the next night, said Dunyazad to her sister Shahrazad, 'O my sister, finish for us that story . . . ,' and she answered, 'With joy and goodly gree, if the King permit me.' Then quoth the King, 'Tell thy tale*" (Burton).

In this version of the opening and closing formula, Burton evinces a sense of humor and clearly enjoys the sexuality of the whole situation. "Her permitted say" is only "permitted" during the night; what she has to say withers in daylight like a vampire. They spend the night "in mutual embrace," which is both a duty and porn. Her sister is a master of irony: she calls Sheherezade's tale "grateful, sweet, and tasteful," three qualities she can surely not be accused of; her first story (in the Syrian manuscript) is cruel, sadistic, whimsical, absurd (killing a giant djinn's son with *date pits*???), and filled with hints of bestiality; her story, if anything, promises even lewder fare the next night. Sheherezade inquires coquettishly of the King whether she may live to tell the story, as if her life is only a trifle compared to the King's possible delight in her modest little tale. The King duly notes this in an interior monologue where he gets a firm hold of himself in the name of Allah and decides, bravely, not to kill her. (Or rather not to have her killed by Sheherezade's own father, who is his official Strangler of Wives.) Next night, Dunyazad exclaims with something resembling enthusiasm, "*O my sister finish for us that story . . . ,*" as if she's already in the throes of orgasmic delight at being allowed to play in the marital bed, and Sheherezade, equally giddy (because she's still alive) answers, *"With joy and goodly gree . . . ,"* whatever "gree" is (it sounds dirty), and the pompous King, his rooster's comb aflutter, gestures indulgently, "Tell thy tale." It is almost a scene from the *Decameron*; Burton's libertine readings and the 18th century shine through these formulas. Burton gets the spirit of the *Nights*: they are entertainment, meant to entertain men, and like all entertainments for men only they are about women, and they are scandalous; at the same time, he is aware that he is writing to a literate audience that has a good deal of respect for the power of women, an audience that might even include women, so he never loses his decorum: like Giacomo Casanova, he flirts, is a bit crude, and amuses all.

"Well, he was an exhausted and hungry monkey,"[48] said Sheherezade, "who wandered in the desert finding nothing to eat, until he came at long last to the shore of a calm sea."

Sharyar remembered the sea that he and his brother, Shahzaman, had come to, where the date tree had fed them, and the Genius who rose from it, and the princess who loved them and took their rings, and he could see it all again.

"Insofar as the sea is limpid, thought the ape (because that's the kind of monkey he was said to be),[49] I could dive in and fish. My arms are strong and I'm fast. I can't swim; it seems as though I once knew but I forgot. He sat under a lone date tree that was very old and years past being able to fruit.[50] The monkey imagined the tree full of dates and he closed his eyes waiting to die of hunger with a mouth full of imaginary dates. When he didn't die, he opened them and saw a ship. It was floating on the horizon on the mirror-smooth sea, its sails limp under the bright azure sky. The monkey saw hope. He tore a thick branch from the date

"An hour before daybreak Dinarzad awoke, and exclaimed, as she had promised, 'My dear sister, if you are not asleep, tell me I pray you, before the sun rises, one of your charming stories. It is the last time that I shall have the pleasure of hearing you,'" and when the next night arrives, *"Scheherezade, at this point, seeing that it was day, and knowing that the Sultan always rose very early to attend the council, stopped speaking. 'Indeed, Sister,' said Dinarzad, 'this is a wonderful story.' 'The rest is still more wonderful,' replied Scheherezade, 'and you would say so, if the Sultan would allow me to live another day, and would give me leave to tell it you next night.' Schahriar, who had been listening to Scheherezade with pleasure, said to himself, 'I will wait till to-morrow; I can always have her killed when I have heard the end of her story'"* (Andrew Lang's 1898 *The Arabian Nights Entertainments*).

Lang is melodramatic and sounds like a Victorian nanny telling a children's story, as well as overacting a playlet: *". . . tell me I pray you before the sun rises . . ."* All this pleading and the imminent sunrise give the scene a tinge of tinsel doom and cardboard mise-en-scène. Only the tearstained handkerchief and the heaving bosom are missing, though they are certainly present, as even his least-informed reader is well aware. *"It is the last time that I shall have the pleasure of hearing you,"* Dunyazad adds for (over)emphasis, a phrase that could not be spoken to anyone under any circumstances, certainly not to her older sister at the possible hour of her death. This stilted formal phrase reveals also that Sheherezade's value to her little sister resides in *"the pleasure of hearing"* her, and one (the reader of this sentence) hears, just below the phrase, a barely audible sssss of resentment, possibly for being asked to assist in the act of sisterly salvation, an act that includes, as we know, certain activities of deflorification and unvirgination totally unsuited to a well-brought-up child with polished shoes. But let us not sell Sheherezade short; she answers her sister quite tartly: *"The rest is still more wonderful, and you would say so, if the Sultan would allow me to live another day . . ."* Well, didn't Dinarzad just say what a pleasure it was to listen to you, Sis, and that *"indeed,"* it had been a *"wonderful story"*? This thing between the sisters overshadows the King's role in the affair: he is, after all, only a man who must get to "council" "early," after which the sisters will be left to their own devices, and you know that it won't be pretty. We are now in another epoch of the long Victorian age, one that belongs tree, and, using it as a raft, he launched himself toward the ship, rowing with his arms. His efforts attracted the attention of the sailors and merchants on board, who leaned on the railings pointing and laughing, greatly amused at the ape's desperate effort. The captain watched the monkey with his spyglass, while the men begged to be allowed to kill it before it reached the ship. 'Let me shoot him with an arrow,' demanded one. 'An arrow,' snickered another, 'that's a waste of an arrow; let me use my slingshot and a date pit.' 'Who needs a slingshot,' boasted yet another, 'when I can easily kill him with a stone?' He pulled a round stone from his pocket, as if he'd been saving it for just this occasion. 'A waste of stone,' opined still another; 'let me just send down my slave boy to strangle him. My slave swims like a fish and is so strong he can dispatch that simian with one hand.' 'I have a better idea,' laughed a brawny sailor, 'let him come on board and I'll bash his brains in with my fist.' One thing they all seemed to agree on was that a monkey on a ship was bad luck, and that if he should make it on board, he had to be killed immediately in some way, the easiest being to throw him back into the sea to drown.

to the English interiors of home life and London clerks, not Burton's sweat-drenched desert.

I confine myself to the Fates' three translations of the opening and closing formulas—a magical number in the *Nights*—though a student could easily follow these through other translations and renderings, after the first European translation into French by Antoine Galland (copied by Andrew Lang) in 1704, and derive insight from the differences. These formulas are abstracts of their historical periods and portraits of the translator-Fates and their intended readers; they are rich in cultural attitudes about how the "West" viewed the "East," and how the distortion that Edward Said called "orientalism" works.

[48] There are many monkeys in the *Nights*, and there was a profusion of them in the bazaars of Cairo and Baghdad, trained to astonish with tricks. There were, of course, even more monkeys in Indian stories, and their almost-human appearance makes them both the ideal companion and the perfect beginner's study in enchantment. Turning people into monkeys and vice versa was a good way to learn magic and to explain, incidentally, a resemblance that was the subject of many a theological argument. As Anselm Hollo (mid-20th-century) said, in conversation with the author, "We have no quarrel with the idea that God made Man, it's only that He made something like a monkey first." Lucy, the 3.2-million-year-old hominid skeleton in Ethiopia, named after the song playing in paleontologist Don Johanson's camp the night of her discovery, "Lucy in the Sky with Diamonds," was the "first woman, a bona fide scientific icon, a poster child for evolution"

(http://killingthebuddha.com/mag/exegesis/why-i-love-lucy/).

[49] By Edward Lane.

[50] At the time of Sharyar and Shahzaman's encounter with the Genius and the princess, the tree had been full of fruit. This tree could fruit at will, dry up, and flower again, because it was none other than the magical Tree of the Knowledge of Good and Evil in the Garden of Eden. This tree makes a number of appearances in the *Nights*, and has been subject to quests undertaken by explorers using textual clues from the Bible and other books. Brook Wilensky-Lanford (http://killingthebuddha.com/mag/exegesis/why-i-love-lucy/) spent two years researching the people "who search for the Garden of Eden on Earth. The search has been full of colorful characters, all extrapolating from verses of Genesis and the science of their day to make their case that the Garden of Eden existed and that they knew where it was: The North Pole, Iraq, Mongolia, wherever. My research has taken me to the Mormon Garden of Eden in Missouri, the Serpent Mound in Ohio, and the Creation Museum in Kentucky . . . Making my way through every search for the Garden of Eden, through every manifesto claiming to confirm some version of biblical truth, there inevitably came

a moment when I realized it was not just a religious quest, but a political one also." For our purposes, it suffices that her most intriguing research leads to a Tree in Iraq (Ur, Mesopotamia): not only did this Tree cause the original Fall of Adam and Eve from Paradise, but it was the reason for the slaughter of British soldiers celebrating the end of World War I and their imminent retreat from Iraq; their celebration caused damage to the Tree, inciting a fatal riot. The Tree stood in Ur in the marshlands that Saddam Hussein ordered drained in punishment for the revolt against his regime following the American war of 1991. Ur, the original site of Paradise, is now being painstakingly restored by new technology (Ur.2), and it is hoped that the Tree will be made indestructible in this incarnation, but in any case this is the Tree in the *Nights*: a date-heap of trouble.

We should probably mention here that this tree-farrago was God's fault. The first humans, Adam and Eve, were particularly *open* creatures: God could have made them *closed*, i.e., unable to pass on the knowledge of good and evil even after eating of the forbidden fruit. But God made a mistake. He endowed the creatures with

"The monkey clambered aboard and threw himself at the feet of the captain, indicating with nearly human abjection and despair his obedience and hunger. The ship was a merchant vessel laden with wares for the port of Basra; it carried silk, leopard and antelope hides, tooled horse and camel harnesses, silver pots, stores of wine and raki, crates of sword scabbards, and well-hidden sacks of silver, gold, and gems. Its captain was a bearded former pirate who had commanded, commandeered, and sunk many ships; he had sailed all the known seas (and some unknown ones) and had killed many men, but never an animal. He was a practicing vegetarian, which meant that he ate almost nothing, except roots cured in brine. He was tall and sinewy like a vine, his face was a narrow crag, and he was greatly feared. He liked the monkey immediately, and when the ship's carpenter said, 'Please allow me to kill it with a hammer,' the captain hit the man across the face, making him fall backward onto the cook, who had been just about to propose using one of his large kitchen knives to disembowel the creature, having cooked and eaten monkey meat before, a real delicacy. Instead, he toppled under the carpenter's weight, and a hush fell over the merry crowd of would-be monkey killers. The captain ordered all the crew to return to their tasks and confined the merchants to their cabins. They grumbled as they dispersed; the carpenter mumbled under his breath, 'He'll give it some tack and sodomize it,' a mumble he was fortunate not to have the captain overhear.

"In his cabin, the captain treated the monkey to some of his best roots. The hungry monkey nearly fainted from disgust when he tasted them, but his hunger was stronger than his nausea, and he ate gratefully, looking with dewy eyes at his savior. Many days passed this way, and the crew became resigned to the presence of the monkey, who became the captain's shadow. The monkey followed the captain wherever he

an oversize communicative ability, the "T-fault," or "the Transmission Fault," as cabbalist Eliphas Lévi called it. It was the transmission (perpetuation, copying) that was egregious to the Lord because it was his own error. He had made his humans unique copies, but instead of putting in some kind of safety device to prevent them from copying themselves, he told them to "be fruitful and multiply." Their sin was not disobedience, since they were as yet unable to distinguish between a metaphor and literalness; the offense was the revelation that God himself had of his own mistake. The only solution was a statute of limitations for his humans, went and imitated his every gesture, so much so that the men began to fear the monkey as much as they feared the captain. The ship's barber offered to groom the monkey, as he groomed the captain, and he did so with great care, combing his matted hair, rubbing coconut oil into it, massaging his muscles, and buffing his nails. The jeweler made him a thin gold chain that the captain fastened around his neck, and sometimes wrapped around his wrist as he searched the horizon with his spyglass before sundown. A harness-maker, who was supervising the transportation of three hundred camel harnesses to the caliph of Baghdad, made the monkey an intricate camel-hair vest and a pair of rabbit-skin gloves. In a short time the crew nearly forgot that the splendidly accoutred friend of the captain was a monkey. The more accepted he was, the more wretched the monkey became. He suffered from being taken for a human; the vest he wore suffocated him; the food made him retch; he was seasick; he suffered from the men's incessant vulgarity; he willed himself to feel nothing, but when he looked accidentally at his reflection in the blade of a sword, he nearly fell on it. His suffering was visible to no one, and, honestly, he didn't know that what he felt was called suffering.

"Three weeks later the ship came into the port at Basra and was immediately surrounded by many small and large craft, full of men ready to trade. There was a hubbub of people calling out in many languages, peppering their greetings with oaths, arguing with each other and not above smacking men on another boat with an oar, or ramming the prow of a vessel shaped like a slipper into an improvised sailboat with a shirt for a sail. The captain loved this kind of seaport, a place where it seemed that language was still new and everyone was trying it out.[51] Among the motley flotilla was an official ship carrying emissaries of the

mortality, hence the haste in which he surrounded *the other tree*—of life and death—with the semidivine guards who, as we well know, failed in even more grievous ways.

[51] Ports were for centuries favorite places for writers to mine rich language(s). One of our favorites is the Levantine Panait Istrati, born in the 19th century in a Romanian Black Sea port, who wrote novels in an odd French mixed with Turkish, Greek, Romanian, Bulgarian, and Russian; he was greatly admired by Romain Rolland. The *din* of ports in literature is almost as loud as the real thing, and it will soon overtake it, as true ports like the one at Basra disappear through being containerized and depeopled. Basra, on the Persian Gulf, was the location of Sumer, the home of Sinbad the Sailor, and another proposed location of the Garden of Eden.

Sultan, who came on board as was customary when a new ship sailed into port."

"What's a Sultan?" asked Sharyar imperiously.

"That's what they called Kings in those days," answered Sheherezade, without bothering to tell him that "those days," the days of the Turkish Empire, hadn't yet arrived.[52]

"After they dispensed with formalities, their commander unrolled a blank scroll and announced that no one would be allowed to disembark until they had written two lines on the paper. The captain demanded to know the reason for this unusual request; he had never before been asked such a thing; a merchant ship rarely carried more than three literate people, a bursar, a log-keeper, and, sometimes, an astrologer or a necromancer. On this ship, however, there happened to be several literate people, including the captain himself, who had whiled away a long period of captivity on the Somali coast by teaching himself to read the Koran, memorizing it, and then copying it from memory. His Koran had been the first and last book he had ever read, bought at the price of a jeweled dagger just before he was captured by pirates; it was a miniature scroll written in a small hand that looked like black sand on a mirror; he had kept it hidden in his long braid of hair, and though he spent the first year of his captivity naked, he had managed to study it; during his second year he had been given a linen shirt, the inside of which he had used for practicing writing. He had never been asked until now to demonstrate his writing skill, and he was most curious.

"The Sultan's envoy explained. The Grand Vizir, who had died the year before, had been a famous scribe who had copied and composed books

---

[52] 1555, from M.Fr. *sultan* "ruler of Turkey" (16c.), from Arabic sultan "ruler, king, queen, power, dominion," from Aramaic shultana "power," from shelet "have power." A wife, mother, daughter, concubine, or sister is a sultana (1585), from It. fem. of sultano, from Arabic sultan. In the 9th century, Sharyar would have known this, even though he was something less than a Sultan, a "caliph," but since he was translated in English as "King," we took the liberty of keeping him true to translation and innocent of his true language, which is sheer perversity.

for the Sultan, books that he then read to his master at bedtime. Since his death, the Sultan had been unable to sleep,[53] and he had scoured the land, sending ambassadors as far as Samarkand, to find a new scribe. His efforts at discovering someone with fine handwriting, capable of copying, composing, and reading aloud, as his Vizir had done, had come to naught, but he had not given up hope. Every new ship that came into port was required to provide samples of handwriting from its crew. The insomniac Sultan, who knew neither how to read nor how to write, nor how to sleep without being read to, having depended on his scribe for these services, had sat gloomily in his vast library for over three years, looking with anger at the thousands of scrolls inside their polished walnut holes, hating them with all his heart but also dying of curiosity and sleeplessness. He had already told himself that if he did not find a new scribe within the year, he would set the library on fire and attack a much larger empire in the East, which was a form of suicide.

"The captain was intrigued by this because he saw suddenly a new course for his life. He was tired of commanding a ship laden with goods like a placid camel, surrounded by the crass company of men who reeked of meat.[54] If he could win the Sultan's favor and become his scribe, he would spend his last years reading and writing, a marvelous occupation that would afford him access to books other than the Koran, which was a fine book, but since he knew that there were others, he craved them. He set himself eagerly to the task and carefully penned these lines on parchment: *Men must kill what most resembles them because what resembles them might surpass them or else remind them of their insufficiencies.*

---

[53] Yet another sleepless person in the *Nights*.

[54] This is what the captain hoped for, but there was another reason: his ship was as tired as he was, and perhaps no longer seaworthy; it was a Chinese-made sailboat built from "as many as ten small boats, for the purpose of carrying out anchors, for fishing, and a variety of other services. They are slung over the sides, and lowered into the water when there is no occasion to use them . . . When a ship, having been on a voyage for a year or more, stands in need of repair, the practice is to give her a sheathing over the original boarding, forming a third course, which is caulked and paid in the same manner as the others; and this, when she needs further repairs, is repeated, even to the number of six layers, after which she is condemned as unserviceable and not seaworthy" (*The Travels of Marco Polo* [Marsden's English edition, 1818], p. 295). The captain's ship was in need of a seventh layer that might sink the vessel, even if he could afford it.

He'd had this thought after he'd saved the monkey from his crew and felt proud now to write it down. It occurred to him that if he'd been a powerful Sultan instead of a humble merchant-ship captain, he could never have expressed himself this way; he'd have written, *First, you kill those you most resemble, and second, you must let no one outshine you.* Power must speak in complete sentences, but absolute power must express itself in imperatives. Allah, who was greater than the Sultan, was uber-imperative: *Give not unto the foolish . . . and those who disobey Allah and His messenger He will make him enter Fire, where he will dwell for ever, his will be a shameful doom . . . ,*[55] he recited under his breath, knowing at once that a Sultan's wrath at being ignored was imaginable, but Allah's 'Fire' was not. The captain was on the verge of a musical discovery, but the envoys were growing impatient.

"Three more shipmates offered to write on the scroll: the accountant, the keeper of the logs, and a ragged dervish who had attached himself to the ship like a barnacle, pretending to know navigation by the stars, astrology, and necromancy. Their hands were illegible, and the captain was pleased when he saw the horrid marks they scratched on the paper. The dervish was the worst of them all: he barely knew how to hold the quill and tried to divert attention from his clumsiness by chanting non-sense with a look of fake beatitude on his face. Everyone laughed at the efforts of the dervish, and the Sultan's ambassador even made an amus-ing short speech about memorizers who pretend to be writers, a plague of which could be found at all hours of the day and night in the bazaars and coffeehouses of every city in the empire. 'They tell stories,' he said, 'that they have neither read nor experienced; they repeat only what they have heard, forgetting beginnings and endings, the morals of the tales if they ever had any, but they never ever forget the reason for flapping at the mouth, which is to astonish the naive and to make them part with their coins. Their only talent is for teasing, like whores who'll lead

---

[55] The Qur'an, trans. M. M. Pickthall, iPhone app.

a man on but demand more money when the desire becomes urgent.' The dervish was abashed at these words because the mention of whores aroused him, and, like all dervishes, he wore only a cloth, which now parted to reveal his arousal, making his hand shake even more, and causing even greater hilarity.

"The envoys furled their scroll and were about to depart, when the monkey threw himself down at their feet and made it known with gestures that he, too, wished to write. This was just about the straw that broke the camel's back, and everyone nearly died laughing, but the captain, who had great affection for his protégé, silenced them all and made them hand the scroll to the monkey. 'If he messes up the paper,' the captain said, 'I will flog him myself, but if, by some miracle, he can actually write, I will adopt him as my own son because he's the cleverest animal in the world.' Seating himself before the virgin sheet, the monkey took the quill delicately between his fingers and started to write without hurry, making the letters flow like a gentle spring in a script so beautiful everyone gasped. As the monkey kept writing, the laughter ceased and was replaced by an awed silence that deepened as his hand moved on. It wasn't only the beautiful hand that moved the watchers, but the sublime content of what the monkey wrote in 'the six sorts of writing in use among the Arabs, and each sort contained an original verse or couplet, in praise of the Sultan.'[56]

"The officials took the scroll back to the Sultan."

And then a milky white light started in the glass dome of the bridal chamber, and Sheherezade stopped speaking.

"When the Sultan saw the scroll, what did he say?" asked Sharyar, forgetting all about the coming day.

[56] *The Arabian Nights Entertainments*, ed. Andrew Lang.

"Please, Sheherezade, what happened then?" begged Dinarzad.

"Dawn is here," Sheherezade said, "if you want to know what happened next, you have to wait until tonight."

This is going to be a major violation of my vow, thought Sharyar, but I must, I must know what happened next. What happens between Kings and their scribes is important, he justified his curiosity to himself. He resolved to suspend Sheherezade's death sentence until next night. He was the King and had power over all subjects, including himself. Allowing Sheherezade just one more day to live was perhaps not enough time for her to be unfaithful to him, but he would have her closely watched nonetheless. At least that's what the King told himself, but in truth, he didn't know how long it takes a new wife to be unfaithful. There was a lot he didn't know, and he was curious, but mostly about the Sultan and the monkey. What he did know was that he had the power to find out because he was the King, and the Storyteller was his.

He found the Vizir trembling outside the door, ready for the task that awaited him every morning, a task so onerous this very morning he had resolved to kill himself as soon as he had strangled his daughter. He was stunned to hear from Sharyar that the strangling was postponed for one day and a night. The King did not explain and the Vizir did not ask, for fear that the ruler might have a change of heart. A tiny green shoot of hope sprouted in his own bitter heart. (Bitter because he was haunted by the screams of the girls he had already strangled, and couldn't sleep. The Vizir's insomnia was different from the King's or from Sheherezade's and Dinarzad's, and as we proceed we will have occasion to classify seven hundred and thirty-three types of insomnia that correspond to as many types of people in the oriental[57] Middle Ages.) Sharyar

[57] The "Orient" was a suspect moniker long before E. Said proceeded to demolish "orientalism" as a colonial excuse that justified European conquest using the huge aggregation of kitsch that had grown around the "mysterious Orient." J. L. Borges was close to the mark when he noted that he could not define the "Orient" any more than St. Augustine could define time: "'What is time? If you don't ask me, I know; but if you ask me, I don't know.' What are the East and the West? If you ask me, I don't know. We must settle for approximations." The Orient and Occident are enmeshed in ways that cannot be separated, and Borges goes on to speak of Alexander the Great, a Greek who became Persian, and Marco Polo, whose travels established a world that is very much part of the topography of our global minds.

then ordered the Vizir to have his daughter watched closely, and the Vizir readily agreed, ordering twenty armed and tongueless Mamelukes[58] to wait outside the bedroom door for Sheherezade.

A terribly frustrated King Sharyar went off to his duties, leaving the two women in bed to finish their toilet and go on to their own daily chores. "That was amazing," said Dinarzad when they were alone in the King's wide and warm bed with sunlight bathing their graceful naked bodies. "Is it going to work more than once?"

Sheherezade[59] laughed, "Forever," she said. (And this is true: it's still working.) Before the servants came in to pick up the marital chamber, Dinarzad, who had assisted in all aspects of the nuptial act, including guiding the King's phallus to its fated place, and then placing her outspread palms on her sister's upraised legs to hold them in their nearly vertical wide V, asked, "And was there a 'greeting' inside?"

Her innocent question cracked up Sheherezade. The "greeting" came from a children's rhyme: "At the joining and the meeting / inside the woman lives a troll / who asks hard questions from a scroll / and if answered rightly sings his greeting."

[58] In the 9th century AD, the Abbasid caliphs of Baghdad enslaved nomadic Turks from central Asia they called Mamelukes (from the Arabic *mamluk*, "owned"). These "white Mamelukes" were more highly regarded than the "black Mamelukes," enslaved Africans who were treated harshly and feared for any number of reasons, including one central to the *Nights*: the size of their penises. (See footnote by Burton and my footnote 23 above.) Mamelukes in the *Nights* are mostly white slaves, but sometimes they are black. The Turkic white slaves distinguished themselves in the service of the caliphate, and eventually one of them, Ahmad ibn Tulun, seized power; in the early 870s took control of Egypt, and by 877 had conquered the Mediterranean coast through Palestine and Syria. The Mamelukes spoke Turkish as well as Arabic with their subjects, the caliphs in Baghdad, and they increased their numbers with new conquests from the fierce tribes of central Asia and the Caucasus. In 1250 the last sultan of Saladin's Turkic dynasty was murdered in Egypt by the slaves of the palace guard. A Mameluke general, Aybak, took power until 1257, when his wife had him killed in a palace intrigue. His place was taken by another Mameluke general, Qutuz, and then came the Mongols!

[59] Sheherezade is an IED. Most commentators and even translators of the *Nights* avoid her (with the notable exception of Sir Richard Burton). Borges, for instance, admired above all the infinite textual possibilities of the *Thousand and One Nights*, and did not concern himself very much with Sheherezade. Other writers were fascinated by the formidable character of Sheherezade, the Storyteller incarnate, but they did not add much of their own to the story told for centuries of the princess known by many names who tells stories in order to stay alive. By the time this Storyteller was written and named Sheherezade, it was late in her archetype's history, and in the history of performers and audiences for her stories. She remains mysterious and dangerous to this day: we still have trouble spelling her name. Oxford University Press has accepted two different spellings, but neither of them is the one most commonly used. Our choice, Sheherezade, sounds, according to DeWitt Brinson, like a cool drink of lemonade on a hot desert afternoon: She-her-ezade™. My reasoning is that her name has to begin with "she" because I think that her history begins as Lillith, the mistress of Adam, and she is also Hagar, the slave-wife of Abraham, the mother of the Arabs, as well as many other manifestations, "she of the night" (as opposed to first-woman, She of the Day). As "she the other" of the night, she is always in danger of being strangled in the morning when the light of day shines on her.

"Did you like the story?" she asked. Dinarzad wasn't sure whether her sister meant the deflowering or the tale, so she said, "The words or the joining?" Sheherezade laughed, tickled, sure that her younger sister now knew more than she had before, because Dinarzad had goose bumps all over and they tingled pleasantly, but in truth her young sister didn't even know an honest word for her womanly opening, since she had only heard it referred to poetically.

The poets of India and Persia have done their best in reaching for images to describe the vulva. They drafted all the flowers, even the prickly cactus. No delicacy was left metaphorically unused, no pleasant scent unemployed. Hafiz spoke of the "red ruby"; Khusrau said, "If there be no pilot in our boat, let there be none: We have god in our midst: the sea we do not need." Rumi: "Drink the wine that moves you as a camel moves when it's been untied." And the Chinese poets had it as "brook," "dew," "flower-path"; everyone agreed that while the Indians and Persians were reaching in their ecstasy for the divine, the Chinese were the earthiest of all. Erudite Sheherezade could have enumerated other poets' euphemisms, but Dinarzad, overcome already by emotions and fatigue, wanted only to hear the conclusion of the story her sister had begun telling. She was dying to know what was up with that monkey-scribe. But when she begged her sister to whisper it to her, swearing she'd tell no one, Sheherezade refused, and reiterated in different words what she had already told her and Sharyar.

"You must wait until tonight, my little pigeon."

But something still troubled Dinarzad: Sheherezade had timed her story to end just before the King fully took his pleasure. She knew this because he had taken himself out of Sheherezade still erect, and Dinarzad had toyed with the royal scepter, something Sharyar did not mind in the least, and when Sheherezade neared the end of her story at the first light of dawn, there was a milky drop that looked at first like part of the light flowing in, but then it thickened like a pearl and came to a standstill, as if it, too, were awaiting the conclusion of Sheherezade's story. To Dinarzad the drop of dawn-milk looked like a tear that she'd have liked to taste. Sheherezade's abrupt ending wasn't very sisterly, she thought, and said so.

Sheherezade laughed again and Dinarzad asked, quite worried, "Why are you laughing so much, Sheherezade?" Sheherezade wiped away tears and said, "You're still a child, Dinarzad." "What do you mean?" bristled the little sister, "I am doing exactly what you told me and so far it's working. You're not dead! And may I add that I helped with the King's, uhm, thing to deflower you, no easy task, poor King!" Sheherezade smiled at her sister's outburst. "Granted, but you also like my story about the writing monkey." "Well, yes," Dinarzad sheepishly admitted, "it's a beautiful story. So how am I a child?"

Sheherezade explained: "It's like this: the story is not about a monkey who can write. It is about a girl who can fool a King. The monkey is a girl because whenever a man, whether it is a ship's captain, a fat merchant, or a bereft ruler, looks at a girl, he sees only her shape, her girlishness, not her talent for scribing or storytelling. When the men on board called out that they wanted to kill the monkey, they were all fighting like roosters to be the first to possess the girl, but when the captain, who was the strongest rooster, claimed her for his own, they quit their claim, and when the Sultan, who was an even bigger rooster than the captain, claimed her, the captain surrendered her without complaint. He could have unfurled his sails and left port, but he would not do that for any girl, because it meant losing money for himself and for the merchants on the ship. Her value was small compared to the bales of merchandise aboard."

Dinarzad was puzzled. "But if she was a girl, not a monkey, she was surely enchanted. Was she, was she, Sheherezade?"

But Sheherezade smiled and said no more. Like King Sharyar, Dinarzad burned with curiosity and could barely wait for the night. After combing Dinarzad's unruly hair, and handing her over to the mistress of the baths, Sheherezade left for her studies, trailed by Mamelukes.

sheherezade's day

She passed before the door of the Hall of the Great Looms and listened to their never-ceasing clacking. This is where her morning usually ended, if she had done her spinning on time. She loved these rooms best of all, but before she could be there with the women, she had to see the Master-Teacher who oversaw her education and handed her different tasks each day. He scheduled her hours with astrologers, physicians, and holy persons who taught divination, explained humors, chanted stories, prayers, and sutras; and music teachers adept with stringed instruments, drums, and clappers. Since the age of six, between eight a.m. and noon Sheherezade had sleep-learned the epics and the sutras, and memorized the Koran and other holy texts; her fingers had followed obediently the sequences of holes, folds, and drum skins whence they drew competent sounds. One hour past noon, after her favorite lunch of one thin slice of lamb roast, ripe figs, and cold honey-water, she met again the Master-Teacher, who examined her about what she had learned in the morning, and she chanted for him the suras of the Koran and the poetry of Rumi,[60] and tormented the instruments. The Master-Teacher then imparted his own wisdom, instructing her in Sufi dancing, the use of knives, and *taquia*, the art of disguise. Only then could she tend to the womanly arts of spinning and weaving.

[60] Rumi was said to have been born in Balkh in contemporary Afghanistan, which was part of the Persian Empire, but some scholars believe that he was born in Wakhsh in what is now Tajikistan. Both these cities were at the time included in the Greater Persian cultural sphere of Khorāsān, the easternmost province of historical Persia, and were part of the Khwarezmian Empire, or the Shahanshah kingdom. Rumi, the poet and perhaps founder of Sufism, has had many lives in translation; each translation, it seems, brings forth new Sufi groups. In English there are several translations, each one with its following: I have myself sat in a Sufi prayer circle and read from a book passed around from hand to hand, prior to *zakr* (twirling); I caused a good deal of awkwardness when I criticized the translation; the devotees misunderstood my criticism of the English version as an insult to God. Banish the thought! God is an original.

For eight years, during the King's long absence, she had been rigorously schooled in the morning but hadn't been fully awake until three in the afternoon, when she joined her girlfriends in the Spinning Chamber and the Hall of the Great Looms. The young girls spun wool and wove carpets, and there, following the turning of spindles and the clacking of looms, other kinds of stories were told, very different from the morning's instructive religious histories, because they were about women and their lives. They talked about men and the court, phantoms, fears, age, and, mostly, the body. The particular uses and limits of the body, male, female, or supernatural, were examined in the light of experience, through gossip dispensed with irony and worldly knowledge by the older women, who winked often, though their tales of childbirth, and other tragedies of the flesh, were not always comforting. Witchcraft and leechcraft were woven with the colored threads of wool into the carpets. Here she learned stories that were timed to the spindle and the loom, and could, if necessary, hide behind the clacking and the twisting like veils that shielded them from being overheard. Sheherezade learned here the art of storytelling: the shape of a story "thickening" and "thinning" was that of a spindle: it pulled in a single thread and spun itself out into a larger and larger shape, round in the middle like a pregnant woman. The cloud of wool from which the thread was spun made a body, the body of a woman full of child, but also a story. The tale-spinner and the spindle that was her body pulled the thread of words unto itself.

The world of stories had begun long before Sheherezade was born, and she was aware of their great weight, piled behind her, above her, and around her, in the form of veils, robes, turbans, curtains, rugs, and flags. A myriad of stories she didn't know waited like mounds of wool for her to spin them. She heard the story of the wandering shepherd Orpheus, who fattened his sheep with the music of the lyre, and she fancied that it was his wool that she spun. Each full spindle was a story, and she noticed that if she told a story while she spun, her listeners would often fall asleep. The dreams that flowed from the singing shepherd passed from the thread in her hand onto her spindle and turned into sleep and dreams again. The long-time-ago and the unfolding merged as she spun:

    spindle and distaff: fibers twisted together to make yarn
    short entangled filaments turned into yarn
    spinning wool
    spinning a tale
    telling a yarn

[61] The spindle-whorl of wood, stone, or metal was a Late Neolithic innovation, but the origin of spinning may be in the Upper Paleolithic, 20,000 years ago; the bone-hook atop the 12-inch straight stick was the Neolithic invention that may have been responsible for the shape of the first story, a projection of the binary, an animated insight of positive and negative charges, of crossroads and transformation. Language developed quickly, but it never doubted its connection to the body until Spinning, also known as the Second Fold. In the Second Fold curiosity became so intense that it doubled the body by its shadow: it thickened the body to make of its shadow a double, another body. Words themselves, still fresh fruits of curiosity, took on doubles as well. Still within the Second Fold, the body-doubles and the word-doubles turned on each other and acquired opposite meanings that coexisted within the same contours and sounds. Curiosity thus discovered its ability to propose new areas for its growing appetite; it conceived a means of reproduction through the question *What if?* Adding other bodies

weaving a web
the world turned

the oldest woman was a spinster
Sheherezade loved her best of all
but about this she had no choice
her yarn wound about the spindle that was the King
whom she had to turn from a killer into a story
his phallus-spindle immobilized in her story-yarn
the distaff held her wool
she held the wool in the left hand
the fiber she drew with the right hand & fastened
in a whirling motion
the direction in which the yarn spun was called the Twist
there was an S Twist and a Z Twist
the Z twist was two spun yarns twisted together *plied*
to form thicker yarn
yarns were made of many plies or used as singles
Sheherezade worked both S & Z twists to make her Story Folds
each innovation a new narrative device[61]
her language made to ease the spinning spindles' chanting
cats purred like spindles and so her story had to spin and purr
her nights spun on the axis of her wheel of fortune[62]

Sheherezade knew that her stories had to arrest the killing of brides to keep the human story going, and as she washed, combed, spun, and wove the wool, she thought of Ariadne and Penelope. Sheherezade stood at some midpoint between them: Ariadne's thread had shown

to the doubles it had already known, curiosity went on to invent the gods, an addition that led to the Third Fold. In the Third Fold we meet the gods and their stories, bodies that opened to human curiosity a wealth of possibilities, but also, inexplicably, a set of unforeseen difficulties. Curiosity began to be constrained by its own finds, which forbade it to look any deeper into them. The meta-beings started ritualizing the stories and imposing a hierophantic routine that might have destroyed the original body forms, if it weren't for the appearance of human heroes who became invested in demolishing the theological order. All of this happened while Spinning faster and faster until the appearance of the Fourth Fold (also known as Time), which was the collaborative work of Prometheus and Sheherezade. The Fourth Fold contains many subfolds, or Wrinkles, in its journey from the demigod Prometheus to the Storyteller Sheherezade, the most important of which for us is the Wrinkle of Numbers that occurred midway between Prometheus and Sheherezade. The Wrinkle of Numbers was the result of curiosity's sudden panic at its own proliferating narrative her lover Theseus the way out of the labyrinth, while Penelope's weaving and unweaving signified her husband Odysseus's absence. Penelope wove a new labyrinth from Ariadne's thread, but then unwove it in expectation of Odysseus's return. The thread and weave were no longer detachable from their stories. Sheherezade's job was to be like Ariadne to make the King believe that she was showing him the way out of the labyrinth of his insecurity and cruelty, while weaving at the same time a labyrinth from which he could never escape to kill again.

powers and the terror that followed: like children scared by the monsters they made up, humans started counting everything, including all the bones in the body, all the veins and organs in the body, and all the animals, plants, rocks, and stars that surrounded it with their own bodies, a numeric incantation to ward off their own spun myths and stay the gods' cruelty. Curiosity retreated into taking stock of what it had discovered about the world; it stilled its growth to count its treasures. When it had counted everything, its appetite awoke again: by that time its enumerative incantations had almost enlisted the human body in an order that bound it as strictly as the gods, an order of ownership, class, power, and numerous other divisions that could be quantified. The human body would have surely disappeared along with the bodies that curiosity had unveiled, if numerology had seamlessly joined theology. If divine restrictions had met numerological dicta unhindered, we would not be writing this book. There would have been no Sheherezade. We would not be curious. Curiosity would have killed itself with its own success. It didn't happen. There was a break.

Sheherezade changed the human paradigm from accounting to storytelling. She did so at the peril of her life and of her afterlife. Insofar as she risked her life for others, she was a hero, like Prometheus. The "others" she risked her life for were the young women of her city. Her name, Sheherezade, means "City Woman." She is a historical hero, a proto-feminist, and a mortal with a biography encompassed by the single word *Storyteller*. The rich menu of afterlives offered by Moses, Buddha, Jesus, Zoroaster, Mohammed, and Rumi, in the Second Fold, was available to her, but she refused these patented Edens for an afterlife of her own, which came to be known as the stories of the *1001 Nights*. The gods punished Prometheus because he was partly their own, but we humans reward Sheherezade because she is wholly ours. We put fire to good and bad uses: we celebrate Prometheus for making roasts possible, and we damn him for putting us in danger of extinction every day of our lives. For the good, we call great gifts "promethean," and for the bad, we cry in tune with gods, "Go, vultures, go!" In sympathy, we wreck our livers early and go to war often. For Sheherezade we have nothing but praise, and we tell, translate, print, reprint, and add to her stories in every language on earth. If the narrative machine that she set in motion ever stops, we will be extinguished by promethean fire. Prometheus was himself a proto-Sheherezade, doomed by his god-half to silent suffering on a rock. The fire he brought to earth was not actual fire, but the knowledge of spinning a spindly piece of wood to make a spark. From spinning-to-make-a-spark to spinning tales stretches a span of time that measures the distance between gods and humans. After making a fire, humans sat around it and started spinning, then spinning tales, the first of which was how Prometheus stole the fire from the gods and brought it down to a special human called Sha-man. This called for a description of the gods and what it is they did on Olympus, and it was Prometheus himself who (haltingly) told the first story: he described the gods sitting around a fire spinning tales, or looking down at the humans below and being so amused by their doings that they couldn't wait for the evening when they could sit around the fire to tell stories about what they had seen. This behavior saddened Prometheus, the half-human, which is why he learned the secret of the gods' fire: to bring it to humans so that they, too, could sit around the fire and tell stories—about the gods. He also taught them spinning in the Late Neolithic. Prometheus was the first storyteller of a certain kind of story, the god-story, mythology. Sheherezade was the second storyteller; she told stories of humans and supernatural beings who had bodies and ventured with them into the physical world; hers were stories of godless magic, the narratives of civilization, the narratives of the founding of cities where City Woman spins tales from the King's bed to save humankind and to increase its power while charming away cruel gods. Her stories were born of the worldly wisdom that deployed magic in the service of the unfortunate, and magic is what stood between civilization (merchants, trade, cities) and the wild (desert, animals, lawlessness). Magic was (and is) perverse, and the stories of the *1001 Nights* detail its malevolent features, many of which have to do with the indifferent play of numbers on which spinning imposes a narrative order.

[62]An intervention from the future made Sheherezade blink: in a docu-fictional film of the late 20th century, called *Ulysses' Gaze*, a washed-out American filmmaker, Harvey Keitel, is searching for a lost piece of film footage that might be the first moving pic-

ture ever shot in the Balkans, "the first gaze," as he calls it. Keitel wanders through the ruins of Bosnia at war (this is documentary), the ruins of the collapse of communism (also documentary), encountering countless Penelopes (fictional) in his search for the missing film. When he does find it, like Odysseus returning to Ithaca, "the first gaze" of the camera captures women spinning. Clad in black from head to foot, Greek women are spinning. This takes place 12 centuries hence, and Sheherezade cannot know what America or film is, but these are not what make her blink (she can imagine unknown continents and undiscovered technologies): she blinks whenever she feels the shock of something

The stories of men were different. Sheherezade thought about Jason's search for the golden pelt and Abraham's sacrifice of the sheep instead of his son Isaac, stories whose metaphorical meanings were stressed by her religious teachers each morning. The golden sheep and the sacrificial lamb had their metaphors polished and proudly put on display, because Jason and Abraham were men with blood on their hands whose legends laid black eggs of destruction for centuries of glory to come. The women who spun the gold thread of Jason's pelt and sheared the sacrificial sheep were not part of those stories. Sheherezade wished that there were some way to add the follow-up stories before the Master-Teacher, but she was still learning to weave and to unweave her own meanings. An infinitely complicated job, this weaving of stories.[63] She first had to make stories that spun off into sequels that were apprehended by the King just like the news of the day before their metaphorical charges went off slowly like the taste of curry after the first bites, and that when the metaphorical aftertaste reached the deep recesses of his brain, their metaphors had to dry up and vanish to become the spindles

occurring for the first time. In the future, when the future will intervene regularly to regulate her excesses of poetry, she will blink no more; she'll smile coyly instead. The tales spin on their spindles indifferent to metaphor, like centrifuges refining plutonium, no longer beholden to theory.

[63] Like a later demiurge from the America that Sheherezade doesn't know exists, Spider-Woman, Sheherezade wove the world, and she did so under threat of extinction.

[64] Spinning wool was not the only kind of spinning Sheherezade did: her Master-Teacher was a Sufi who taught her to spin-dance. She spin-danced when she needed to clear her head. Histories of ideas started being written as soon as humans had more than one, though they had to wait for the idea of writing before they could. By the time writing was invented, there were already thousands of ideas and histories of ideas memorized in many languages and through many techniques by storytellers; there were also philosophers preoccupied by the production of ideas from observation both of the physical world and of storytelling. Ideas born of storytelling and ideas about it multiplied and sped up in keeping with the pace of *spinning*. Tales were (and are) spun, a rotation that increases the word-field and spins off new word-fields. Oral narrative *rotates*, a motion that, like that of celestial bodies, creates fertile magnetic fields and makes it possible to measure time. (Or to establish temporary measurements based on the speed and rhythm of the story.) Long before writing imposed symbolic orders and laid out the first infrastructure for histories of ideas, the neural pathways that generated, transmitted, recorded, and incorporated ideas were multiplying in the *1001 Nights*.

It's true, Sheherezade's head hurts from spinning, but she is obligated to keep spinning because she is the first of her type, a producer of the infinite within human time. Human time and its duration were the result of multiple ontologies, and not subject to a paradisiacal *before* and a doomed *after*. A good story was one that purposefully violated the frontiers between the real and the surreal, the actual and the imagined, the physical and the magical, but submitted paradoxically to the limits of human time. There is no discernible chronology in the *1001 Nights* outside the one that the stories established themselves according to internal rhythms, but calendars and the sensible agreements of society continued to function on the basis of the two formal units agreed upon at the beginning: day and night. Even when we can't know how a story ends, night must follow day and day must follow night. From the for new and spicier, but more realistic spin-offs. There were now only two enchanted listeners to her spun tales, Sharyar and Dinarzad, but in the future there lived many wide-eyed spectators to her spinning, not that Sheherezade cared much about the future. Still, those awed witnesses of her construction lived in the future already, as her Fates had clearly foretold, and they surrounded her occasionally like a shimmering fog. It was enough to make your head spin, thought Sheherezade, spinning faster and faster as her Qadiri Master-Teacher taught her.[64]

The morning that she had miraculously survived after her night with Sharyar, everything shone more brightly. At first, everyone who encountered her thought that they were seeing a ghost, and fell shaking to their knees; when she laughed and told them that she was alive, they praised Allah and cried, "You have delivered us," but Sheherezade pointed to the tongueless Mamelukes and shook her head. "Not yet, not yet," she whispered, but the word spread quickly nonetheless, and the palace was shaken by premature joy. The women of Al-Adl went

very first story told, before Sharyar and Sheherezade even enter the picture, we have stepped into the world of Story and begun to wander through a labyrinth from which there is no exit, a labyrinth that generates itself, proving that human existence has always unfolded within a story, that we are being narrated even as we follow the narrative deeper and deeper into its own self-generating world. The storyteller and the listener are already part of a narrative machine before the problem of Sheherezade's body (or bodies) is even posed. Sheherezade's storytelling body becomes a source of new bodies even as it settles in and becomes more embodied the more stories it tells; at

the end of the *1001 Nights*, she *may* be the mother of a flesh child, Sharyar the listener having become the willing agent of her (and his) physical perpetuation.

In the Judeo-Christian-Muslim world, the first idea, which caused humans to be banished from Paradise, had a history before the banished humans were finished tumbling to earth. In this system, the second idea was, in fact, the history of the first idea. What happened, why it happened, where it happened, and, finally, what happened after it happened, were questions that generated different stories that agreed only when they were finally written. The agreement was that *it* happened in a garden, and as to what that *it* was, the consensus was only that between the first idea (self-consciousness) and the second (the Fall) occurred the event(s) that created *history*. The first idea was catastrophic (or providential), and its recollection created *time*. How much time passed between the first idea (self-consciousness and the mirroring of that self in the body of another) and the second idea (the awareness of time, or history, and mortality) is a question that Augustine pursued in language as he attempted to understand what *time* is, but whatever it is, it was a catastrophe. For Augustine, anything that was not *in principio* is suspect, the fabulation of a freed verb *facio*, thus the first line of Genesis: *In principio fecit Deus . . .*

"*A catastrophe happens—the desperate form revolution takes at the level of desire—and the ball breaks for the middle of the plate where the welcoming interior of a woman awaits*" (Ghérasim Luca).

The "original sin," which we have compounded many times, is wanting to reproduce, to make copies. This is the difference between the First Woman, Eve, and the Second Woman, Sheherezade: Eve knew both eternity and time, and she would never have known time if she hadn't asked, quite reasonably, why are there multiple apples (or dates) in the Tree? Sheherezade never knew eternity; she knows only time and it seems reasonable to count apples (or dates), and days, and nights. The question occurred to Eve because the apples (or dates) were the only multiples visible in the narrow Edenic foreground. Her question was answered all at once by a cacophony that Eve, who was one of a kind, did not have the organ to perceive. To her the birds' chorused answer sounded as incomprehensible as her maker's injunction to not eat of the apples (or dates). Since they were the only multiples around, eating *one*, or less than one, a *bite*, could not remove anything *forever*, as eating Adam, for example, or that thing hanging from Adam, might have done. If she ate one apple (or date), there were many others. Everywhere else she looked, there was only singularity. One cloud, one god sitting on it, one Adam and his unit, one each of freshly named creatures and plants, one snake, one Eve, silently past her and their resolve was still as firm as ever. One day was but one day. Another night was coming.

Sheherezade prepared for it by thinking about the monkey who wrote beautifully in many languages. He was the world's most accomplished linguist and calligrapher: his script was sheer beauty, a beauty that she felt in her body, and it made her dizzy. She felt the letters of the alphabet glowing and filling her flesh, going deeper in. "In" was the first word. *In the beginning was the Word.* Thanks to that word, we now live in a storied world, Sheherezade's body told her. Somewhere in the storying of the world she was bound to tell, humans were allowed to live. Perhaps that is also where they were born, she surprised herself thinking. There are certain folds in the layers of narrative where the human form and its storytelling are spun. There was no chronology here that she could see,

her body. And all these things, including herself, were filled with seed, ready to "multiply" and "flourish" (as per God's Orders No. 2 & 4), but she lacked the knowledge of how exactly to do that, information locked inside the forbidden apple (or date). She asked Adam, but since he, too, had been forbidden to eat of the fruit and moreover was still hurting from the lack of rib from him ripped that had become this questioning woman, he could not answer. Happily, there was a knowledge-delivery device under the tree, either a snake or an *amanita muscaria* mushroom, and of this she partook the information that led her to the apple (or date), the bite, the discovery of paradox (how could she and Adam be "fruitful" and "multiply" if they were forbidden the techne of reproduction?), and the subsequent first night of full-bore-garden-of-Eden-whoopee, which in itself may have shaken and detached Eden from the rest of Mesopotamia and God's anger. God, in Middle Eastern godlike fashion, did not speak to Eve directly, because she was a woman, so he directed his rhetorical interrogation at Adam, who snitched on her on the spot, but this gave him no Lordy brownie points because they were *both* banished from Eden. In their tumble downward, Eve looked up and was amazed at how narrow her field of vision had been: there were *lots* of multiples above— there were four rivers, for one—and they'd been there since the moment of Creation, and each thing that appeared singular to her when she'd lived in Eden, was in fact stuffed with the multiplicities of myriads of seeds; in addition to the seeds that contained each thing in miniature, every thing had not just one shadow, but many shadows, and all that she had perceived as singular was plural to the max, so much plurality it was impossible for her to say whether there had *ever* been an original, a *one*, and these things she saw were also the stars.

Adam, who had also partaken of the mushroom, was still puzzled by God's anger and herm's inflexibility in allowing for extenuating circumstances after he'd snitched, but he had learned that, god or no god, anger or no anger, he had transgressed against God's *original* creation, which was himself, Adam, and also the many other lesser originals that had been given him by God to lord over in Lord-like fashion. Sin was the making of copies after the manner of apples (or dates). In Eve's defense, thought Adam, maybe there were *two* apples and she couldn't tell the difference between them, a difference very clear to Adam now, as he, too, tumbled downward, namely, that one apple was filled with the knowledge of good, while the other was filled with the knowledge of evil, but you couldn't tell that just looking from the outside. To know that each apple was singular, that even though one looked like the other, it was not, was a knowledge vouchsafed to Adam by God as a matter of primogeniture. To one like Eve, who came second, two might even be "many," because one who does not have singularity from the beginning, cannot know that it is singular. For all Adam knew, Eve might think that she herself was two, Eve and Sheherezade. Number Two acquired many names in different accounts: Lillith, Spider-Woman, Penelope, Sheherezade, Ariadne. God was the only being who knew what a copy was because he copied himself to make Adam. If Eve thought that there were two apples (or dates) she had a 50-50 chance of "sinning" with good or with evil; not that it matters now, as they both tumble down to earthly exile, though Adam would like to know which one she bit into, just for his own satisfaction, not because of the result, which is already written in the book, and it's the same no matter which way you look at it: eternal exile and endless reproduction.

even though she had learned histories, memorized Hindu gods, copied the successions of Persian rulers, and numbered the verses of the Koran. These histories existed simultaneously in her memory, a generalized knowledge; they could not be said to have happened *then* or *later*: they inhabited a *now* that she would use as a narrative matrix, since her monkey's work was writing stories, beginning perhaps with the first story she told at night and theorized during the day.

king sharyar's day

After leaving his astonished Vizir in charge of ordering Mamelukes to watch Sheherezade, Sharyar went to the council chamber and began receiving supplicants in order of importance. It

To Eve none of Adam's reasoning mattered: even if there was only one apple (or date), it contained a pair of opposites, so it was multiple even in its apparent uniqueness. She wasn't hallucinating: more than one voice spoke from the apple tree. From one to many in one bite, and that's *that* story. Her story. Adam would never know the full extent of the multiplicity she saw now, and she would never convince him, for the rest of their corporeal existence, that she could be trusted with the faith in singularity that was as much part of him as God.

God, lonely and original, made a human companion who mirrored him in all respects except for the know-how of making more of himself, a knowledge he enclosed inside one or two apples (or dates) in order to remind himself, in case of amnesia, how to keep making him. Apples (or dates) are the Lord's memory sticks. We don't know why he made Eve; maybe because he had already made two of everything else that didn't resemble him, and he felt that he was being unfair to his copy if he gave him no companion. After God made Eve from Adam, he made himself an Eve too (or he'd not have had a true copy), and so he also became a she, a Herm, and it is thus that Herm will be referred to from now on in this book. Herm knew, because Herm was All-Knowing, that the secret of reproduction could not stay en-appled or in-dated) long. The snake-mushroom under the tree was singular for only the tiniest conceivable quantum of the smallest fraction of time, as was Adam's penis and Eve's virgin vagina, and the creatures of land and sea and whatever else Herm had created during the week-long dream of creation, but the only way for them to stay unique would have been for them to be stupid, and then they couldn't be like Herm and that was inconceivable. For God, the only *significant* singularity in the *story* of Genesis occurs just before Eve bites the apple (or date); suspended in that prebite moment is the last breath of singularity—that moment is suspense itself—and it is the only moment when God truly enjoys herm's creation. If Herm could suspend the story at that point, freeze Eve forever before that first bite, the Genesis would never go past the point of God's total ownership of the universe, and Herm might change herm's mind and go back to the nothingness before Creation, when there was no story and Herm was just an *it*, not even a *he* yet. But once set in motion, to herm's divine regret, Creation could not be stopped. The original sin of reproduction was God's very own, and humans, as it turned out, were not even, strictly speaking, copies, but translations, retellings. Herm found hermself alone, again herm's creation convulsing downward out of control. The only communion God still had with herm's creation was when things collided in such a way as to create *suspense*; at those narrative cruxes of unknowing, indecision, pause, sudden expectant silence, God could still feel within hermself the pulse of herm's creation. The resumption of narrative ejected Herm again, en-appling (or in-dating) herm's demiurgic self until the next moment of Suspense fractured the logos. Inside the apple (or date), God thought of many things, but herm's chief thought concerned the hatching of a plan to suspend all creation forever, so that Herm might be part of it again. To this purpose, God became a student of suspense, of narrative and narration, of coincidence, synchronicity, singularity, misjoining. In other words, Herm became a student of the one thing that hermself was incapable of: conceiving of disconnection. God was in exile. Herm listened to Sheherezade as carefully as Sharyar did, but in self-reflection Herm was represented by Shahzaman, who wandered the desert having these thoughts, on account of the Two.

is not easy to rule an empire, and Sharyar's was no small empire, if there is such a thing. In fact, Sharyar's empire was, on the morning after his first night with Sheherezade, the largest empire the world had ever known, including that of Alexander the Great, and there would be no greater empire until Genghis Khan's. Situated by history between Alexander and Genghis, Sharyar was preoccupied with his recent traumas and desired nothing more than to hold his lands until his urge to conquer[65] returned. His advisers, foremost his trusted Vizir, were of the same opinion: Sharyar must govern and hold until his woman-induced madness passed. The not-yet-quite-digested and sudden addition of the kingdom of Samarkand, left in his care by his brother, Shahzaman, was an administrative nightmare to the Vizir already managing the enormous lands and peoples of Persia, India, and China. On the other hand, the generals of Sharyar's armies, driven mad by the boredom of peace and the punctilious prose of the Vizir's rule in the King's absence, had taken to religion, and were now urging Sharyar to enact their faith by marching in Allah's name over all the rest of the world. The warriors had already quarreled with the Vizir when he pointed out to their dismay that the empire was home to four hundred and sixty-five religions, some of which, like that of the Hindus, paid homage to countless gods, and that to these people, Allah was either just a god among many, or a principle rather than a god, and that it was only in the form of a divine principle that the other religions might be persuaded to accept Allah, the newcomer. The enraged officers held secret meetings with their dervishes and founded a secret society willing to die for Allah's victory. Sharyar was not yet in danger of being assassinated because his return to Baghdad was still relatively fresh, and the addition of Samarkand required that many of his best soldiers reside in that country until it was secured, but they did intend to assassinate the Vizir as soon as possible,

---

[65] Some of Sheherezade's scribes write that she told her stories at the court of Caliph Haroun al Rasheed, but among the many others who have placed Sheherezade between the covers of a book within the sheets of a royal bed, there are those, like this author, who prefer that mythical King Sharyar of Baghdad remain the only identified despot.

and in this they had the fervent support of every mother of girls in the land. The plot was difficult to carry out because the Vizir, a Persian, had hundreds of ears and eyes peering from every curtain-fold and every corner, and had had himself duplicated by look-alikes and by cleverly placed mirrors. His spies called him Zoroaster, after his god, but his enemies never spoke his name, preferring to spit instead and cross their eyes whenever either he or Zoroastrianism was discussed. The Vizir's only weakness was his daughter Sheherezade, and news of her marriage to the murderous King was greeted with joy by the generals. The demise of the Vizir, after he was compelled to strangle his own daughter, was only a matter of time. A very short time. Among themselves they were already splitting up the empire into their own kingdoms.

Sharyar had no intention of making up his mind. The glory of the wars he'd been dreaming of while begging on desert roads did not seem so urgent now, but neither did the unending labor of entering nightly into the bodies of girls untouched by men and too scared to laugh. While the ambassadors and every other sort of petitioner bowed before him and presented him with long and tedious necessities of the present, Sharyar reflected on his odd new wife, an abstract effort for which he was ill prepared. Sharyar was most interested in questioning the Master-Teacher, who had overseen Sheherezade's education in his absence. The Master-Teacher was very old and ill, but he mustered all his strength to report to the King:

"In Your Highness's Absence," the Master-Teacher said, "the girl was a poor student, more interested in spectacles than learning. She remembered the names of actors and storytellers, but if she was asked what a story is about, what it means, or what it teaches, she hid behind her scarf. When I insisted nonetheless on examining her, she recalled nothing about the hierarchies of the kingdom or the divisions of angels, but was quite detailed about the tight spots that animals and the lower orders were sometimes forced into and, somehow, escaped from."

"I don't care about that," Sharyar exclaimed impatiently. "What I must know is what stories she knows and how they end!"

"I do not remember which stories she watched or read," the Master-Teacher said, "but I know that she took particular delight in misshapen creatures, hunchbacks or genii, or human-animal hybrids who often sacrificed limbs or eyes in order to survive."

He is very slow, this old Master-Teacher; I'll have him delivered to the executioner as soon as he tells me what I need to know, though, in truth, I don't really know what I need to know.

"About her stories," the Master-Teacher said, choosing his slow words carefully, "there was no mercy or forgiveness in them, only the occasional good bestowed in a dreadful fix; everything else had to be redeemed by action. Those who did not speak well while in danger, perished. Of course," the Master-Teacher said, "when she became my pupil, there was no definitive Sheherezade yet—she was only eleven years and six months old—but I did dread to think what would come of her when she grew into a young woman! I tried to cure her of her foolish imagination, and I was careful to make her memorize and recite.[66] As for her character, I cannot say that she is pleasant or polite; I can even say with some certainty that she is not: she is irritable and brusque, often high-handed (though sometimes she regrets it), she is often petulant and impertinent, and if she appears occasionally well bred, it is only because she is too sleepy to be rude. Allah only knows what she's been doing during the night to be so sleepy at her lessons. Her impatience was always great, and she couldn't wait to escape from me and her other

---

[66] Burton: ". . . the books, annals and legends of preceding Kings, and the stories, examples and instances of by gone men and things; indeed it was said that she had collected a thousand books of histories relating to antique races and departed rulers. She had perused the works of the poets and knew them by heart; she had studied philosophy and the sciences, arts and accomplishments; and she was pleasant and polite, wise and witty, well read and well bred." Well, we dislike contradicting one of her Fates, but such excessive literary labors sound more like wishful thinking, and if she did indeed absorb and collect at such a prodigious rate, it would have been many decades later when, as an old woman, she had time on her hands. What is certain is that the *1001 Nights* are a deconstruction of male conceits intended originally to save girls from men's jealous wrath, and they resulted in the deconstruction of the male persona in its entirety, to make the world safe for the imagination. It is doubtful whether this grand operation had any use for vast quantities of medieval knowledge.

exasperated teachers. She seemed to be waiting for something, Your Highness, and I fear that the barrier between us was great; it was as if she were somewhere else, on the other side of this life . . . she sometimes shook with impatience like a bedsheet on a line blowing in the breeze . . . an embroidered scarlet sheet of silk from China that flew behind her when she rode her horse . . ."

The Master-Teacher was starting to ramble poetic, and Sharyar dismissed him unexecuted.

When it was night

and Sheherezade was in bed with the King, Dinarzad said to her sister, Sheherezade, "Please, if you are not sleepy, tell us more of your lovely little tale to while away the night." The King added, "Yes, let us hear the conclusion of the monkey-scribe's adventure." Sheherezade replied, "As you wish." Dinarzad had played many delightful games during this night also, and was very sleepy, but she was just as interested as Sharyar in the outcome, and had not forgotten Sheherezade's instruction to ask for a story an hour before dawn.

"The envoys took the scroll back to the Sultan, riding with great haste to present their find, astonished at the beauty of what they held. The Sultan saw from his window the fast pace of his envoys and had a pleasant premonition. When they unrolled the scroll[67] before him, he was speechless with astonishment: it was a script so mellifluous it surpassed that of his regretted Vizir and perhaps that of the greatest scrolls in the imperial library. He called for the finest horse in his stable to be caparisoned[68] with a splendid saddle draped with his departed Vizir's robe encrusted with gems, and twelve of his most valiant officers in parade

---

[67] The Scroll is a phallus that opens like a vagina.

[68] Lang, *The Arabian Nights Entertainments.*

dress to make haste to bring the writer to him. The envoys laughed heartily at this show and exclaimed nearly in unison, 'But Your Highness, the writer is a monkey!'

"'Well, hurry, then, and bring me the monkey!' shouted the Sultan, adding for good measure threats and imprecations. The laughter died and the party took off for the ship, where they were met by the silent crew and the visibly saddened captain who had hoped to adopt the monkey as his son, but now saw that he had been overridden. The monkey put on the robe and rode at the head of the delegation to the palace as all the people in the city crowded along the route laughing and pointing at the brightly robed monkey in the saddle. The monkey looked neither left nor right, as if riding a royal steed were a habitual matter.[69] All the laughing spectators pointing and jeering were speculating loudly as to what this monkey was doing and what it could possibly mean. The monkey pretended not to hear any of it, but to himself he said, 'I am not capable of withstanding the tsunami of meanings headed my way, but come what may, I am not the monkey they call Shakespeare.'[70] So spake the ape to himself.[71]

"The Sultan met the monkey at the gates. The monkey dismounted and performed in correct order all the bows owed a Sultan. He was led to the blue-tiled private chamber where the Sultan dismissed everyone except for the Chief of Eunuchs[72] and a young slave. He bid the monkey sit before him on a divan with

[69] We interrupt this majestic procession to bring you an important announcement: the monkey hates adjectives. By his reckoning, if one were to remove all adjectives from stories written and unwritten, the resulting shrinkage would save one million years of human time. Unfortunately, he is in no position to communicate his insight because (a) he is a monkey who is about to escape his predicament (that of being a monkey in the human world) by the use of his quill to pour forth adjectives in praise of the Sultan and all that the Sultan finds admirable, and (b) the descriptor of his essence, "monkeyish," is itself an adjective in use by humans well into the future for the purposes of symbolizing many things, including the origin of humans themselves.

[70] At this point the announcement that interrupted the procession was itself interrupted by a telephone call from friend and poet Dave Brinks in New Orleans, who, upon hearing that the monkey is heading for the palace, tells the story of his uncle Dave who had brought a monkey from "Sock America," as he called his imaginary South America. He took the monkey to school, where the monkey behaved well until teased into biting a girl, and then "the monkey had to go" and Uncle Dave quit going to school. "And also," my friend Dave said, "I have a plastic monkey on the dashboard that is very dear to my four-year-old son Blaise. I asked him why he needs to make sure the monkey is always there, and Blaise said, 'In case we get lost.' That," Dave added, "is totally right. If we get lost we'll always know where we come from as long as the monkey's there."

[71] While the monkey speaks to himself in our rendition, in Sheherezade's telling of his story he speaks in the first person throughout. For instance, speaking of his journey from ship to palace, he says: *Everyone came out, crowding to gaze at me and enjoy the spectacle. By the time I reached the king, the whole city was astir, and the people were saying to each other, 'The king has taken the ape for vizier'"* (Haddawy). We are taking advantage of the time that has elapsed since Sheherezade's tale, which was still close enough to the events in question to quote the monkey verbatim, to tell the story in the third person, thus placing both Sheherezade's storytelling and the subjects of her stories in the same approximate time period, SST (Storytelling Standard Time).

a fruit-and-flower-laden table between them. The slave brought delicate appetizers to eat, and the monkey ate sparingly and elegantly, not at all like most monkeys, including himself when he had been very hungry, before being taken in by the captain. Manners, thought the monkey, aren't hard when you aren't hungry.[73] He let a lightly smoked pickled oyster with a dash of ginger brush his palate. Before the arrival of the main dishes for which he composed verses, he reproached himself briefly for not having foreseen the appetizers. There are, of course, an infinity of descriptions for reality before, during, and after one experiences it, and an infinite variety of verse forms for these descriptions. All the monkeys and all the people writing and talking at once would be unable to either catch or match the flavor of any reality, which is why language is language and life is life. The monkey was very pleased at having thought this because it absolved him of any sin of omission he might commit in the future, while pretending to versify reality. He drank the wine the slave poured from a silver pitcher, and when the Sultan downed his glass, the monkey gestured for it. The Sultan handed it to him, whereupon the monkey dipped the quill lying next to his plate in a red berry and wrote on the Sultan's empty glass the following verse: *'I was once only a red berry become now warmth in my King like a small sun*

[72] This Chief of Eunuchs was, next to his Vizir, his most trusted friend. After the death of his scribe, who had been more than a friend, he had come to rely more and more on his minister and his eunuch. At the morning meetings, the Vizir was accompanied by an imposing official with an uncertain job description, corresponding roughly to something like Inspector General, who delivered a monotonous list of facts and figures that were, doubtlessly, most important, but hard to listen to without falling asleep. The Sultan was never sure what this man did, but knew that he could rely on him for accuracy, a quality that his eunuch, though infinitely more amusing, did not possess. His eunuch reliably lent an ear to any confidence without blushing, whispered honeyed consolations, or poisoned or honey-poisoned gossip, into his ear, and exhibited an arrogant and crude attitude toward anyone below his Sultan. In later ages the eunuch would be known as a "court jester," or a "fluffer." The Inspector General and the eunuch were opposites in every respect, and the scribeless Sultan teetered between them.

[73] Such good manners he had! Before the dishes even arrived, he wrote some verses in praise of them, in this way cleverly letting the Sultan know what he desired, mourning the fate of the animals and plants sacrificed for the repast, and indicating with delicate skill his gastronomic preferences. Haddawy renders these verses thus: *"Wail for the crane well-stewed in tangy sauce; / Mourn for the meat, either well-baked and fried; / Cry for the hens and daughters of the grouse / And the fried birds . . ."* and on to *"two kinds of fish,"* *"two loaves of bread,"* and *"eggs rolling like eyes"* that *"fry in their pain."* For good measure the monkey throws in some *"pickled greens."* There is cruelty in those eye-like eggs rolling in pain, but there is little else that betrays the fact that the writer is a monkey, not Craig Claiborne. Sir Richard Burton has them partake of a different versified menu: *"Wail for the little partridges on porringer and plate; / Cry for the ruin of the fries and stews well marinate? . . . And omelette round the fair unbrowned fowls agglomerate . . ."* and he has therein also *"meat pudding"* and *"pot-herbs."* Even if we account for the changing tastes of 20th-century gourmands (Haddawy) and Victorians (Burton), we note that both translate the apology to the things eaten; this is a universal custom: the world over people ask forgiveness of those (or that which) they are about to consume, a graceful human habit that transferred badly to the customary Christian thanksgiving prayer that thanks the Lord for the food, not the animals and plants that gave their life for it. In passing, we bow to simplicity: Burton was just too high on fancy language to reach us; those ruined "fries" are funny, even if he didn't mean "french fries." Haddawy comes closer to making a contemporary salivate, but his plainness isn't right either: we are talking about a poeticking monkey here, not your average restaurant review; to future translators we recommend some of the Menu Bards, also known as "Servers," who now present in lovely language the menu specials in new American restaurants.

released at last from its skin.' He wrote this verse in a circle just below the rim, and no matter which way the Sultan turned the glass, the verse read the same forward and backward.[74] The wine had now spoken to the Sultan from itself and through a line of verse, a pleasure that he had never before known.[75] Next, the monkey took a peach from the fruit bowl and wrote on it, *'I will pass through a Sultan's lips and I will be forever remembered for having been written.'* The Sultan laughed and took a bite. Peach juice and ink dribbled into his beard. 'You will remember me forever for being bitten, peach!' he laughed, and tossed the peach to the Chief of Eunuchs who laughed and took a bite, too, and tossed the peach to the slave boy who likewise took a tiny bite as juice dripped down his chin, and then he tossed it back to the monkey who took the last bite on which the word 'written' was written.

"'We have eaten your words,' cried the delighted Sultan, 'now we must go to the library.' The Chief of Eunuchs led the way through a copper door down a marble hall to a vaulted chamber where tens of thousands of scrolls were lined up side by side in polished wooden tubes that rose to the high vaults tiled with a mosaic rendering of the night sky. Light came in through colored glass windows, tinting the maze with various degrees of thickness and transparency. The Sultan beamed with pride: 'Behold the scrolls I have collected from every place in the world where there was writing. Only Alexander's library compared to this!' The potentate, the monkey, and the eunuch stood there, bathed in the richly hued light, surrounded by the world's writing, and the ensuing silence was significant.[76]

---

[74] Haddawy calls the glass a "flagon" and renders the verses thus: *"For my confession they burned me with fire / And found that I was for endurance made, / Hence I was borne high on the hands of men / And given to kiss the lips of pretty maid."* He is clearly talking about the "flagon," not Joan of Arc and her legacy, but I wonder whether the monkey, drunk already, did not begin to articulate his long-repressed lust, which, as we shall see, will soon be sated. Burton has no qualms about getting right down: *"With fire they boiled me to loose my tongue . . . / And honey-dew from lips of maid I sip,"* which sounds to us like cunnilingus and Coleridge.

[75] In those days, as in ours, anything articulated for someone else was increased in value if repeated in another medium; in the days when storytelling was at its height, storytellers competed with each other to see in how many media they could say the same thing, and so theater was born; in our day, the dumbing down of stories for film and television has given birth unfortunately to the dictum "Tell them, show them what you told them, and tell them what you showed them that you told them."

"'In the end there will be as many people as there are words,' the Sultan sighed.

'Or syllables,"' the eunuch emphasized.

Allah forbid, thought the monkey, but instead wrote dutifully down in his notebook: 'As many people as there are words.' He carried this notebook everywhere, always careful to differentiate what might please his master from the mere usage of language. The interesting thing about this notebook is that it existed entirely in his mind;[77] he couldn't have carried or owned a papyrus, so he made a picture of a scroll in his mind and wrote in it without moving his hand: all he had to do was to close his right eye for it to appear.

"'Where will all those people fit?' the Sultan wondered.

The monkey said, 'In the future there will be several people inside each human body.'[78] He looked up at the library scrolls as the thought of a closely calligraphed future overwhelmed him.

"'All is one in Allah,' the eunuch said reverentially.

'That is true,' the Sultan added, 'All humans are emanations of the One.'

"What is sad, thought the monkey, is that the multiplication of people will drive them farther and farther away from the One. There will be as many people as there are words, and they will keep distancing themselves from the Creator, if only by the mere increase in their numbers. During his wanderings, the monkey-scribe had noted the existence of many enchanted beings—he being one of them—but by far the eeri-

---

[76] When we still hear this silence in the future, we are tempted to put on sackcloth and ashes and throw ourselves into a live volcano: few of those scrolls are still extant. Still, for our purpose, a narrow one, granted, the one important scroll to survive was the 14th-century compilation titled *The Book of the Thousand Nights and a Night*, which introduces the Storyteller Sheherezade who must tell a story every night in order to stay the hand of Sharyar, the tyrant who marries a new wife every night and then has her murdered next morning.

[77] It was an iMindbook.

[78] They will call this process "marketing."

est had been creatures that were changed from humans into automatons; some of them were only part human and part mechanism, while some others were composed in various degrees of stone, wood, crafted wheels and springs, and whatever remained of their flesh."

"That is frightening, Sheherezade!" cried Sharyar, who felt his hand go cold over Dinarzad's smooth warm midriff. "What could possibly be the purpose of such monsters?"

"The purpose of these creatures is to multiply in order to consume the words that they themselves produce in greater and greater quantities. The monkey feared that the future beings created by words would eventually obscure the horizon completely, making it impossible for people to see more than the person right in front of them." But Sheherezade reassured the anxious King by adding that the monkey immediately calmed himself by thinking that he did not need to fear because (1) he wasn't going to be alive in that future, and (2) automatons were not separate from people, since their purpose was not to destroy people or monkeys. People would become automatons only from the involuntary need to keep producing and re-producing, which was the same purpose that the Creator must have had in mind when he'd first started the ball rolling.

"'There is no need for fear,' the monkey told the Sultan, 'because I have myself been enchanted and transformed, and Allah is great,' and he congratulated himself silently on his good luck.[79] And he kept writing everything he thought might please the Sultan, but not everything he thought of. Just as, Sheherezade added to herself, I am not telling you everything, my King and sister, because you would lose interest if you knew it.

[79] If you call "good luck" the inability to speak and to be transferred only from flesh to flesh, not from flesh to metal or a combination thereof. The monkey thanked Allah for his not being a clock.

III

"'The Sultan was overcome with awe at the possibilities of entertainment offered by his myriad of scrolls, and the by-now nearly forgotten sweet balm of sleep, and the monkey was overcome by fatigue at the thought of reading them. The eunuch felt the pain of becoming orthography, or rather of being orthographed as a means to pause within the endless story. It is then that the Sultan had a great inspiration."[80]

But morning overtook Sheherezade, and she lapsed into silence. As the day dawned, and it was light, her sister, Dinarzad, said, "What a strange and wonderful story!" Sheherezade replied, "Tomorrow night I shall tell something even stranger and more wonderful than this."[81]

"You cannot stop now!" shouted Sharyar in a voice that echoed in eternity. "I must know what the Sultan's inspiration was!"

Sheherezade would not be persuaded, and, with the tiniest smile, accompanied by a salty oblong tear that fell on her breast, she offered her long white neck for strangling, but the King waved it away as if it were a fly. He'd seen enough strangled necks, and while, granted, Sheherezade's was delicate, pretty, and throbbing with life, he'd rather hear the end of her story than her last breath. He absentmindedly stroked Dinarzad's dainty foot and rose to be dressed, leaving the women in his bed to their matinal tasks.

sharyar's dilemma

That morning, while having his first ibric of sweet hot coffee, and before his ministers arrived, Sharyar realized his dilemma and was horrified. He understood that he would never climax again

---

[80] The Sultan's great inspiration: the power of power is to tell an infinite story by means of a finite product, a scroll. Or, to put this in the light of administration: the finite instrument of the law must work the same everywhere every time.

[81] Haddawy.

until he climaxed inside Dinarzad, and that he could never climax inside Dinarzad unless Sheherezade finished her stories. Only at the moment that Sheherezade concluded her tales, but while she was still speaking the last few words, would he be able to release the dammed effluvium of sperm that had gathered inside him from the night that he had married the Storyteller. Not that he hadn't tried: from the very first night of frustration from the lack of both narrative and sexual conclusions, he had attempted to obtain satisfaction from any number of comely slaves and palace girls, and even from the eunuchs best known for orally gratifying his harem. He had even tried to bring himself to a conclusion by means of his well-oiled hand and a book of erotic miniatures, but it was all in vain: at the very instant that surrender seemed possible, he felt rising within himself the question, "And then what happened?" and his hot lava cooled as if ice had been dumped on it. Certain that he had been bewitched, Sharyar summoned physicians who manipulated his body in a number of ways and burned herbs and steamed him with piquant spice. He was subjected to spells and given strong infusions of hashish, wine, and opium, and slathered in scented oil by eight nude Nubians with strong fingers—all for naught. In addition to his increasing frustration, his inability to climax was a matter of state. His seed was needed to ensure the production of heirs, and subtle and not-so-subtle hints began to be heard from abroad by his spies, who spoke of foreign Kings greedy for his empire, laughing about his condition. Whether he liked it or not, he had to follow Sheherezade to the end of her stories and let her live, or he'd never find the peace that called to him from inside Dinarzad.

when it was night again

and Sheherezade and Dinarzad were already in bed with the King, having been undressed way too slowly, in Sharyar's opinion, by the slave girl and eunuch appointed to the task, Dinarzad said to her sister, Sheherezade, "Please, if you are not sleepy, continue the tale of the Sultan and the monkey-scribe because I shall never sleep again if you don't," and she wiggled herself into the King's lap, taking hold beseechingly of her sister's hand. The King added, "Yes, let us hear the conclusion." Sheherezade replied, "As you wish."

"I must now describe better the foodstuffs that the Sultan ordered for his sumptuous lunch with the monkey-scribe . . ."

"Wait!" cried Sharyar, "didn't you already tell this one?" He looked ready to turn her over to the Strangler. How dare she repeat herself? Repetition was permitted only in prayer and poetry: stories should get on with it.

"My Lord," Sheherezade replied firmly, "it is necessary to reintroduce some of the story because I have purposefully omitted the lunch-fare, so that we might grow hungry and order the cook to bring us the very same delicacies in bed!"

In truth, the King was a bit hungry because his impatience to hear the rest of Sheherezade's story had decreased his appetite during the day. Now, he was truly ravenous, he thought, admiring the rosy buds of the girls all perky before him.[82]

"So lunch was brought," continued Sheherezade, "and the monkey-scribe praised the 'crane well-stewed in tangy sauce,' the 'boiled and fried . . . hens . . . and grouse,' the 'two different kinds of fish . . . served on two loaves of bread,' the 'eggs like rolling eyes' frying 'in their pain,' 'the porridge,' and did not fail to append to this gastronomical laudatio a few verses concerning the appetites of the soul and man's fate. When dessert came, he 'took a peach and wrote on it some verses in praise of the Sultan.'[83] The impressed potentate called for wine, and the butler brought out 'a choice wine in a glass flagon.' The Sultan drank first,

[82] A feeble attempt to imitate Persian love poetry.

[83] Writing on fruit is an ancient art that I have myself rediscovered in a 2009 poetry workshop at Louisiana State University. See http://www.insidehighered.com/views/2009/01/16/codrescu.

then offered the ape-poet some, and after he had again kissed the correct spot of ground between the royal legs, he wrote some new verses directly on the glass of the flagon, to the effect that he had passed the test of fire, and that, having endured it, he was celebrated and could now kiss the lips of pretty maidens."

Summoned quickly, the cook woke up the kitchen servants, and a replica of the story-lunch was produced and delivered to Sharyar's bed before you could say the marvelous verses in praise of it. Dinarzad and the King fell on it wolfishly, but Sheherezade went on.

"The Sultan's astonishment grew, for he had never heard such cultivated verse. He set a chessboard between them and asked the monkey whether he played. Once again, the ape kissed the ground between his feet and nodded yes. The first game was a draw; then the scribe won the second and third games, and the Sultan bowed to his skill. The monkey then dipped the pen in the inkwell again and wrote directly on the chessboard a quatrain so beautiful the Sultan felt compelled to send for his daughter so that they might enjoy this poetry together. While waiting for the eunuch to fetch his daughter, the Sultan delighted in the verses that had two armies contending in the day, but when night fell, they slept together in one bed."

Sharyar ordered the Chinese chess set brought to the bed, after the remains of the sumptuous lunch were removed and all three shone with the fat of happiness that they licked from each other's fingers. Sheherezade offered her hand only reluctantly, but Dinarzad kissed the King's hand eagerly and even licked between his fingers like a cat. The Chinese chess set, given in tribute by a vanquished Chinese lord, was an intricately carved landscape of valleys and mountains with rivers and streams of gold-and-blue water running through them, and two whole armies, one ivory and one scarlet, standing to attention on either side of the border, which was a mountain.

"How do you play this?" Dinarzad exclaimed with wonder.

Pleased at her outburst and her licking, Sharyar closed his eyes and let himself feel, and when he had felt sufficiently, his penis rose in the direction of the ivory army and several horsemen moved forward.

"Now it's your turn," he said.

In no time at all, Dinarzad closed her eyes and felt inside her a power that she was certain could move some of the army. Indeed. When she opened her eyes, three scarlet warriors had moved and were heading at full gallop for the ivory soldiers. Sheherezade looked as if this game was none of her concern, but several pieces moved on the chessboard none-theless when she picked up again the thread of her story, which proved to the King that the chess-maker had indeed been brilliant when he'd set lust in place as the motor for the game's motion.

"When the Sultan's daughter returned with the eunuch, she saw the monkey-scribe and quickly veiled her face. She cried out, 'O Father, have you lost your honor that you expose me to men?' The properly astonished Sultan said, 'But this is not a man, Daughter, it is only a monkey. From whom do you veil your face?' She then replied, 'From this young man who has been cast under a spell by a demon who is the son of Satan's daughter . . . He whom you think an ape is a wise, learned, and well-mannered man, a man of culture and refinement. He was turned into an ape after he killed his own wife, the daughter of Timarus, King of the Ebony Islands.'

"At the Sultan's inquiring look, the ape nodded that, yes, this was indeed the case. The Sultan then questioned his daughter as to how she knew, and she replied, 'O Father, there was with me from childhood a wily and treacherous old woman who was a witch. She taught me witchcraft, and I copied and memorized seventy domains of magic, by the least of which I could within the hour transport the stones in your city beyond Mount Qaf and beyond the ocean that surrounds the world.'

"The Sultan said, 'O Daughter, may Allah protect you. You have had such a complete power all this time, yet I never knew it. By my life, deliver him from the spell, so that I may make him Vizir and marry you to him.'

She replied, 'With the greatest pleasure.'

Then she took a knife inscribed with Allah's name in Hebrew letters, drew a circle on the ground with it, scooped up a handful of dirt and blew over it, saying some words, and wrote with her finger on a bowl of water . . ."[84]

But morning overtook Sheherezade, and she lapsed into silence. Then Dinarzad said, "Sister, what a strange and entertaining story!" Sheherezade replied, "What is this compared with what I shall tell you tomorrow night, if the King spares me and lets me live!"

The King shook his head and said, "Today we are all going to stay in this bed, do nothing but eat, drink wine, play chess with our secret powers, and listen to the rest of your story, Sheherezade!"

Sheherezade, at this point, seeing that it was truly day, and knowing that the King always rose very early to attend the council, stopped speaking. "Indeed, Sister," said Dinarzad, "this is a wonderful story." "The rest is still more wonderful," replied Sheherezade, "and you would say so, if the King would allow me to live another day, and would give me leave to tell it to you next night."[85]

[84] The reader of the *Nights* has doubtlessly noticed that much of the magic performed in the stories involves writing on water; spells written on water outnumber by far writing with other elements. Water writing has the advantage of speed, of disappearing quickly, and of traveling farthest. All four elements have their share of magical writing in the *Nights*, leading us to this formula: Four Elements + Writing = Magic. Sheherezade has made of writing not just a tool to be used by the four elements, but also a fifth element of its own, born of having employed the elementals to carry messages.

[85] Whenever Sheherezade repeats herself, she makes it so: her repetitions are spells, the most primitive form of spelling, but effective nonetheless; if one were to sketch a scale of spells, one would begin with the spelling of her name, all the way to the powerful formulas writ on water or with fire that cause great physical transformations; the *Nights* is rife with spells, some of them famous, like the secret formula that opens the treasure cave to Ali Baba, "Open, Sesame." Spells must be exact: Ali Baba's brother is killed when he misremembers the cave-opening words; Sheherezade also uses rhymed poetry and prose to induce spells on Sharyar and her millions of listeners since. The spelling of her name alone yielded this many Google hits on December 20, 2008: Sheherazade, 1,080,000; Scheherezade, 176,000; Sheherezade, 52,600; Sheharazade, 2,910; Shezerade, 1,120; Shezarade, 368; Sheherizade, 299. For our purposes, she is Sheherezade, despite vox google populi.

The King realized that Sheherezade was more interested in living another day than in lolling about the bed like the lazy drunkards who lived in Baghdad's seamier quarters. He tried to persuade her to go on, but to no avail.

Sheherezade truly really perceived the dawn of the day and ceased to say her permitted say. Then quoth her sister to her, "O my sister, how pleasant is thy tale and how grateful; how sweet and how tasteful!" And Sheherezade answered her, once again, "What is this to that I could tell thee on the coming night, were I to live and the King would spare me?"

So the King spared her.

in the king's absence: sheherezade.1

When Sharyar and Shahzaman wandered in the desert and Sheherezade was but a sapling, her best friend was her horse, Abd al-Hakim. The silk of her scarf had been secreted by silkworms in the endless mulberry forests she often saw on her rides. She saw other things, too, but barely noticed them because she spent all her free time conversing with her horse. Abd al-Hakim had belonged to a defeated caliph and spoke Arabic, Chinese, Hindi, and Persian. She knew those languages herself, and a few others, and she believed that she possessed fragments of a secret language that she could speak only when she didn't think about it: this was God's language, written and spoken before Babel. God's language was what holy men and prophets sometimes spoke after drinking hashish-wine. The words of God's language are what the world is written in: everything that can be seen, sensed, imagined, or told is part of the very long sentence God wrote when creating the world. How she came to know bits of this language is a mystery, and she didn't even know that she was studying it because something in her was trying to discover the *fold-drive*. She thought best on horseback, where there was no barrier between her and Abd al-Hakim, who was not only learned and well traveled, but also funny and wise. For instance, one day when mounting she spoke a bit of the illuminated tongue without knowing it, and Abd al-Hakim asked: "What did you say?" Sheherezade was startled to realize that she had just said, "Up and away we go!" in God's language, and she told him so.

"How do you know that what you speak is God's language?"

"Look, horse," said Sheherezade, exasperated, even though she knew well that her Abd al-Hakim was only engaging her in Socratic dialogue, "I know it because all the words we speak are only sparks from its original flame, but what I just said was all fire."

"*All* words?" quoth the horse, feigning incredulity.

"Yes! Why else would we 'give our word'? Why else would we value honor above all else? We tie our word to our actions; therefore each word is an oath. Why else would we hold a naming ceremony for each child? The word of everyone's name is an oath that binds it to God."

"Well, I am a horse," the horse said, "and it is true that I am not nameless—my name is Abd al-Hakim, and I speak besides—but aren't our oaths as decayed in practice as the words descended from the original flame?"

"Yes, unfortunately. Still, there are words that are more sacred than others, that are heavier, that contain more of the first fertility, more seed, words that are more like pomegranates than shoes, words like 'God,' 'Allah' and 'love.' These words bind a creature more closely to creation, but in truth all words are just as full and grave, but we don't see it. I rarely see it."

"i see it sometimes," abd al-hakim said mirthlessly

Each time she dismounted, she entered the palace a little sadder and more thoughtful. One particular conversation with Abd al-Hakim left her even more thoughtful than usual. Her horse had said, "Why are you people so afraid to die?" It was a heavy question for such a young girl, but as we know, young girls are often very eager to answer or at least to think about every question, as if all questions are part of a cosmic exam.

"That's a hard question, horse," replied Sheherezade, "but I think that it has something to do with numbers. When people look at the hourglass, the sand is never aligned to the line drawn on the glass; it's either below or above it. I think that this means that they are still alive and they are reassured, but they also become afraid to look at the hourglass in case the sand is aligned with the line. They fear that when that happens, they will die."

Sheherezade saw herself often as the savior of her sister, Dinarzad, who was only nine years old—nine and two months, to be exact—and was a quiet girl who worshipped Sheherezade, her protector from their earliest days when Dinarzad, frightened by the dragons emerging from spuming seas, and beautiful princesses locked in the darkness at the bottom of pools of blood or squeezed tight inside glass bottles, sought refuge in the crook of Sheherezade's arm and snuggled against her until she fell asleep. Sheherezade's body was Dinarzad's sweet narcotic, the source of a healing wave of sleep that kept her safe. When Dinarzad became old enough to ask profound questions, around the age of six, she asked Sheherezade whether the stories they saw performed in the Great Hall were real, and whether the terrible things that happened to the princesses in the story could happen to them. Yes, Sheherezade assured her, such things could indeed happen to them, but in the end they would not be harmed because she, Sheherezade herself, had powers, courage, and cunning superior to those who'd harm her. To prove this, she told Dinarzad the *real* story of how these things were: whatever story the storytellers, using masks and dances, told them, Sheherezade retold later, in their bed, and in her retelling, things were made well again, and the world was there in the morning.

Dinarzad developed two kinds of listening: she listened in one way to the recitals performed at court by people older and larger than her, and in another way to Sheherezade's retelling of those stories. When she told Sheherezade about the two kinds of listening, Sheherezade replied that since there are two kinds of listening, a dutiful, scary one, and a hopeful, trusting one, there are also two ways of telling a story, and that she specialized, particularly for Dinarzad, in promoting the second kind of listening by telling the second kind of story, the *retold* story.

Like all children (see Melanie Klein),[86] young Sheherezade was often caught in the rhetorical traps of her inexperience when she told an adult a story intended to explain where she'd been and what she'd been doing. Aware that whatever she'd been doing had taken place in the absence of the questioning adult, she felt a giddy sense of freedom, physically manifested by a handful of tiny light arrows exploding in her solar plexus. She felt that she could say *anything*. So Sheherezade proceeded to retell a story by eliminating the narrative defect, and ended up telling another story. The smoother story was superficially intended to firm up the veracity of her first account, but was, in fact, an application of her skill in narrative sinuousness, and proof that she could learn quickly. A series of narrative inconsistencies were eliminated by trial and error by Sheherezade in her childhood. Her *alt-story* thus served a dual purpose: fooling the grownups and comforting her sister.[87]

[86] Melanie Klein (1882–1960), Austrian-born British psychoanalyst, devised therapeutic techniques for children. She found that the objects of an infant's desire were parents, in whose absence the infant would create imaginary objects that she would manipulate in *play*. Such objects, carried into adult life, were pathologies to be cured, in Klein's view, but, in our opinion, these alternative realities created by children within the absence of caretakers became reality itself when the parents' worlds vanished, as they inevitably did. We live presently in the descendant of a reality that was once a world of imaginary objects in play, an alternative reality that we created when we became older than our parents, and which is being transformed by our children into a new reality that will be *the* reality when we disappear. Many such "realities" have succeeded each other since the original absence that must have created the first play of imaginary objects. Those objects are no longer imaginary; they are already in museums, part of the history of the materialization of imaginary objects through the free play of children's fantasy. Objects not physically recovered by archaeologists survive in stories. Sheherezade is of the utmost importance because she greatly speeded up the manufacture of alternative worlds through her innovations in narrative technique. Let us make a brief intervention from the future here, because our understanding of narrative development has grown. The retold story was actually *another* story, an *alt-story* (by no means a *sequel*, like every other story), an alternative story that Sheherezade had been developing since early childhood.

[87] It is worthy of note that R. Burton was a "resolute and unblushing liar" in his childhood, and in his own words (cited by Edward Rice in *Captain Sir Richard Francis Burton: The Secret Agent Who Made the Pilgrimage to Mecca, Discovered the* Kama Sutra*, and Brought the* Arabian Nights *to the West*). Rice also quotes Burton's reasoning: "I used to ridicule the idea of my honour being in any way attached to telling the truth. I considered it an impertinence to be questioned. I could never understand what moral turpitude there could be in a lie, unless it was told for fear of the consequence of telling the truth, or that one would attach blame to another person. That feeling continued for many a year, and at last, as it very often happens, as soon as I realized that a lie was contemptible, it ran into the other extreme, a disagreeable habit of scrupulously telling the truth whether it was time or not." Note here how B. Clotho passed on to his charge the integrity of the imagination, the pride of one's own story, pride attached only to splendid gratuitousness, and how, as soon as a taint of the "real" might attach to it, in the form of self-interest or harm to another, it became more noble, whatever the consequences, to tell the truth. This Fate gifted Sheherezade from the very beginning with a reversal of the values that society likes to attach to such notions as "lie" and "truth." Life is more elevated for being an act of the imagination, while truth, a pedestrian convention, is to be used only under circumstances when the lie might adversely affect the heart and spirit of another.

While the process is common to all children, the topos of Sheherezade's world was different: she moved in a maze of uneven heights edged by erotic (brightly colored) statuary that emitted perfumes (of India, China, Persia), and within equally rich color-and-scent structure(s) of spiral stairways, layers of carpets, round rooms with hidden doors, windows that opened onto secret gardens, fountains splashing on abstract mosaics of polished stones, libraries of stacked goatskin and rolled-up papyrus books written in bright inks. Her stories could never be verified, for lack of a straight line of sight. Everywhere her listener looked, he encountered only roundnesses, trompe l'oeuil spaces, optical illusions. There were so many places to hide in the surroundings of Sheherezade's childhood that any adult intent on catching the child fabulating would have to have been a great psychologist, familiar not only with the brilliance of children, but with the secrets of perspective in an environment that consciously toyed with expectation. This was a willfully aesthetic world created for her own pleasure and that of her intimates, the opposite of any rigor in the application of the law, which was her father's job.

Sheherezade's father, the Vizir, was no obstacle to her early training in fabulation. While he held a quill above a legal parchment, absentminded, he readily accepted her stories. He attributed some of her lack of restraint and the unexpected turns of her childish fabulation to her origin. Sheherezade's mother was a Scythian captive, one of the last nomads to have eluded the grasp of Cyrus the Great's empire and that of Darius III, and even that of Alexander the Great. This Scythian band was renowned for its wildness, its canny strategies of escape, its courage, and the beauty of its women. When the Scythians were captured, the King of Kings and the Vizir were first to choose among the maidens. The King's Scythian wife was tall and graceful, and was going to be unequaled in fierceness and passion by any of his other wives, not excluding the youngest and comeliest. As for the Vizir's wife, he knew that she carried Sheherezade in her womb, but did not disclose this to anyone, because he loved her. When Dinarzad was born of their union, she was never told that Sheherezade was her half sister, the spawn of savage nomads. The Vizir's wife, Sheherezade's mother, rode into the desert shortly after Dinarzad's birth and never returned. The distraught Vizir loved his daughters even more then, and he saw her mother's fire burning in Sheherezade, who greatly resembled her.

There was an army of women charged with her proper upbringing, women of different ages, some of them slaves, others servants from noble families. The constant variety of her caretakers allowed her to practice her fancies, though as the Vizir's daughter she was well monitored in the daytime. Even her horse rides were watched from the city towers by hawkeyed guards. The only time she truly had to herself was the night. And so night became the playing field of her imagination, the time when she could explore the palace: she peeked behind curtains into the hidden gardens, moved objects slightly out of the way, just enough to befuddle their owners, especially her father, who could never find his inkpot; she watched the ministers and their harems sleeping or frolicking; she heard intimate conversations, some of which involved plans and plots; she observed unobserved the poets and the scribes working late into the night with furrowed brows. She liked sitting cross-legged before spiders daring each other to weave the most fantastic webs; she watched the night-guards drinking raki from gourds with half-dressed beardless boys in their laps; she even descended through secret passages into the dungeons where chained men screamed all night; she sometimes passed them water and bread through the bars, and in gratitude they told her their stories of bad luck, and how the world *really* was; at times she found her way even further down, under the dungeons, to dim ossuaries that stretched many miles, and she'd stepped lightly on the bones of the dead, like a bird, listening to roving rats and slithering snakes; and after each such night, she crept back to her chamber at dawn and slept for one hour, until her slave girl woke her up and carried her sleepy body to the baths. In the baths, the other girls in the palace, who'd slept well all night, splashed and laughed, wide-awake and rested, unaware that in a very few years they would become the brides of King Sharyar, and would lose their lives the morning after they married him. So full of life were they in the mornings of Sheherezade's youth, she barely knew what to make of them as they tried to draw her into games she was too sleepy for. Even though she couldn't quite bring all of herself to them, she felt great affection for her lively naked contemporaries whose tiny bumps, where breasts would eventually grow, made her laugh.

another day of royal prose

All day King Sharyar saw scrolls and ordered edicts to be written on scrolls, and he saw that it simply did not matter who wrote the scrolls or read them aloud to him. The human body, he noted, was best suited to writing, but an ape with hands and fingers could also write. So could other creatures with toes or fingers who could hold a pen, and instead of his chancellors and scribes bent over paper and inkwells, conducting the writing of the empire, he imagined apes and dogs and cats and birds. And what if these human bodies holding his vastnesses together by means of writing were not human at all, but enchanted animals condemned to take human shape and write. The King was moderately superstitious, but he did not doubt the existence of magic and its powers to cause shape-shifts. He himself was both a powerful King with a body hardened by war, hunting, and the desert, and a man haunted by the infidelity of his wife and the wearisome oath he had taken to kill every one of his brides. The jealous murderer was one and the same with the ruler of lands by means of scrolls, invisible to the naked eye, and perhaps not even human-looking. Maybe he the proud King and Sheherezade's husband did not even share a body, thought the King, looking at his reflection in a window: the King was tall, tan, muscular, weather-beaten, scarred, and merciless, while the husband was a fat little meatball, a soft uncooked kebob who'd prefer to stay in bed, listen to lascivious stories, and drink rather than rule. He thought that he could make out the shape of this meatball just behind him, but the image didn't displease him. He couldn't wait until he got back to bed to hear the rest of Sheherezade's tale at the soft urging of her sister, Dinarzad, the deflowering assistant, whom he had begun to fancy. Would he have taken that ape into his service and made him his Vizir? The King liked to think that he would have, because both the captain of the ship and the Sultan in the story had shown nobility of character and the foresight to disregard the despised shape of a monkey to see the skill and genius under the hair and monkey limbs and brows. The ability to see beyond the form was what distinguished a leader from the herd, but would either of those wise leaders have acted as they did if the ape had been but a mediocre scribe? The ape's brilliance was doubtlessly part of their discernment. And if even apes were distinguished by their skills, why weren't wives? The King arrived at an uncomfortable conclusion: if wives were not all the same, then killing them as if they were, was wrong. Perhaps he ought to kill only the dull ones. He had already killed some very shapely ones and he regretted it, but in those cases, he had never thought past their form. Sheherezade might be shapely, but if the truth be known, he had barely looked at her, so captivated was he by her story. His daily life consisted of enforcing the authority of writing, but his night had been taken by storytelling. Was there a contradiction between the two, something fundamental, a break between the oral night and the written day, something that made the ruler and the husband suffer separately from their effects? The story of the ape was about writing: the ape was hired as a calligrapher and a reader; he had applied for the job with verses written in many scripts and languages that showed, no doubt, his courtly Chinese education; he had written poetry on glass like the Egyptians, on fruit like the Romans, and on a chessboard, like the Persians; then the princess started disenchanting him with words written on water and a steel dagger inscribed with the name of Allah in Hebrew characters. Was the need for writing so great that a King would hire even a monkey? Well, of course. He thought of his own empire and how essential writing was to its functioning. Treaties and letters were the core of his power, a tightly rolled scroll made up of millions of words on countless documents, a core-scroll that rotated at the center of the palace, in the center of his own body: he himself was the vessel within which was housed the rotating imperial scroll. King Sharyar drew himself up straighter, the better to feel the surge of the moving wheel of paper within himself, and the better to hear its rolling hum, its surge of accumulated agreements over centuries of war and increase of wealth; he closed his eyes and saw a tower of numbers also written on the scroll inside him—words of law, property, and succession mingled with numbers denoting precise amounts of tribute, and measurements of grain, gold, silver, and slaves. Then the meatball took over, and he couldn't wait to get back in bed to curl up with Dinarzad and enter the body of Sheherezade's story. The scroll of power within himself started unrolling as an apish hand overwrote it with magic formulas and symbols. Sharyar tried to stop it, but he felt nauseated and couldn't; different styles of calligraphy, strange languages, and oddly truncated sentences appeared over the laws, histories, and accounts of his empire.

The Vizir, summoned quickly to his side, thought to distract him with a report from the keeper of the royal zoo, who complained that, for no discernible reason, all the King's monkeys had begun masturbating obsessively and simultaneously, covering the floors and the walls of their cages with semen. The zookeeper wanted some instruction, but the Vizir had no remedy. Sharyar did laugh at this, and shrugged his shoulders. He suggested to his Vizir that the zookeeper should equip the monkeys with scrolls that they might stroke just as they did their penises, with considerably less messiness. His own advice had a salutary effect on himself, and his appetite returned. He retained the Vizir by his side and ordered the cook to bring them again the precise menu that the Sultan had served his ape-poet in Sheherezade's story, and that he had already eaten once in the middle of the night and licked from the sisters' fingers. They ate "crane well-stewed in tangy sauce," "boiled and fried . . . hens . . . and grouse," the "two different kinds of fish . . . served on two loaves of bread," the "egg like rolling eyes" frying "in their pain," "the porridge," and for dessert they had a bowl of peaches and grapes. Sharyar remembered the oysters from the first telling, and had some of those with the grapes. Taking a sip of his wine, he asked the Vizir who was currently the court poet.

The Vizir had to ask a dervish who had to ask a musician who had to ask a eunuch who inquired within the harem, and in no longer than it takes to peel a grape, the current poet was found and brought before them. The trembling hunchback shaking with fear, with eyes rimmed by sleeplessness, and the smell of stale wenching about him, bowed so low he had difficulty rising again. The King had him seated at a safe distance on a pillow and asked him to partake of some of the delicacies before him. The poet leaned forward and dove greedily into the cooling porridge and the wing fat, slurped loudly three oysters, and emerged with a face full of leftovers. "Now write us a poem about what it is you ate," asked the King. The poet feigned surprise, as if this request were some kind of joke (being a court poet he had often been asked to commemorate battles and praise visiting dignitaries, but he'd never written a line about anything he'd had actual physical contact with); then, seeing that the King meant it, he rolled his eyes upward where Allah did not help him, and then, finally, he asked for paper. "No paper," said the King, pushing the fruit bowl toward him, "write your verses on this fruit." An inkwell and pen were set before him. While the poet fidgeted, the King went to the war room to consult with his generals before maps, and when he returned, the poet had barely scratched a half-word on a grape. On the instant, he commanded that the poet be beheaded, and he told his Vizir to find him a new poet by next day, or else he would suffer the same fate as his daughter Sheherezade, who was sure to die the very next morning.

The panicked Vizir sent messengers to the marketplace, where the many scribes earning a living there dabbled in verse as well. How can it be, wondered King Sharyar, that this Sultan, King like myself, could have a grown daughter, a young woman, who learned to be a witch and know seventy arts of magic without her father's knowledge? He had no daughters—indeed, he had no children at all, because his brides of one night had not given him any, nor had the original and unfaithful wife— but if he had, he was sure that he would have known what they were up to. The King felt a longing for a daughter whose secrets he could know. If he'd had a daughter, he would certainly be informed of her studies.

He ordered the chief Carpet-Weaver, who was reputed to be a witch, brought before him. The woman, wrapped in black from head to foot, so that only one of her eyes was visible, kneeled on the carpet and kissed the required spot between the King's legs.

"Old woman," bellowed the King, "do you teach your witchcraft to the daughters of my nobles?"

She denied the dreadful accusation with a violent shake of her head, a less than believable gesture, so the King threatened her with instant death if she did not answer truthfully. "My sovereign and light of all our souls," the Chief Weaver said, "I wish that you'd kill me now and let one young girl live in my stead. All us old women, and the married ones, the mothers and the widows, wish that you would kill us and not our daughters. We wish that peace would come to your angry heart and that you would marry a virgin as beautiful as there ever was among us, and that you would spare the rest. Your killings of brides have depleted the kingdom of women, and we will soon perish from sadness and lack of wombs."

The King did not expect such a vehement political speech, so he had her beheaded at once, without receiving an answer to his question, though he was sure that all the daughters were secretly learning witchcraft. He reasoned that if witchcraft was practiced chiefly by means of writing, the best way to prevent its effects would be to allow no young woman to write. He ordered (again) all schools to close their doors to girls. He commanded also that a spy stand close to every crone known to be a witch, and report to him every morning. For every one of these actions undertaken by the upright King that he was, he felt a weakening of the meatball husband who was burning with curiosity to hear the rest of Sheherezade's tale, and could hardly wait for night to fall so that he might go back to bed.

Unknowingly, he had executed the leader of Al-Adl, who was none other than the Chief Weaver, and Sheherezade was elected its leader that same day.

an hour before dawn

Dinarzad said to her sister, Sheherezade, while Sharyar tried to stuff her entire adorable left foot in his mouth, "Sister, if you are not sleepy, tell us one of your lovely little tales."

"The princess drew a perfect circle in the dirt with her dagger on which the name of Allah was inscribed with Hebrew letters. In the circle she wrote in Kufic characters: *'Come Brother from your cozy dorm . . . to have that final fight about form.'* Then she closed her eyes and chanted spells in a language even the monkey-scribe did not know. In a short time the world turned dark and the darkness grew and grew and thickened like honey around them, so that it was hard to breathe, and every time the Sultan and the scribe drew a breath, it was as if they were breathing inside a sealed cave. They felt a large animal coming through the dark, and soon they smelled him, a sweaty large cat whose shiny yellow eyes pierced the darkness. It was a large lion who landed on his paws facing the princess.

"The lion roared, 'You have betrayed me and broken your oath! This is how you repay me, wretched creature of wiles and sloth? Have we not sworn to never cross each other?'
'Dog,' cried the princess, 'son of the daughter of Eblis, the most inept Genius in these parts, do you think that you frighten me by taking this lion shape?'

"There was a small measure of regret in the beast's remonstrance, but none in the princess, who pulled out a hair from her head and straightened it to make it into a sharp steel sword. She lunged at the lion, who opened his mouth intending to bite off her head like an apple, but the girl cut him in half with the sword. The two halves went flying, covering the King and the scribe in blood, but the lion's head remained and turned into a large scorpion that scuttled up the princess's dress, making for her throat. As it climbed, it uttered words in a strange language that the princess countered with her own. Before the scorpion could reach her neck, the princess changed herself into a long black snake and lashed at the scorpion with her tail.

"They fought a bitter battle for a long time, chanting all the while, long enough for the astonished Sultan to admonish himself for knowing little of his daughter's powers. Had he known, he'd have enlisted her aid in moving the capital from the arid South into the Delta; with her help he might have finished his palace that now lay two-thirds completed like a pyramid with a missing marble face; or he might have employed her to vanquish the invaders who had killed his entire labor force. And he would have exhausted only a small number of her seventy arts. Magic is wondrous indeed, but its domains are so guarded his own kin hid it from him. Once it appeared that neither the scorpion nor the serpent could win the battle, the scorpion turned himself into a vulture, filling the chamber with the stench of corpse, and the princess followed, becoming an eagle with sharp talons, and she flew after the vulture out of the palace.

"The King, the scribe, and the eunuch ran to the window to watch the battle in the sky. The two could be seen now and then as a whirling ball of feathers, then flew so high they vanished, taking their battle to other worlds.

"They so resemble each other, thought the scribe when he first saw the fighting birds, they are like two scripts from the same tree, two languages of the same thought, two words on the same tongue. The princess and her nemesis are equals. Great Sultan, I fear for her.

"Just when the most dreadful outcome seemed possible, the mosaic tiles on the floor split open and a huge piebald tomcat came snarling and hissing through, followed by a black wolf. The cat and the wolf fought each other with claws and fangs and dreadful chants. At no time during their pitiless combat did they cease chanting. Please note here, [said Sheherezade], that fighting is about form. Each form of fighting has its roots in the shapes of fighting beasts, and each beast has a secret language whose words it hurls at the other, and this is a lesson I'm giving you gratis, O great King, busy like a black wolf with my little sister Dinarzad's catty purring.

"When the cat saw that he was losing to the wolf, as you apparently seem to be doing, dear Dinarzad, she turned into a worm and burrowed her way into a pomegranate that lay by a fountain, a pomegranate formerly known as a wolf. The fountain was in a corner of the hall, like all the interior fountains of the palace, but the fountains outside were at the center of courtyards and gardens, a beautiful architecture that entitled the father of the princess to call himself one of the inspirations for the Alhambra, which was going to be built by one of his grandsons. The pomegranate swelled until it became the size of an enormous striped watermelon, out of which jumped a much smaller wolf who turned into a snow-white rooster. The swollen pomegranate rose into the air and burst, scattering seeds everywhere. The rooster started picking them up as fast as he could, reminding the scribe of a melancholy night when he'd been a human prince and had gone out in the snow up the old mountain in the city of his birth, and it had rained gold coins that he had gathered quickly just as the cock was doing now. He had loaded his pockets and hat with coins, but when he got home he found only melted snow in his pockets and hat, and the gold coins turned out to be scraps of starlight. The rooster seemed to have gathered all but one of the scattered seeds, and then turned to the King and the monkey-scribe and flapped his wings hard and crowed as if asking, 'Are there any more seeds left?' They looked but didn't see any, although one was hiding under the ledge of the fountain. The rooster saw it and rushed to get it, making a piercing and unroosterlike sound, but the seed rolled out of his way into the fountain and became a fish . . ."

A ray of milky dawnlight entered through the dome, and Sheherezade said, "I see dawn coming, and you must now wait another day to see the fight," and Dinarzad, red with pleasure like a pomegranate, said, "I can't wait, dear sister, please finish now," and Sharyar moaned and begged her, "Sheherezade, please go on, this is what you say every morning just before the pleasure of a conclusion overtakes me," but Sheherezade just laughed and did not utter another word.

and yet another royal day

Sharyar was determined to break the spell Sheherezade cast on him every night. Having delayed killing her, he now felt obliged to hear her out, but this did not mean that he would allow himself to be made indefinitely curious, kept in suspension like a ginger-root in an alcohol jar. He ordered his spies to redouble their efforts at finding out all there was to know about the girl. This order set off a flurry of informational frenzy among the spies, and testimonies were obtained through torture, bribes, and tattle telling. Just before his afternoon siesta, Sharyar was handed

the findings: scroll two, in your majesty's absence

Sheherezade was not a very diligent student, the author of this report contended. She preferred riding her horse to sitting before her masters. She told friends[88] that she felt well suited for heroic physical feats, but was easily bored by words. She was not a master of

---

[88] The friends were protected by false names in this report, a precaution that with the passing of years has become quite unnecessary.

martial arts, she could barely concoct a poison or a potion, and she was awkward in the application of leeches. She knew how to read but had no interest in writing. She admired beautiful penmanship, but did not practice. When she rode her steed outside the city walls, she often returned hungry and bruised, and told no one where she'd been. She liked colors and spices. Spectacles were performed nightly at court by costumed actors lit by the embers of brass braziers and torchlight, mostly for her entertainment. Her father, the Vizir, preferred the quiet of the library in the evening, but Sheherezade and her friends enjoyed these spectacles, which were about princes and princesses who are enchanted, disenchanted, and reenchanted, genii, dragons, magical fish,[89] hidden treasures, lost and found keys, and (always) great danger from which they escaped through magic (mostly), but also luck (often) and courage (sometimes). The dei ex machina were everywhere, but because there were so many, there might as well have been none, concluded the author of the report, who obviously fancied himself a theater critic. If everyone either has a superpower or will have one in the future, he continued, interest is bound to decrease proportionally.

"Aha!" exclaimed Sharyar.

The stories performed at court before Sheherezade's gang of mischievous girls, were serials. The actors and the storytellers were well-known persons from the marketplaces of Baghdad—each one with a criminal record—who earned their living by introducing characters whose adventures continued the next day and the day after and the day after that. The only difference between their spinning yarns for the riff-raff and doing the same for the princesses was the translation of the extreme vulgarity of the market, by means of euphemisms, symbols, and metaphors, into barely acceptable performances that fooled no one,

---

[89] Two hundred and thirty nights later, Sharyar woke up suddenly as if he'd been living under water like a dreaming fish, and demanded loudly to know how Sheherezade knew such stories. She shrugged both moonlit shoulders and replied, "I can't say. The zeitgeist finds me useful, I don't know why. I'm a mollusk. I filter a lot of tales through my bivalves; maybe it likes the way I do that." Even if Sharyar had known what the word "zeitgeist" meant, he'd have found the answer unsatisfactory. Prodigies are like that: they can speak hundreds of languages and have no idea how they do it.

least of all the girls, who knew all that hid under them. Thus a chess king could stand for a satyr for the drunken rabble and a respected monarch (ostensibly) for the not-so-innocent children of nobles. In any case, these storytelling actors incited curiosity, and much speculation revolved around what was going to happen next. Sheherezade often guessed right, but if the storyteller was truly gifted and surprised her, she rewarded him with gifts of fruit or gold.

It is true, the writer of the report went on in a more contrite tone, that these vulgar stories were not the only ones performed at court. There were also sacred stories from the Hindu temples, which, being about exemplary sacrifices and slaughters of a pedagogical nature, terrified the spectators, causing some of Sheherezade's friends, but never Sheherezade, to tremble and have fits. The sacred plays had been performed the exact same way since time immemorial, but these young people had no way of knowing it, and they returned for every sequel, dying of curiosity, as if the gods had been created for their amusement that very day. Dervishes attended these plays too, curious to see how other gods explained the afterlife, miracles, and the order and numbers of angels, and there were often heated debates about their meanings that lasted long into the night. Some of the followers of less spectacular gods than the Hindu tried their hand at writing spectacles that explained their beliefs, an endeavor that on the face of it was not difficult, except for the maddening fact that in telling their stories they had to ensure the return of the audience by leaving unfinished even the simplest tales. The followers of Allah, for instance, resolved this infuriating narrative requirement through the repetition of prayers that had to be recited over and over and could never be completed because there was always one more repetition that merely carried the prayer forward once more and moved closure out of reach again. In the lack of resolution there was both resignation and faith (God's will be done) and a healthy focus on earthly matters of family and commerce. When Allah's word comes to rule the earth, prayer will become mandatory one hundred times a day, so that no impious thought will find time to cross a person's mind, and all disobedience to Allah and his earthly representatives will be erased, the writer of the report noted, sure that such radical ideas would find an echo in its Exalted Reader. They did, sort of. Sharyar was too new to Allah to love his mullahs, but he sure enjoyed his secret police. No story, holy or naughty, advised his secret policeman, had an end for this crowd of spoiled youths led by Sheherezade, and tongues tattled.

You have no idea, Your Highness, what this city allowed within her walls in your absence: it was as if a serpent were crawling in day and night from the stone chambers of Egypt through Hindu temples and Persian altars to slither into the souks of our beloved Cairo and the markets of our blessed Baghdad. Riding on this serpent came multitudes of foreigners, barbarian storytellers who set up tents everywhere and chanted, sang, danced, and somersaulted, often accompanied by vipers, parrots, tigers, and elephants. The wide-eyed people of our city wasted their money every night on actors who outdid one another in vice and color. These liars have endless imagination about how to empty our pockets of piastres and pledge our souls to unclean marvels. All those people conquered by your father, the King of Kings, Shahanshah, managed to smuggle their stories back to your city, not just the tribes of India, Greece, Persia, Tibet, Samarkand, or China, but nameless and countless others who worship blood and animal spirits. They have revived the appeal of theo-anarchy through stories, so that our Crescent Moon and Star must ascend and descend alongside Kali's many love-skilled arms, Zoroaster's two faces, Mithra's taurean blood, long-buried Roman and Greek idols, and cat-faced goddesses with onyx eyes. As our Persian Empire grows to rival the Roman Empire, it must uphold the glory of Allah against these stories released into Baghdad like djinns from uncorked jars.

But back to the Subject, the reporter admonished himself: Sheherezade knew that Baghdad was the goal of all traveling tale-bearers, and she never ceased pestering her father, the Vizir, about bringing these novelties to the palace. When some of us complained in a letter, the Vizir claimed that he had brought our concerns before Sheherezade, and that she had replied (a mere child!) that she knew that a great battle was being waged in an invisible world for the exclusive attention of her Absent King Sharyar, the ruler in whose stead stood her father, enforcing his laws and imagining his directives. I do not even know what to call such nerve: arrogance does not suffice. She, and the Vizir, I might add, have made use of the shadow of Your unseen Highness to rise above us, but she had no fear of her father, so she was truly without the rule of law.[90]

Sharyar was only half-reading the report of his contemporary spy. He could barely wait for the sun to set so that he might go back to bed with long and a few decades more after the murder of the Divine Imam Ali. The struggle between the Prophet's Sunni nephews and the Shia avengers of Ali's death is still raging.

[90] Speaking as a historian now, I can't state with certainty exactly when King Sharyar read this report, but Sheherezade's Fates, intent on translating and then out-translating each other, ended up in near agreement to place the perusing of the scrolls of **the findings** in Baghdad around the 9th century CE. That time would have been 100 years and a few decades after the death of the prophet Mohammed in 632 CE, and as

Of this timing we are of many minds. Sheherezade is well known and "needs no introduction," as presenters say when they have no idea who it is they are introducing. In Europe we have seen her in plays and the opera, swayed to her in a Strauss waltz, and leaned forward to better hear Rimsky-Korsakov's musical depiction; we saw her dressed in rock'n'roll drag belly dancing in every city; we viewed her in paintings and sculptures; a vast body of "oriental" views highlighted her sensuality, eroticism, all that Europeans once called "the mystery behind the veil." Nor was she seen substantially differently in the Arab world, where she is sometimes admired for her cleverness, but always prized for sensuality.

Giving Sheherezade a biography is risky, and the writer of the report was aware of it. She certainly had a body and no one contested it, least of all us, the people of the future, who have seen it, as we noted above, in ballets, operas, dramas, and movies. She is the Tale-Spinner whose tales contain many bodies, wronged and righted creatures of many origins, earthly and unearthly, the bodies of Geniuses (or jinns, djinns, iffrits), Kings and princes, and, above all, women of every description, from fresh maidens to crones (or virgins and witches). Many of her subjects are locked (temporarily or perpetually) within the bodies of animals, the length of their sentences determined not by the gravity of their crimes, but by the cleverness of the woman who frees them. Her stories are a crowded world where many human and animal languages are spoken, languages from whose words come new bodies with stories from whose words come other bodies and so on, a generous and constant spawning of language and flesh, flesh and language. These bodies and stories occur at the same time in different places or over time in one place, but one thing does not change: Sheherezade's own body, from which multitudes issue, is imprisoned for 1001 nights in King Sharyar's bed. Her tale-spinning naked or fetishistically costumed body is then employed for centuries and projected into the future to her biographers, who must then decide whether this Sheherezade was indeed the one who had grown up in Sharyar's absence, lived freely before Sharyar's return, acquired form and intelligence under her father's benevolent care, saved womankind, demonstrated the power of stories over killing, systematized en passant the virtues of mercy, forgiveness, generosity, innocence, caution, and love, or just a device to unify a collection of stories printed in a book. One of her mid-20th-century biographers, J. L. Borges, inclines to the latter: "To erect the palace of *The Thousand and One Nights* it took generations of men, and those men are our benefactors, as we have inherited this inexhaustible book, this book capable of so much metamorphosis." Borges goes on to review the many translations, all of which have added something to the stories of the *1001 Nights*, something marvelous that wasn't there before, and he notes how much of the West, in the form of the adventures of Ulysses and Marco Polo, is part of the *Nights*, and how tenuous and indefinable notions of "East" and "West" are.

This biographer does not share the first part of the Borges hypothesis, the "cathedral" theory, but agrees with the indefinability of East and West, and knows for a fact that stories from Homer and Marco Polo were part of Sheherezade's repertoire, because her mother had been a nomad. Sheherezade herself was not just real, as we have already seen, but we shall go on and watch her grow in the King's absence, as evidenced by the above report, and other sources, without another thought as to her unreality. We will follow her until she appears written in history, first in a 9th-century mention, then in the tales collected in the extant Syrian manuscript of the 14th century CE, now in the Bibliothèque Nationale in Paris, and we will pursue her into our own time.

Sheherezade and Dinarzad and find out what happened when the Sultan's daughter disenchanted the enchanted scribe-ape.

An hour before daybreak Dinarzad awoke, though she hadn't been sleeping since Sharyar was using his tongue to draw intricate alphabets between her thighs, which she translated into moan-language, and exclaimed, as she always had, at this hour, "My dear sister, if you are not asleep, tell me I pray you, before the sun rises, the follow-up of your charming story. It may be the last time that I shall have the pleasure of hearing you," and she wondered herself at why she had said "I" instead of "we," as if the King, with his head buried between her thighs at that moment, did not matter. And maybe he didn't, because he couldn't hear.

"The pomegranate seed turned into a fish that swam quickly to the depths of the fountain," said Sheherezade, "but the rooster dove in after it, and when it touched the water, it, too, became a fish, a bigger one than the one that had escaped. For two hours the two fish chased each other in the water, surfacing and resurfacing, the bigger one almost swallowing the smaller, the smaller escaping at the last moment, and the Sultan, the scribe, and the eunuch held their breaths watching the battle and did not draw air.

"Suddenly two columns of fire rose straight out of the pool and in a flash reached the domed ceiling. The flames wrestled all over the room, blackening the walls and starting small fires in the corners. Fearing that the whole palace might catch fire, the Sultan called his guards, but at the sound of his voice one of the columns of fire twisted in place and rushed toward him, singeing his beard and his skin. He would have been burned to death on the spot if the eunuch had not thrown his body in front of his sovereign and burned instead. The monkey-scribe rushed to the side of the burning eunuch and tried to put out the fire by jumping on it, but the fire singed off his fur, and a spark flew into his right eye, blinding him. The other flame, hovering exhausted near the ceiling, descended to defend them and, with the last of her powers, flared brightly and swallowed her antagonist.

"She then turned herself back into her princess form and rushed to the side of her father, the Sultan, who lay badly burned and moaning in pain. She could do nothing for the eunuch, who had burned to death and was now only a handful of embers. The scribe rolled on the floor and put out the fire in his fur with water from the fountain, but he remained blind in one eye.

"'Victory!' shouted the princess. 'At what price!'

"'Daughter,' the Sultan called out weakly, "Now do what you set out to: please turn the monkey into the prince!'

"'The princess, trembling with fatigue, reached for an empty pitcher on a table and started for the pool, but she tripped and the pitcher broke. In the meantime, the palace guards had come in, roused by the Sultan's shout, and looked in astonishment at the charred scene around them. The princess ordered one of them to bring her a cup and to fill it with water from the fountain. When she finally held the cup of water in both hands, she blew over it, rippling the surface, brought it close to her lips, whispered a few words to it, then set the cup down on the floor next to a heap of ashes that were all that remained of the enemy Genius, and she sprinkled some of them in, and then wrote with the index finger of her left hand on the water some words that the scribe could not make out. Even had he known the language, he could not have read it because he was changing at that very moment, metamorphosing from a monkey into a tall youth. Allah be praised, he murmured, as he felt himself straighten out, his muscles and skin stretch and fill out, and his head stand on strong shoulders. He had lost sight in one eye but was otherwise the man he had once been.

"'Unfortunately,' said the princess, 'you thanked the wrong entity, and I must die now.'

"The scribe, now a handsome prince, realized his mistake in the instant, and fell to his knees to thank her. The princess turned to her father, the wounded Sultan, and said, 'Sire, I have won the battle but it has cost me my life. I might have been saved if any of you had noticed the pomegranate seed that I failed to collect. It contained the soul of the Genius. I had to resort to fire, a weapon we were equally skilled in, but as you can see, in the end I knew more than he did. As it is, the glory of knowledge will serve me for naught because one of the sparks from the Genius has entered my heart and is killing me as I speak to you. I might also have been saved if this handsome prince, whom you had intended to be my husband, had thanked me first and Allah second. He didn't, and that spark, which was the love I bore the Genius long ago, found my heart and pierced it. You have gained a human scribe but have lost your supernatural daughter.' She shouted suddenly, 'I burn! I burn,' and fell into ashes atop the heap of the Genius's ashes.

"'There was much grief, as you can imagine, and I can see by your tears, little sister, that I have touched your heart; either that or Sharyar, who looks as red as fire, has touched you in a place that brought forth tears." Both of these guesses being true, Dinarzad felt bad for a moment, but not as bad as the old Sultan who lay waning from his loss and his wounds, or his scribe who tried in vain to heal the Sultan's sorrow by reading to him from his scrolls.

"For a whole moon, the Sultan heard nothing of what the scribe read to him, as he mourned his daughter. The lost seed haunted him as if it were his own seed out of which his daughter came. The distraught young prince-scribe read and read, though there was little in the scrolls that interested him now, and his voice reached the Sultan only as a distant murmur. The prince anxiously awaited the King's return to health in order to know his own fate, which was going to be very different from what he believed it to be . . ."

Sheherezade, perceiving a tender ray of sun announcing the coming of dawn, said that they must wait until the next night if they wanted to know what happened next, and King Sharyar, aimlessly stroking Dinarzad's upraised buttocks, regarded with wonder his Storyteller, not understanding how it was that he, the great King Sharyar, could be left wanting like this, unfulfilled and unspent, at the whim of a storytelling sorceress. "Please, Sister," begged Dinarzad, raising herself a bit from the bed for her buttocks to meet the King's open hand that had begun rhythmically and aimlessly slapping them, but Sheherezade would have none of it, and they parted once again, the King to his kingly chores and the women to their womanly ones.

in the king's absence: sheherezade.2

By the time she turned twelve years old, her storytelling hypnotized people to the point where they disappeared into her stories, which also gave her time to disappear altogether. She then became invisible as her listeners became all ears; closing their eyes while opening their ears, so that she could become invisible, had been Sheherezade's greatest trick to date, an autumn day in ancient Persia, one full year before the King's return from the desert.

The night of her discovery of invisibility, Sheherezade modified her roaming so that she might encounter the people she had previously hidden from: palace guards, insomniacs, scribes, inventors, and alchemists. She bumped into them deliberately, and when they asked what in Allah's name[91] she was doing in forbidden quarters so late at night, she began telling one of her trap-stories, a tale that started ordinarily enough with an explanation of what she was doing in that place at that time, and then became more and more fantastic and more and more absorbing, until she saw the eyes of her questioner begin to close and she saw his ears open and grow out of his head

[91] We are using Allah here again (and throughout) to harmonize the oral Sheherezade of the fresh Islamic caliphates to the written Sheherezade of Sassanid Syria around the 14th century CE. The writing has it that her storytelling occurred in the caliphate of Haroun al-Rasheed, an Islamic kingdom, and that Arabs identified with her stories and came to think that they were both the description of their cultural evolution and the portable wealth that nomads and warriors could carry with them on their camels. But the *Nights*, as noted before, belongs to more than the Arabic language and the glory of Baghdad, namely, storytelling itself and how story is the universal means of generating beings who then tell more stories. We may be arranging a bit of time-travel for Sheherezade now and then because the vagueness of facts allows it, and because a great swath of history from 333 CE until 1300 CE involves empires, wars, nomads, steep mountains, deep valleys, and regions whose imaginary worlds are present everywhere in the *Nights*: we will not surrender her to either history or geography, and certainly not to 19th-century nationalism.

For a good portrait of an oriental palace guard, see *A Palace Guard*, painted in 1892 by Austrian painter Ludwig Deutsch (1855–1935). This guard, armed with a pistol, is obviously a later incarnation of the ones who watched Sheherezade, and if we subtract the pistol we have a true likeness.

like the petals of a large flower. When she was sure that he was well enrapt by the story, she vanished. Sometimes the story went on during her absence, and a few times she managed to return just before the story ended and the listener opened his eyes. She didn't always manage this trick of timing, though, so she was sometimes late and in danger of being caught, but she always managed to escape. There were quite a few palace dwellers who believed that they had dreamed her. In any case, none of them came forward to discuss the matter of the young Vizir's daughter putting them to sleep with a fancy tale. Nor did any of them confront Sheherezade, who looked as guileless in the daytime, at her lessons or chores, as any noble young lady might be expected to be. The few of her night-stung prey who sought some recognition in her eyes met such a wall of sheer opaque innocence, they dared go no further.

As her nightly encounters became more frequent, Sheherezade began to plan them better. She cut silk dresses decorated with patterns of numbers and symbols if she thought that she would encounter algebraists or alchemists. For astrologers she wore the constellations embroidered or painted or patterned into the material of her dress or veil. For the night watchmen she devised a tight body-fitting costume emblazoned with swords and bows and rivulets of blood. To those she met it seemed as if her appearance had been born of their own occupation, and they were, then, that much more certain that they had dreamed her. As Sheherezade grew more daring in her exploration and her disguises, she began layering her patterns so that those she encountered might discern the pattern of a wall decoration of the very room they were in: in addition to being bewildered by the symbols of their profession, they now saw the shapes also of the space where these nocturnal meetings occurred. Now they were sure, more than ever, that it had all been a dream, and Sheherezade, who was on familiar terms with most of the dream-readers and oracle-wielders in the palace, began to hear the most fantastic stories of a ghost who haunted the palace, taking on the appearance of a young and beautiful woman whose dream description varied greatly from one dreamer to another. Sheherezade's skills for disguise grew as her body seemed to demand more and more excitement, complexity, and danger. She now created clothes for herself that were layered so they could be shed to reveal a different design or pattern, one that was more startling and harder to decipher by her chosen audience. At times she tested the limits of her new body by engaging her fascinated listeners in a game of touching and guessing; with their eyes closed and their ears wide-open, the watchmen and the scholars groped blindly toward places on her body she guided them to, as she instructed them how to touch her and told them what they were touching and what they were experiencing, all as part of the storytelling. There were some close calls: some of these men were rough, particularly the soldiers, and sometimes they burst right through the skin of the story to take hold of her body in ways that scared her; at those times, it seemed to Sheherezade that something deeper than the pleasing music of her words had been activated. She suspected that she was coming face-to-face with the sheer cliff-walls of some truths that her body was not yet ready for. Every time this happened, she blamed her narrative skill and worked harder to improve it.

There were certain repulsive stories that she sometimes told, and many stories that had repulsive moments in them. She noticed that her own pleasure increased at those moments, as did that of her listeners. She started to foreshadow repulsive (meaning scary, vivid, and gory) moments, watching her listeners' expectation grow, physically, like a thing. She sometimes thought that she could touch this swollen expectation, but she knew that if she did, there would be a violent and possibly uncontrollable reaction. She held the repulsive moment suspended instead, until the curiosity she had incited had grown a body of its own that made jerky motions around her and her listener, like a shadow gone rogue, and then and only then she vanished. She knew, from the close calls, that revealing the repulsive moment at the point of the greatest expectation was not wise. These repulsive moments, which dwelt in the seams of her story, like knots holding together different parts of the fabric of her costumes, were there to be desired, not to be released. Sheherezade understood suspense. She was not quite thirteen.

"The world I move in during the day does not contradict the one that exists at night. This is why I cannot claim to be troubled by the fact that humanity lives only half the time. I no longer say that I dream, because the quantitative difference between the two phenomena of day and night also implies a qualitative one."[92]

Thinking of the ties or binds in the fabric of her time, no longer divided into day and night, Sheherezade reasoned that their energy could be used in more varied ways than simply increasing expectation and creating a drunken shadow in the night. It was as if she had four bodies now: a diurnal one, observable and obedient, performing the tasks expected of her; an evening one that comforted Dinarzad; a nocturnal one that moved in and out of men who worked at night; and a dream-body that existed in the uneasy awareness of the night-men who could not say for sure whether or not they had dreamed her.

When it was the next night, the King, sandwiched like a salmon slowly poaching between Dinarzad and her sister, Sheherezade, could not sleep for fear that his resolve might wane, but it was his manhood that was waning despite the choreography of Dinarzad, who had become something of an expert, so he was relieved to hear her say, "O my sister, finish for us that story . . . ," and she answered, "With joy and goodly gree, if the King permit me." Then quoth the King, "Tell thy tale!"

"When the Sultan's beard grew back and he was able to speak again, he faced the prince, who had been reading to him for the many weeks of his illness, and then he looked about and saw that the prince had covered the walls of the royal chamber and every statue, table, utensil, and even the edge of the pool where the terrible fight of the fishes had taken place, with beautiful writing.

"'What is this?' he demanded angrily. The prince-scribe answered that when the Sultan slept he had stopped reading and had written instead.

---

[92] Ghérasim Luca, *The Passive Vampire*.

Having used up all the parchment supply in the palace, he had continued writing on the surface of every visible object, including the staff, until the entire palace and all its servants, not just the Sultan's chamber, had been covered by the fine writing for the sake of which the Sultan had brought him from the ship and ended up sacrificing his own daughter.

"'And what does this writing say?' cried the distraught Sultan.

'Some of it is in verse and some of it is in prose,' said the former monkey, who was proud of his work, 'and if read from room to room and spoon to fork, dress to tunic and turban to shoe, it is a long tale composed of many smaller tales.'

"The Sultan now saw that all of his faithful, including the doctor who had tended him, were covered with fine scrawl as thin and intricate as spider thread, and he questioned them angrily as to why they had allowed themselves to be written on like clay tablets without will; they responded that the Sultan's own love for the scribe, which had caused so many misfortunes, had made them afraid to deny the prince. With a terrible voice that could be heard in all the palace, the Sultan commanded all to disrobe and enter the pools of the palace to wash their bodies clean of writing, and then to scrub every surface until no trace of the calligraphy remained, and then, when they had cleansed themselves and the palace of the calligrapher's madness, they were to remove all the scrolls in his great library and throw them in a bonfire and mingle their ashes with those of the Genius who had killed his daughter. He also ordered that his daughter's ashes be carefully gathered and placed in a gold urn over which a marble tomb would be erected. While everyone bathed and scrubbed, the servant charged with gathering the ashes of the princess cried out in despair that she couldn't find any. The dejected scribe-prince, who had witnessed with astonishment the Sultan's fury, confessed that, having used all that could be made into ink in the palace, he had drawn his own blood and mixed it with the ashes. He had dipped his quill in this substance and had composed a text entirely with red letters above the doorsills, pithy sayings that condensed the wisdom of all knowledge.

"The Sultan gathered all his remaining strength and said to him, 'You have killed my daughter and my eunuch, you have nearly murdered me, and you have dishonored all of us and our death with your compulsive habit of substituting letters for feeling! I would have you executed now, but I am going to let you go your way for fear that in your death-agony your blood will pool into ink and start writing of itself! Leave now, wretched ill-fortune, and never set foot again in my kingdoms!'[93]

"The distraught prince, blind in the right eye, went out the gates and shaved his head, put on a coarse robe, and became a dervish, sworn only to the spoken. Never, he vowed to himself, would he write or read again. After many years of wandering in the desert he met two other dervishes who were blind in the right eye like himself, and, intrigued by the coincidence, they joined together and came to the great city of Baghdad in the middle of the night. The city was shuttered and dark, and they had just about made up their minds to sleep in a ditch when they spotted a house with light seeping through heavily drawn curtains, and they heard music coming from within. Resolved to try their luck, they knocked on the heavy and beautifully ornamented gate.

"Above the gate written in letters of red gold were the words, '*Whosoever enters here must never question what he sees or speak of whatever he has seen.*' No sooner had they read this than the gate was opened by a young woman whose body, clad in crimson silks, was sinuous and wavy and milky and gave off a scent of rare oils and ripe persimmons. The dervishes, overcome by her beauty, begged for a place to spend the night. I must ask my sisters, she said, and, leaving the door open a

---

[93] What had happened was that the prince's reading could not compete with the opium given to the Sultan to alleviate his pain. Opium gives you dreams so strong no story can penetrate. The nervous system of language can't hack the poppy dream. What had worked for the Sultan in the past, the flow and music of his scribe's voice, no longer worked in his world of pain: nightmares ruled there. His new scribe, with all his marvelous gifts of writing and reading, who had been miraculously transformed into a prince by the sacrifice of his daughter, was a distant voice on the far shore of the sea of pain. The Sultan desired to be rid of this voice that reminded him of the most abhorrent thing in all the world: transformation. As he watched images tumble and transform in his sleep, he knew that language, with its own power to transform things into one another, had been his gravest error. If the masters of metaphor—his scribes, the magicians, his daughter—had been illiterate and ignorant, he'd have had little trouble sleeping. He wouldn't have been a Sultan either, certainly not a Sultan in a story told to a King by an enchantress.

crack through which they could glimpse a merry party in a room with a splashing fountain, she disappeared within."

The ray of sunlight that announced the coming of dawn pierced Dinarzad's long and pretty neck on which Sharyar's teeth had left a mark, then pierced the one drop of dew at the top of the King's manhood that always heralded the beginning of his ultimate pleasure, and played over Sheherezade's lips that now closed, determined not to utter another word until next night. "Please, Sister, please," Dinarzad begged in vain. "Oh, oh," moaned Sharyar, "you must speak or die!" "If I do speak, I die," laughed Sheherezade, and lay still until all the hearts in the royal bed quit beating like race horses whipped to a frenzy, and they had no choice but to surrender to the day and await again the coming of another night.

in the king's absence: sheherezade.3

Thirteen-year-old Sheherezade, a preteen in the Middle Ages, falls prey to insomnia and anorexia. There are times when she sleeps in the saddle as she rides through the mulberry forests, and times when she thinks that she is dreaming. Nonetheless, she loses considerable weight, a frightening occurrence in Baghdad, where becoming a woman means acquiring curves. The interior of the palace is designed primarily to encourage the coming into fullness of woman and of adding flesh to the exercise of power. The thin people, the stick figures of peasants and outlaws, live around the castle walls, pressing their bodies for warmth against the narrow openings in the thick plaster. Their piercing cries penetrate the night inside the castle now and then, joyous when an old camel with a sheep inside is broiled over flames to celebrate a birth or a holiday, grieving when death, hunger, cold, and sand reduce them to agony. Thus the skeletal appearance of the rabble and begging monks is well known to the residents of the palace, and Sheherezade's weight loss does not go unnoticed, nor does her pallor. Just as her flesh is expected to wax curvaceous, her coloring is expected to glow with the ruby hue of health, but instead she acquires a slight yellow tinge. The Vizir orders her to the spell-caster, the first step in a series of measures; if she doesn't improve, she'll be sent to a doctor and treated with leeches; there are other steps after that, horrible to contemplate, so Sheherezade decides to cooperate.

She confessed some of her adventures and her insomnia to the kingdom's best renowned spell-caster, an oracle who lived with snakes beneath the floor of a shrine. The oracle saw through her as plainly as if she were looking at a lit crystal. Sheherezade waited for advice, her heart beating fast from expectation and some dread at the roiling serpents. At long last, the oracle laughed. "You, Sheherezade," she sibilated, "have one thousand and one bodies, five hundred in the past, five hundred in the future, and one right here before me, moist with terror and excitement." When Sheherezade, careful not to step on any of the oracle's slithering friends, pressed her as to the meaning of her sleepless existence spent in the perfecting of storytelling technique, the oracle became grave, and in a changed tone of voice, portending Allah-knows-what frightful events, she advised: "Take thee to the gold and crystal and cloth shops and learn the motions of crafts, because you are charged with increasing the pace of time." And then the oracle fell asleep, leaving Sheherezade to her work. She prescribed no diet, a great relief, because Sheherezade had her own manner of supplying her body with food, having added pomegranates and oranges to her lunch, and, to please her father, now and then a bubbling hot flat bread spread thick with chickpea paste.

Just after her thirteenth birthday, Sheherezade achieved a sudden understanding that sought and found objects in need of it. She directed her insight to narrative, logic, and ontology, things that she felt compelled to articulate. On the surface, her childish desires remained the same: like many of her friends, she believed that she had a gift for performance and was going to make a name for herself in the streetplayers' dramas or in the sacred plays. The secular plays were regarded as unworthy of her station, the domain of lowborn actors who had been trained since birth and often maimed in the interests of gymnastic excellence, but those plays seemed to her to be greater examples of the art than the retellings of god stories. Sometimes the actors were the same, in which case the flaws were with the material. Now and then a gifted noble fled the palace life and joined one of the traveling companies under an assumed name. These defectors were the secret heroes of her girl gang. Sheherezade saw herself dancing in a whirl of silks before rapt audiences in a marketplace. She sometimes danced late at night before the empty throne that was awaiting Sharyar's return, and the ecstatic imaginary auditor applauding her was none other than Sharyar himself. Watching the acrobats and dancers, she knew that she had much more to learn, and she became angry, exercising her body until it hurt everywhere. Sometimes she rode Abd al-Hakim out of the city at such great speed they could barely converse when they stopped because they were both out of breath. Her desire for stardom was mixed with inexplicable anger, perhaps because she suspected that her stage might in the end be narrower than the market or the Great Hall. At least during her lifetime.

She didn't know, as we do, that her stage was going to be a bed, a narrow stage indeed, but her audience was going to be practically all of literate Humanity. She wouldn't have believed that she was destined for a heroic fate whose object she hadn't quite refined. She had pledged herself to Dinarzad's safety, but there was more. Ridiculous, she told herself, that I should feel the certainty of my heroic role, when the only fight I can see myself waging is on behalf of Dinarzad, whom I should be looking out for anyway since she's my little sister. Still, the certainty of her heroism kept growing every day, without any visible change in the object of it, and in addition to being a hero with an unclear cause, she had the not-quite-sensical belief that she must learn even more about telling stories.

Something about her origin troubled her: when she asked her father, the Vizir, about her mother, he told her only what she already knew. One day her mother had returned to the desert. The Scythian nomad had been relegated to silence by the palace, and there was little to be learned from those who'd known her. Her Master-Teacher kept a stony silence, and even the eyes of the women who had been her mother's attendants and companions clouded over when her daughter asked about her. Sheherezade formed the opinion that her mother was *the story that could not be told*. This was an opinion, merely an opinion, she told herself, and her pride would not allow her to fully believe it: there was no story that Sheherezade could not tell; therefore there was no story that could not be told. If such a story existed, it had not been told either because the right words had not been found, or because no storyteller great enough to unfold it had ever lived. Even if the story didn't exist, Sheherezade reasoned, her gift for telling would bring it into being. In other words, she silently exulted while riding Abd al-Hakim to frothing speed, if she had no mother, she would story herself one.

Sheherezade didn't exactly know why she was becoming so absorbed by narrative technique, since she had already achieved privately a great many victories; her nightly forays had become so much a part of the city's dream lore, she often heard herself described as ten feet tall, having eyes that were in actuality deep wells containing the enchanted souls of men who'd fallen in by looking too long; she heard that she had long golden hair unheard of in Persia, that she was naked, wearing only tiny gold bells on her ankles while her breasts put forth a blinding light, that she was black like ebony and her fingers held serpents; she heard herself described as a goddess, a Genius, a djinn, a demon, an iffrit, a demi-serpent. It seemed that each of her stories had given birth to a new body for each of her listeners. Perhaps I do have one thousand bodies, laughed Sheherezade to herself.[94]

She knew that her dreams of acting stories were unrealistic; she would never be allowed to perform on any stage because she was the Vizir's daughter. A Vizir's daughter was fated to marry a prince and learn to master a household of concubines and domestics. She had seen many rich merchants' and nobles' households. Some of them functioned discreetly and quietly in an atmosphere of dignified indifference, while others were loud and raucous, occasionally violent, and distinctly happier. Running such a complex machine did require good skills, but she felt herself utterly unsuited to such a task. From these family interiors she had learned only that telling a good, instructive story with accurate timing often made the difference between goodwill and cruelty. The ability to quip, offer a fable or a parable, or even offer a pointless but charming tale had the occasional benefit of avoiding violence, but she had no intention of employing her gift for domestic harmony. To entertain the powerful, the condemned must speak,[95] which is laudable, thought Sheherezade, but banal.[96]

Her memory was reasonably well trained by her Master-Teacher through repetition of sutras and suras, and she liked to encase in a phrase any detail of interest to her, as if putting a pretty stone or scarab in a jewelry box. These phrases she set in her Memory Room, a structure she had built all by herself, without having read any of the ancient Ars Memoriae, thus unaware of the theaters of memory used by the

[94] Note from the future: A thousand and *one*!

[95] This means of obtaining a pardon is extended in the European Middle Ages to writing. If the accused proves that he can write, he must be a clergyman, thus safe from the death penalty. This benefit of clergy was introduced by Archbishop Thomas Becket and conceded by Henry II in 1176 in the aftermath of Becket's murder. It exempted clergy from trial or sentence in a secular court on charges arising from a range of felonies and offenses. This exemption extended from tonsured clerics to include nuns, and later it was granted to all who could prove themselves literate by reading a verse of Scripture when charged with certain violations of the law. The reasoning was that literacy was the accepted test of clerical status. Benefit of clergy was abolished by Parliament in 1827.

[96] *The future (wearing slight grimace):* Her gift was no deeper than that, but she didn't know how deep that *was*. In her day, as in ours, an exceptional gift was practiced by the recipient, but the gifted rarely knew what they had; their talent was analyzed by others. The Prophet, for instance, had fully exercised his gift of transmitting the Word of Allah, but did not stop to question what he was channeling; that was left to the commentators. Sheherezade did not doubt her ability to weave a web of magical story, and she did not deploy any kind of intellectual-critical faculty, the organ for which would not be developed for centuries yet. Her mother's Greek side might have equipped her for this, but such double vision would have deprived us (the future) of a job. *Qui sait?* In any case, even without analytic insight, Sheherezade knew that her gift was threefold: she had memory and imagination, and *something else*.

ancients to store knowledge. Her Memory Room resembled Sharyar's bedchamber, which she often secretly entered, though it was heavily shuttered awaiting his return.

The Vizir had once surprised her in the forbidden bedchamber, but instead of punishing her, he told her one of the great secrets of the architect who erected the palace for Shahanshah, the King of Kings: the domed oval bedchamber was symbolically constructed to reflect all the empire's religions, from the prayer wheel on the ceiling occupied by bright-colored Hindu gods, to the fountain before the carpet-bed that shot a clear jet of water resembling the beard of the monocular desert God's prophet. Surrounding the bed stood statues of nude gold Sivas and Greek deities. Above the door was a tablet written in a beautiful hand with golden letters, a story from the Koran. Black-and-white Zoroaster, erect like an exclamation point, stood in the midst of a black-and-white army of figures holding swords. The Vizir showed Sheherezade the hidden springs of clever mechanisms that allowed these marvels to move and even speak.

After this tour, her father drove her from the room, with an admonition to never enter it again. She came back the very next night through a secret window and leapt atop the high carpet-bed where Sharyar himself had once happily frolicked with the wife he had murdered on this spot. There was a small opening in the black marble dome above the bed that let in a ray of a star that pierced her. She then lay in Sharyar's bed, pretending to be dead while the King stood above her. She imagined him weeping, thinking her truly dead, but then she let out her breath and laughed, and the King whipped her buttocks with the knotted cord of his robe and then called his pet tiger to come to the bed and lick her from head to foot, and ordered her not to laugh. If as much as a chortle escaped her, he would command the beast to rend her. In order not to laugh, Sheherezade recited the sutras and the suras she had memorized, and let their grave contents choke off the urge to burst into laughter at the unbearable tickling of the tiger's tongue. Sometimes she was able to hold off until the great cat grew tired of licking, but there were moments when she burst out in mirth, releasing a gushing stream of golden urine on the carpet-bed. At such times, the great danger that she was in caused her to leap through one of a number of tiny escape holes that she made sure to build into her game, just in case. After she had successfully escaped from Sharyar's shuttered and guarded bed-room, Sheherezade, her heart pounding, went about the business of being a well-behaved Vizir's daughter, assiduous in learning and present for duties. Each time she escaped from the tiger in the King's bed, she had better recall of the room, and she used her memory of this forbidden bedchamber as a special place to store ideas she found worthy of remembering. During the many nights that she indulged in this game, she told the stories that later she told the real Sharyar, the stories that stayed his hand from killing her. What Sharyar eventually heard for one thousand and one nights were *re*told stories, alt-stories of the sort she used to tell Dinarzad to soothe her.

Sheherezade's imagination was of another order than her memory. While memory looked back into the past, imagination looked forward into the future. What she imagined took place in the present when she imagined it, but when she told it, she used the past tense, as if it had happened in the past. Sheherezade did not use, and couldn't have used, the word "imagination," because even if she'd been familiar with the Latin, she didn't think of her imagination as making "images." "I image" was not what she thought she was doing. She thought of her gift as a three-headed serpent: "the lie with three heads," as she once described her facility to her Master-Teacher, who asked, rather exasperated, why she insisted on providing luxuriant details in a story that was obviously of her own making. The three-pronged lie was as follows: wishing, drawing, and activating. If she wished to leave the present for a place of pleasant reverie, her wishing furnished her instantly with characters and a place to repair to; she then drew each detail of the creatures that inhabited the place, and she took care to sketch them using a fine brush; when everything was visible to her mind's eye, and she was satisfied with their numbers and features, she activated the scene; her characters would then begin acting, doing things that surprised her. She watched them fly, leap, intrigue, hide, argue, plot, become animals, speak unknown languages, and a myriad of other fascinating activities that she could never have thought of all by herself. Her only intervention, after she had set them in motion, was to rein them in now and then, using an imaginary leash, because the adventurous creatures tended to get out of hand, doing things that quite frightened her. She did hate having to pull on the leash because she saw it for what it was: a braided rope. If she saw the leash, it meant that others could see it, and she found it shameful to hear the words "she's pulling on the leash," which was the Arabic equivalent of "you can see the strings." Sheherezade was adamant about the suspension of disbelief; she required this from herself when everything took place in her mind, but she felt even more strongly about it when she let others in. Her capacity for lying was infinite, and she did not mind letting her fancy play to exhaustion within herself. The truth, she had already noted, was fairly well respected and formally required by the people surrounding her, so she was mindful of the border between her imagination and the requirements of society. When her inner world was put in words out loud, it ceased to exist in its fullness, losing color as it gained veracity. At that point it almost ceased to exist. Her Master-Teacher knew this, which is why he taught her dance, prayer, memorization, and *taquia*. Her other good teachers were the ones who pointed out rocks or metals and named them, but her best teachers were the weavers, the carvers, the jewelers, and the scribes, who taught her the motions of their skills accompanied only by the barest and most economical words needed for the practice of their crafts. Outside these teachings, which were all about what her body was capable of doing, words had a whole different mission; they were ultralight materials that hardened into the mind-worlds she wished, furnished, and activated. The future agreed to call this faculty "imagination," using the Latin, but Sheherezade saw it as *time*. There was the time of her life, the time of her fancy, the time of the telling of her fancy, and, as she would find out, the time for the *necessity* of the telling of her fancy, and the future, where the carriers of her fancy live.

Then, aside from her memory and imagination, there was *something else* that we will provisionally call *the fold*, which is what she was pursuing, studying, glimpsing. The *fold* was the manner in which words were hinged to time in order to make one story attach to another; we could also call this a *drive,* the mechanism that propelled words to gain dimensions, first as a story, then as an oft-repeated story traveling the world through storytellers, then as a three-dimensional object performed for an audience, and finally, after having gained sufficient circulation and weight, as *flesh*. Flesh was story in all its dimensions. Yes, Sheherezade discovered that words could be made flesh; storied characters became alive through telling and then stayed alive as long as they were told by others, dying only when they stopped traveling, when their seed dried up and their bodies shrank to nothing. The human body, her own body for that matter, was both a story-body and a flesh-body, and there was no telling where one ended and the other began; they were identical at all points. What she was seeking to discover was the *fold-drive* where the transfer of word to flesh took place, the infinitesimal point (the smallest she could think of) where a small tentacle exited the word to latch on to the next word with a protein.

The Master-Teacher, who oversaw her religious education by making her recite over and over the holy writs, taught her that the Word becoming life was a divine operation, *the* divine operation, and that people like actors have no business trivializing the Word by telling shameless stories. This teacher, with his knotted Assyrian beard, despaired of the proliferation of storytelling actors about the city and predicted doom for the kingdom if their practices continued. He did not know that the Vizir's daughter, with her distracted gaze somewhere above his beard, thought of God as just another storyteller, and that she intended to become the human operator of the *fold-drive* that was so far still Allah's exclusive property. Happily, her Master-Teacher had no foresight, though he was wise, and was only trying to keep the Logos from the abuses of storytellers. He died many years later, after reporting to Sharyar about his difficult pupil. He took to his grave certain facts about his pupil, facts that have remained hidden to this day, given her penchant for invisibility, the grandeur of her project, the confusion over her origins, and the complexity of her transducers.[97]

sharyar's day

Today, Sharyar already knew, he was not going to be happy. Sheherezade had gone too far and her history was too complex to allow it to continue. Perhaps the time had indeed come to destroy her before she could enmesh him any further in her stories. He was becoming entranced and ensorcelled, a not unpleasant state perhaps, but it induced lassitude, languor, and feminine weakness. His desert-hardened flesh was becoming soft, and many parts of his body, such as his ears, which he rarely thought of, became sensitive to the touch and aroused the rest of him at the simplest breath of a woman. His knees, his toes, and even his eyelids followed suit. It was as if his entire skin were becoming eroticized while tiny bolts of craving traveled from his hips into his heart and then to his mouth, drying it, and causing him to drink hashish-spiked wine constantly. It was no way to run an empire, as everyone could see. His generals regarded him with pity, and even his Vizir, overjoyed at first that he had spared his daughters' lives, began to fear him less, and started ruling as he had before Sharyar's return. Slowly, the snake-charmers and houris began returning to Baghdad, and women forgot to veil when they went out,

---

[97] A transducer is a device, usually electrical, electronic, electromechanical, electromagnetic, photonic, or photovoltaic, that converts one type of energy or physical attribute to another for various purposes including measurement or information transfer (for example, pressure sensors). In this instance, we are using the word to also mean a device that converts Indian-Egyptian stories told and written in Arabic prose-in-verse via Greek-Western renderings, into *bodies*.

despite the alarmed cries of the preachers. I will have her killed tomorrow after I hear the end of her story about the scribe-prince, Sharyar swore to himself. He could not see how a mere girl, no matter how well versed, could hold him in thrall. After all, he had suffered dreadfully, and Sharyar recalled, in order to steel himself and stiffen his resolve, just how things had come to this pass. It was thus with more than passing interest that he received from his spies

the findings: scroll three

Sheherezade's mother was a captured nomad, reported this researcher, who had been roaming the desert and sailing the seas with fellow nomads; they navigated by the stars and lived inside tents they folded in the morning and put up again at night. Sheherezade's mother had roamed Asia and Europe on horseback and aboard ships. She was a fierce, always-willing-to-die-fighting nomad chieftain who spoke fast and forgot little: she was both Mongol and Greek. The Mongol side drove her at great speed, and the Greek side kept the surfaces of things in sight. She rode for a time with a pirate crew.[98] Her stories, chanted to Sheherezade in the womb, were in many languages redolent of thick cinnabar-scented smoke; they featured warriors with one long braid down their backs and shaved eyebrows, saintly beggars who took revenge after being abused by caravans, brothers who turned each other into animals by means of spells, rocks that were doors to enchanted cities, swords that came to life, and other objects and monsters that violated all that most people found physically, biologically, and existentially proper; Sheherezade's mom's stories oozed the pestilential scent of swamps, deserts, and seas beyond palaces and cities, and were bereft of any decent moral worth whatsoever, even when they sounded (deceptively) instructive.

---

[98] I like to think that if she rode with Genghis she was partly responsible for destroying the earliest version of my hometown, Sibiu, in 1334.

[99] Let us interject here, from the future, that the author of the third scroll of **the findings** is absolutely right. If Sheherezade had been entirely of the palace, the number of her stories would have been 1000, an even number like the business of any well-ordered house. The numeral 1 pointed to nomad wildness, an exception that she embodied because the numeral 1 was her mother. God is also unique, a 1, which is why the faithful always make an uneven number of prostrations and apply uneven dots to their eyes. God likes uneven numbers, and the first to know this preference of the unique God were the nomads, among whom her mother was known to be a great accountant. She had witnessed the Second Fold,

Her mother had often ended her stories abruptly when their camp was surprised by a sneak attack before dawn, and had to leap on her horse to escape, but she always reprised them next night wherever they made camp. Some of her mother's stories were meant to inspire her fellow nomads to form new war parties to avenge those killed the previous night. The languages of her telling were all mixed up because she did not know that they were separate languages, though she was aware that the people she often fought and conquered wanted to keep them separate; she simply took languages the way she took treasure and slaves, and used them whenever appropriate. This is of great importance, Your Highness, because your wife also speaks many languages learned in her mother's womb, and, if you so desire, we can have them translated for you, so you will not be surprised by foreign assassins. (This reporter was clearly trying to ingratiate himself with Sharyar, but he may have been a sincere servant who had heard of the generals' intrigues.) When your wife Sheherezade became herself a Storyteller, her gift came easily because she had learned her craft at her mother's breast.[99]

which was when the shamans foresaw the One God of Abraham. From that vision to the manifestation of the One God in history, time turned and folded in on itself, pulling millennia into that fold. The Second Fold creased the human brain by speeding up time to harmonize with the speed of the warrior herd and the growing curiosity and impatience of humans thirsty to know what lay beyond conquest, within the objects they had looted, the treasures they held, the earth they trod, the air they drew into their lungs. The men on horseback and the exiles fleeing bondage were folded within an algebra in the time of Sheherezade's mother.

"The Numbers may vary in function, in combination; they may enter into entirely different strategies; but there is always a connection between the Number, and the war machine . . . When Greek geometrism is contrasted with Indo-Arab arithmetism, it becomes clear that the latter implies a nomos opposable to the logos: not that nomads 'do' arithmetic or algebra, but because arithmetic and algebra arise in a strongly nomad influenced world" (Gilles Deleuze and Félix Guattari, *Nomadology: The War Machine*).

We believe that one of the reasons for the nomads' algebraic affinity is simply the impossibility of carrying on a conversation on horseback because the winds snatch the vowels and return the sounds to the riders' ears all scrambled, as in the game of Telephone. That sound distortion and the sheer numbers of riders, plus the vast numbers of the conquered, and the difficulty of being able to account at any given time for people and objects, gave birth to an X that was algebraic and chromosomal. We tend to think of language now as a self-referential system of signs, but we have to imagine a time when language had no "self" referent because there was no "self" to direct it to, no interiority to address. All words were pointed outward at a listener, and they were issued in the form of a prayer, a story, an order, or an account. All words were public to varying degrees, from small circles to auditing masses. Stories had no existence until there was an audience for the storyteller who then channeled them and began broadcasting. Where she channeled them from and how they formed was going to be one of Sheherezade's preoccupations when she began having difficulty with the pronouns "I" and "you," a difficulty that emerged every time she thought of the *how* of stories. Sheherezade's study of the pronoun problem predated all others, having been conducted as a basic test of "I," the

When it was the next night, said Dinarzad to her sister, Sheherezade, "O my sister, finish for us that story . . . ," and she answered, "With joy and goodly gree, if the King permit me." Then quoth the King, "Tell thy tale."

"The three dervishes with the shaved heads and blind in the right eye were met by an astonishing sight in the candlelit room of the house they were asked to enter. Two beautiful girls, dressed in silks that allowed for glimpses of flesh from which emanated intoxicating perfumes, surrounded a naked muscular youth lying on his back on a bear fur. One of the girls brought down a horsehair whip over his thighs and magnificently erect endowment. Another spit a mouthful of water on him. The young woman who had admitted the dervishes pointed to a bench and bade them sit; then she removed her outer garment and stepped forward dressed only in a wild wolf skin, sank to her knees, and bit the youth's lips, drawing blood. She then turned to her guests, with blood dripping from her mouth onto her ivory-white throat, and asked them once more to respect the injunction written above the door to ask no questions no matter what they saw. At this, the one-eyed dervishes nodded their assent, and the sisters left the youth on the bearskin rug and

storyteller, and "you," the listener, before the study was subdivided for better focus between "I," the person, and "Thou," God, and then "I," the lover, and "you," the beloved. For Sheherezade, this was not the subject of her doctoral dissertation, but a matter of life (her own). The question for her was *What story can I tell to stop you from killing me?* It was clear to her that the story in this case was different from her mother's. Her mother told stories without the threat of imminent death, but Sheherezade's stories were bounded by "I," the teller at the beginning, and by "you," the killer at the end (Sharyar). This was a narrow channel to navigate, and what flowed through it was worth her life, so the answer lay either in an increase of force as she pushed the story through its narrow passage, or an enlargement of the pronouns, an operation for which there was no precedent because there wasn't yet a psychological language. How she solved this dilemma is also one of Sheherezade's great discoveries, an important revelation that leads to the Third Fold as surely as the sperm is called to the egg. Her answer to the question *What story can I tell to stop you from killing me?* became even more urgent for the generations that followed (and forgot her solution). *How would I use words to stop you from killing me?* received many answers in history, each answer perfectly suited to the situation and to the times, but generally divided between (1) *talking crazy* (for centuries, until the Enlightenment, killers were queasy about dispatching crazy people), (2) *begging for mercy* (this never worked), and (3) *inducing curiosity*. This last was ½ of Sheherezade's answer. Curiosity was great in people in her time, and though greatly diminished in ours, it still works. The other ½ of her answer was, as we shall see, contained in the stories themselves.

turned to them. They removed the wanderers' tattered clothing with the greatest care, and they bade them to step into a fountain in the middle of the room. When they did this, they found the water pleasantly warm, and the three sisters proceeded to wash them slowly, lingering long in the seams of their bodies, especially in those folds of flesh between their testicles and their buttocks, but also in the pits of their arms and under their ears, and when they were satisfied that the dervishes were clean enough for their taste, they pressed tonic unguents on their skin and fanned them with palm leaves, making certain that their erect manhoods received the greatest number of fannings. After this bath, the dervishes were carried by servants to a baldaquin bed covered in furs, and were joined there by the sisters and the youth, who had risen from the floor. The servants, who were also young, comely, and mostly nude, held swaying lamps above the bed, gradually extinguishing wicks until a gentle chiaroscuro enveloped the room."

"No! No! No!" cried King Sharyar thrice, "If the sun dares to rise now, I'm having it put out by my soldiers, like an eye!"

Sheherezade laughed at this, and continued:

"One of the dervishes, as you know, was the prince who had been a monkey-scribe and had been enchanted and disenchanted. Finding himself in a large bed with a multitude of pleasing bodies, he was tempted to forget his past, but just then there was a loud knock at the gates.

"One of the sisters, the same one who had let the dervishes in, jumped up and said, none too pleased, 'Oh, I will answer, Sisters!' Being the youngest, she was the answerer. She put on a saffron robe that covered her but carelessly, and rushed ahead of the servants who, strangely enough, disappeared. She cracked the gate open a bit. Two cloaked strangers stood there, and one of them said, 'We are two merchants traveling through your city at this late hour, and we cannot find lodging. Hearing merry sounds from your house, we thought to beg your hospitality.' The two strangers waited outside, craning their necks all the while to see what they could inside the room through the crack in the door, while the girl went back inside to consult with her sisters on whether or not to let the guests in. There was a bit of discussion: one of the sisters was of the opinion that the seven of them were pleasingly distributed as to sex, and that two more strange men would upset the balance. Another was of the opinion that two female servants could step in to help with the guests. We have a rule about that, the other said, that we do not allow the servants our privileges. They went back and forth on this, but in the end they agreed to let the strangers in.

"The youngest sister, who'd had a good look at the strangers, sensed that they were powerful men, only disguised as merchants, and that in reality they were princes. She led them in, taking care that they saw the baldaquin bed even as the other girls drew curtains around it. The musicians hiding behind other curtains changed the tune they had been playing, and started plucking their dolorous instruments in a manner more suited to a welcome than to an orgy. The two merchants entered, graciously thanking their hosts, and were even more aston-ished when the other two sisters emerged from the bed, removed their cloaks, and led them to the fountain to bathe. The two new guests, one young and handsome, the other old and thin, allowed themselves to be washed, and the girls saw from their finely chiseled features that their guests were indeed of royal blood, just like the dervishes they were hid-ing in their bed."

"And indeed they were royal," said Sheherezade, "they were none other than . . ." but just then the sun rose over the roofs of Baghdad and sent a hard golden arrow into the room where Dinarzad, overcome by a wave of lust that felt as if she were being baked in hot sand, and a disheveled King with a glistening scepter open to its utmost, collapsed in a heap and exclaimed in unison, "Not again, dear Sheherezade, not again dear wife, please, please . . . ," but Sheherezade, her own body pulsing with familiar sadistic desires, said brusquely, "You must wait until tonight, my shiny audience covered in fine beads of jeweled sweat, to hear just who these marvelous royal guests were . . ." And she would not be persuaded to speak no matter how hard they prodded, begged, and threatened.

failure of the middle class

Word got out in Persia and beyond that the Vizir's daughter, Sheherezade, who had married King Sharyar, had lived longer than one night, many nights in fact, by telling riveting stories. The news was greeted with a mix of emotions: the army chieftains who had hoped that a Vizir weakened by his daughter's death might be easy to dispose of, were bereft; women of every class and age breathed a collective sigh of relief that could be felt as an actual breeze puffing up the cloth on all of Baghdad's clotheslines; the storytellers, actors, snake-charmers, musicians, and acrobats in the marketplace proclaimed Sheherezade their patron and dedicated poetry and spectacles to her. The merchants met to confer.

Remember Hassan, the Merchant who understood the language of animals, and was saved from death and his wife's curiosity by the speech of a rooster? By the time that word of Sheherezade's miracle started getting around, he had become immensely rich and respected, so much so that he was elected head of the merchants' guild in Baghdad, and then head of all the merchants of Persia; his personal seal guaranteed free passage for goods, and he had power over ships, caravans, and oxen carts going to market. It was he who called a meeting of merchants to adopt some kind of position about the King's situation. The merchants were pleased by the status quo and felt that they needed to help Sheherezade fabulate for as long as possible because she had brought stability to the empire. Their interests benefited immensely from the King's lack of desire to conquer new lands and unsettle the trade routes now seemingly secure. This was Hassan's opinion, but there were dissenters.

The meeting took place in the same house, much enlarged and grander than before, where he had been ready to say his goodbyes to the world. The heads of guilds pulled up in horse-drawn carriages, some of them ornate and proud as befitted the goldsmiths, for instance, others more modest and outwardly shabby as befitted the beggars' guild. Also allowed into the conclave was the King of Thieves, but only after he swore not to steal anything from those present, an oath he didn't honor because his honor would have been impeached had he not tried, but he returned everything good-naturedly, so all was well. Other respected merchants who dealt in less than honorable goods, such as the premier Madam of Baghdad, were invited also, because in those days barely a century since the birth of the Prophet, there wasn't yet a distinction between the middle class and the criminal class if they had similar incomes, just as there was little or no persecution of followers of Jehovah, Jesus, Shiva, or Zoroaster by the faithful of Allah. The issue was wealth, a blessing that the Prophet himself had approved both before and after the Revelation, which distinguished him, Allah be praised, from fanatics of every stripe who translated their lack of success into renunciation of the world. In this, the gathered were agreed, and after the King of Thieves returned all the money pouches and jewels, they were greeted by Hassan, the master of the house, who came in preceded by his rooster, the animal he had made his Vizir after his narrow escape from stupidity.

After they had all been seated on fur-covered divans, servants brought majoon, date and cheese plates, fried meats, poached fish, hot pita breads and carafes full of wines and raki. The servants who brought these to the lips of the lounging guild-masters were dressed at the special request of the Merchant's wife in the skins and feathers of the animals who had contributed so greatly to their present happiness: oxen, mules, dogs, and chickens, a domestic menagerie straight out of Aesop. The fare was rich and festive, and the smell of the scented youth under those skins and feathers added greatly to the pleasure of the welcome.

The discussion began, reasonably enough, with an attempt to ascertain what was true about the rumors of Sheherezade's prevention of her decreed fate through storytelling, and what was not, and when the majority of them agreed that the rumors were substantially true, the talk turned to the sort of tales Sheherezade told. The head of the Silk House suggested that they were stories of fascination, kin to spider's webs, and that the King was paralyzed within; the representative of the potters pointed to the prevalence of jars in popular tales, jars containing imprisoned genii, thieves, treasure, and oil, and proposed that the King had been jailed within a jar of words spun by the enchantress; the normally taciturn and dark chief of the coal and iron guild responsible for furnishing metal to the weapon-makers, was certain that Sheherezade had alchemically altered the King's body to harden it into an alloy that became pliable only in her hands; the Madam of the whorehouses of Persia laughed at all these guesses, and said that Sheherezade, together with her sister, Dinarzad, made a triangle with the King, a pyramid from which he could not withdraw without collapsing, a pyramid composed of small particles she called "bombykles," which were the smallest but strongest known glue in the universe and emanated from Mons Veneris; the chief of the house of goldsmiths and jewelers said that it was a plain case of two young women creating a setting for the precious substance of the King's sperm, the two of them composing a sort of ring or brooch; the jocular captain of the acrobats' guild said that the King was practicing tightrope walking over the chasms of Sheherezade's stories, which were very perilous; the musicians' delegate drew several sounds from his zither and slapped his tambour to signal either his agreement or his disagreement with what had been said so far; the last to speak, the King of the Beggars, said that it was plain as day that King Sharyar was a beggar who couldn't get enough of Sheherezade's scraps, but that when his pride awoke, he'd punish her properly as he had first sworn to do. Each delegate spoke from the perspective of the material herm traded in, so that it became clear, after they had all spoken, that in their material interests, the merchant class were all of one mind.

The Chief Scribe of the Marketplace then asked permission to extend this understanding to society in general, and to propose that, thanks to their interests, there now lived in the empire a middle class that was dependent on and loyal to the goods they provided. This middle class, he hoped, would defend them when the time came, as it inevitably would, to clash with the warriors and the fanatics.

The Madam of all the whorehouses in Persia then expressed her doubts as to the loyalty of the middle class. "Yes," she said, "they profit from our goods, they come out at night and partake of my girls, but when dawn comes and their crier yelps from the tower, they pretend that they were praying all the time, just as these good-smelling girl and boy servants pretend to be chickens and oxen."

The Chief Potter agreed, saying that after they all exclaimed in wonder at the beauty of the wares, these artifacts were among the first to be smashed by crowds incited to zealousness by preachers or generals, but mostly by preachers, he corrected himself, because the god-crazy and the bloodthirsty worked hand in hand against contentment and ease.

The Master Beggar and the King Thief both expressed agreement and noted the usefulness of their followers in this scheme of things. "When we beg, we increase the value of what people possess," quoth the Master Beggar, "and we thus increase respect for those things that in private use are only what they are."

"And we," cried the Thief, "increase that respect tenfold by depriving people of those things which, until they are absent, mean little or nothing!"

The only serious disagreements came from the delegates of the makers of metals and weapons, the weavers of rich fabrics, the gold and jewel craftsmen, and, surprisingly, the Chief Scribe. "While it is true," the Elect of Gold and Preciosities began cautiously, "that some of the religious shun ornaments, we get a great many orders from houses of worship and priests because, happily, they see divine reflections in the expensive beauty of our products, and, if the truth be known," here he lowered his voice, "these servants of Allah and the other gods are even more vain than your average harem wife." There was hearty laughter at this, and he continued, "And the most vain of all are the leaders of armies and their soldiers, who adorn themselves and their weapons in every manner, even embedding precious stones in their wounds. In times of war we sell more scabbard jewels than at any other time; isn't that true, sword-maker?"

"I have little to add," said the weapon-maker, "it is quite clear why we disagree with peace and prefer conquest, but you are not entirely clear about your own interests. If there is no destruction of your wares, there will be no need to make more. Making more is what keeps you going because you always make more than what anyone needs. I am only baffled as to why the Chief Scribe is on our side."

The Chief Scribe ran his long fingers through his beard and sighed. "It is true that most of our business comes from writing letters in the market to loved ones or ones who are far. It is true that the better scribes make a living at court, keeping the books, writing down the laws, and translating the King's directives into acceptable languages. At the same time," he sighed again, "there exists among us a better class of scribes, among whom are superb calligraphers and philosophers, whose hands are stilled when their minds are at ease. Without revelations or war, their minds refuse to move, and so do their hands. If the peace we all seek came to pass, the happiness of the middle class would simply smother our best minds. As Chief Scribe I should be speaking for the majority, but as one deeply enmeshed in the workings of language, I have a duty to speak for more than communication and writing materials."

There was the tiniest moment of silence, imperceptible perhaps to anyone who wasn't there, before a clamor broke out. Everyone started shouting at once: "You think you're the only one mindful of the ambiguities of your materials? Don't you think we also have our purists and idealists?" and so on, until the Merchant had to intervene personally and remind everyone that the meeting was about the median, the average, the norm, not the whims of the overeducated, and that if they were going to help their members in any way, they must ensure stability, and that meant keeping Sheherezade in business. Thanks to her, the empire was stable, he reminded them, so let's get back to what matters.

After all this discussion, the assorted merchants and guilders, agreed with surprising ease that Sheherezade's stories, whatever their effects, were morality tales, having to do with right comportment, with more kindness toward women and animals, and that all of them, no matter how fantastic or how illegal, proved the primacy of cleverness and wits over hot-bloodedness and slow-thinking. Examples were proffered from stories then circulating, stories that might not have been the ones Sheherezade told every night, but which couldn't help but be related because there were only so many stories structurally in existence, human history being still young, and, besides, the influence of opiates, hashish, wine, and raki made some of those present sleepy and others agreeable.

The Head Locksmith, who had been quiet until then, as befitted his trade, gazed directly at his nemesis, the King of Thieves, and said: "Each of us knows many stories. Each of our crafts and trades has its own stories told and retold. Some of these are wise. Some are clever. Some witty. Some funny. All crafty. Layered. Internal. External. Occasional. Universal. Each. I speak not as a locksmith now, but as an open source. Let us take our stories, the best of them, and pass them on to Sheherezade so that she may never run out of stories. There is danger that, left to its own devising, the spring of her imagination could dry up. We must replenish the spring. Inspire. Water her source. Sheherezade must not be allowed to dry up for even one hour."

All agreed, though the Chief Scribe only reluctantly. He was already thinking of copyright, though he didn't know it. He did know that something separated the stories of Sharyar's wife and all the other stories of the empire's subjects from the labor of his members, but he didn't yet know what vast abyss there stood open between the oral and the written. That was the future's self-reflection.

It was thus decided to continually replenish Sheherezade's store of tales from every sector of the middle class via the vast network of their customers, women, teachers, and palace servants, who came into contact with her. There should under no circumstance be any interruption of the flow of stories. They vowed to watch closely the religious dogmatists, the warriors, and the poets, who repeated themselves incessantly and thus dammed the flow with their edicts, hadiths, suras, sutras, calls to action, and rhymes.

Unfortunately, after deciding this, the merchants failed to assign a number of their own to watch each of those damming obstacles, and their lack of vigilance eventually translated into the triumph of god, war, and poetry for long and unhappy periods in the future. This was not so much an oversight as the result of a lack of time; few tradesmen or craftsmen could find the time to spare for watching their enemies; they preferred practicing trades and crafts instead. They failed to create their own secret police because the very idea of police belonged to the enemy. They created agreements instead, pieces of paper called contracts, that they trusted the scribes to make permanent through their skill. But the Chief Scribe had warned them: the higher the value of the scribed document, the less certain the loyalty of its instrument.

They failed also to heed the weapon-maker's warning about overproduction, so they did not see either the value of destruction or the necessity for inspiration, whatever its source, which increases people's appetite for consumption and creates craving for more. Instinctively, they knew this because there wasn't a man or a woman present who did not secretly bribe mullahs and soldiers to occasionally interrupt production: scarcity brought by destruction also encouraged craving.

Nonetheless, the stories flowed uninterrupted to Sheherezade, and as long as they did, there was peace and trade flourished. In fact, there was such a wealth of stories flowing, many of them had to be stored for the future, and there were a myriad of stories left over at the end of the *1001 Nights*, a surplus of stories that were going to be used in surprising ways. Sheherezade's method of interrupting the stories was akin to the workings of revelations and war, but it didn't exhaust the immense supply flowing to her from all corners of the empire.

An hour before dawn, after an exhausting battle had brought all their three bodies to a near standstill, Dinarzad, now a woman in all but age, begged Sheherezade, "Conclude, dear sister, or this night will never end!" "It is true," Sharyar said warily, "I have ordered the sun not to rise today." And Sheherezade laughed and said, "Very well, then."

"After the royal guests were washed, dried, and perfumed, the curtains of the baldaquin bed were pulled back to reveal the naked dervishes and the beautiful young man within being kneaded like dough by exotic servants with fiery eyes. The sisters led the two new guests into the bed, which became larger to accommodate them, and the sisters climbed in, undulating like perfumed serpents.

"The disguised prince, who liked to go incognito among his subjects, was not shy about getting into bed. As the serpent-girls started to disrobe him, he saw one of the dervishes looking fixedly at him with his one eye. Then he knew. He saw in the eye of the dervish that the dervish knew him as well. He willed himself to silence, but the word escaped him nonetheless: "Brother!" he said.

"Your brother, Shahzaman, for that's who he was, embraced you warmly and said, 'I have found them, my beloved Sharyar! I have found the wizards who make people in pots. I have been to the future, and I was told by the wizards that your wife Sheherezade will be a hero for centuries, even in a time when people no longer believe in heroes. The wizard said that Sheherezade may even be the last hero, because her storytelling skill is what makes the perpetuation of human beings in his time *still* possible, even though sexual reproduction in the future is at the bottom of the list of all the known means of perpetuation, which, in that future, include something called cloning and ICSI (intracytoplasmic sperm injection). What makes her a hero, the wizard said, has nothing to do with sex, but with something that is inside sex, namely, curiosity, which is the one ingredient that human beings need in order to exist, in that time as well as in ours. People, he said, will continue to reproduce, sexually or by other means, only if sufficiently entertained. The stories that your wife Sheherezade tells through her knowledge of the secrets of suspense, are the *best* entertainment of your day, but, strangely enough, in the future, in a world of myriad media, they are also the *last-resort* entertainment. In that future that I have visited, O Brother, people are entirely dependent on the stimulation of entertainment. After they have separated sex from reproduction, the necessity for reproduction is itself in doubt because people have become immortal and therefore immensely bored. Choosing to reproduce has become a matter of calculated reason. There are no accidents, no hazard. Their technology puts forth endless stories of experiment, failure, and success, but none of them contains the drunken dance of the imagination that made your story so blindly spontaneous up until we saw each other again a few minutes ago. This would be the end of one story cycle, or the end of one type of human, *homo circum*, if it weren't for the fact that your wife Sheherezade will never let us know what happens here in the bed of these three sisters from Baghdad . . .'"

"What are these dreadful stories?" Sharyar cried weakly, still unable to find release in the warm folds of Dinarzad's body.

"A series of exits," said Sheherezade, in a voice unlike her own; "they are connected escape tunnels. Each one opens into another so that first I, then Dinarzad, then all women, then all humanity may escape!"

"Escape from what?" Sharyar moaned.
"From flesh, the 3-D story," said Sheherezade.
"Escape from whom?" Sharyar cried in anguish again.

"To tell a great story, leave them hanging," laughed Sheherezade. "To write a great story, violate the tenses," she added.

"Fine," Sharyar said, resigned to eternity, "who were the royal guests in the bed of the three sisters?"

"O King, great King," sighed the Storyteller, "I thought that you'd have guessed by now. One of them was the Vizir, my father, and the other one was you."

Then the sun broke in through the colors in the window and it was day forever after in the great Persian kingdom.

the problem of containment and why a baby won't solve it

Anthologists, translators, and writers, scholars and admirers, have the daring and energy to deal with the beginning of Sheherezade's stories, just as beach-goers in spanking new bathing suits have no problem strolling on the beach of a vast ocean. They also have no problem imagining the now-placid waves turning violent and funneling upward into the shape of an angry Genius. They are not bothered by shipwrecks and storms; they do not shrink from the creatures of the underworld who inhabit the waters. Scholars look on the ocean of Sheherezade's stories as a huge text ready to be mined for the salt over the fish they will have at supper that evening in the elegant resort where the conference is taking place. The admirers, a.k.a. readers, were children once, if they aren't when they first hear the bed-bound enchantress's tales, and they revel in the pleasure of remembering and placing themselves in her magic worlds with shivers of delight. Translators, who are also Fates, have the privilege of looking closely into her language, almost as if they were looking inside her: it's an indecent operation, which is why mostly crude men who don't shy from eros and danger can go through with it. Writers, shy creatures, are mostly content to steal a jewel or two from the treasure, to turn it for profit into a story of their own, without mentioning the source. (Umberto Eco, you know who you are! I only name you because, unlike all the writers who do little but scavenge on ravaged cultures, you also found a theory to dignify your dumpster diving.)

Anthologists have a greater problem than do all the *Nights'* lovers mentioned above. They cannot simply stroll on the beach, or go for a dip. They must contain the ocean. It was resolved, since the earliest known anthology, the 14th-century Syrian manuscript, that the stories ended when Sheherezade gave birth. The first anthology has it that she had three babies: *". . . in the course of time Shahrazad bore Sharyar three children and . . . , having learned to trust and love her, he spared her life and kept her as a queen."*[100] A baby (or three) makes for a reasonable, if expedient, conclusion, and it's not an anthologist's job to imagine what might have happened if Sheherezade hadn't had one (or three) babies, and thereby fell silent, relieved of her narrative burden. Concluding in the birth of a flesh being is justifiable historically as well: after all, history is the story of the murderer impregnating the victim. The resulting being will, hopefully, be less tyrannical and, through knowledge of history, kinder. Your baby-partisan might also muster to his defense the near certainty that Sharyar was only a cover for the murderous father, the Vizir, and that it was the Vizir, in his guise as Sharyar, who both raped and threatened to murder his daughter. In this version, Sharyar never returned from the desert, and the Vizir hired an impersonator to take the King's place. Worse things have happened.

We take the unpopular position: there was no baby. Sheherezade was never pardoned, and Sharyar never learned to trust or to love her. She was compelled to take to the tyrant's bed every night and she hasn't left it yet. She is still telling stories. When she revealed to Sharyar that the one-eyed dervish was none other than his brother, Shahzaman, Sharyar drew himself up sharply, but then he fell back on the pillows when Dinarzad looked up from where she had been dreaming. If there was a chance that Sharyar might have a moment of self-reflection, it would have been here, while meeting himself inside a story. As it happened, he fell back under the spell of Dinarzad and failed to see the cosmic crack that the story had just opened for him: instead of going in and rejoining himself in the story-world, he chose to fall prey to the flesh crack that so enthralled and frustrated him. Readers, I can hear you now: you dirty Platonist! You scurvy-riddled pox of a monk! Religious desert rat! Misogynist!

[100] Haddawy.

Hold your horses. I am Sheherezade's lawyer: she is weaving from words the world we humans have, to allow it to continue.

And now we are at a crossroads, sitting on the jaiyan stone: does the human world continue through animal reproduction or through ongoing, linked stories? Which comes first: the Storyteller who turns the word into flesh, or flesh that becomes conscious of history?

I believe that in a hurry to conclude their performances or their books, the anthologists invented a baby (or three) and conveniently forgot that Sheherezade practiced birth control by means of the sunrise: Solar Coitus Interruptus. Her sister, Dinarzad, took what she could of the King's libido, a libido that was competing with his curiosity. (And Dinarzad's curiosity, too, because even though she'd heard many of her sister's stories, she still couldn't guess what happened.)

Sheherezade went on telling her stories, which were fertile and sexy and caused many babies to be born from their heated charge, but she herself stayed put. This is the terrifying news. The stories could and did, of course, go on without her, spawning a web that is greatly increased and speeding up, but it is still Sheherezade telling them. Readers, take a deep breath.

Such a preposterous proposition has consequences: among them is the thought that Sheherezade herself is inhabiting a billion storytellers in our day, as many storytellers as there are cameras. Does that mean that she has become a camera? Not at all. There are more stories than cameras; there are as many as there are words, to paraphrase the monkey-scribe, or perhaps even more, because each image is composed of one thousand words and millions of colors. The new cinematic, telephonic, cellular, semiautomatic story-deliverers of our time are all inhabited by Sheherezade herself, the real Sheherezade.

What do you mean what do I mean by "real"? I mean the flesh-and-blood Storyteller who began storying in Sharyar's bed and who was never eclipsed, though efforts were made by many professionals to submerge her into her stories by making her mythical rather than real. In this effort, her admirers resembled Sharyar, who vowed to kill her but never could, because her stories kept coming and he had become addicted to them; he couldn't eliminate his provider.

Another piece of dreadful news with serious consequences is that, while Sheherezade remained singular and busy, Sharyar subdivided into a billion Sharyars. Having missed the narrow opening provided by self-reflection and choosing Dinarzad's instead, he *shattered*.

Instead of having just one King and a younger sister as an audience, Sheherezade now services vast masses of Sharyar-shards who demand more and more stories to pass their more and more capacious and jaded Nights. What is worse is that all Time has become Night because electricity has eliminated any distinction between night and day. Our cities are lit at night by the brightest suns, and your 1001 Nights, City Woman, have become too many to count.

But enough of the news, and more of the consequences:

As the thirst for your stories grows, Sheherezade, the salty sweat of your dear sister, Dinarzad, grows proportionally as well: the young giver of pleasure must now please a billion Kings. I know you're wondering why you got her into this, but know as well as I do that you can't get her out without collapsing the universe you wove, because she holds it in place with the weight of her body.

Your ever-faster (and saltier) narration has led us inevitably to a Fifth Fold. In this Fifth Fold, your shape-shifters are numerous, and I mention only supermen, vampires, and zombies, to give you an idea. These creatures preserve the suspense that you employed to such great effect in those long-past centuries at the beginning of your career, but in a much-abbreviated form. Clark Kent changes his suit very quickly inside a phone booth (which doesn't exist anymore) to turn into Superman; vampires, until recently, still had to wait all day to go out because the sun silenced them (as it did you), but of late they are one bite (a mere beat) away from going from human to vampire. The same goes for werewolves, ghosts, geniuses, djinns, genies, and all the rest of your repertoire. Some metamorphoses don't even have the luxury of a temporary pause, let alone one as long as a sigh or a deep breath, because in this fold we can no longer appeal either to dawn or to gender. Whereas Sharyar the King was a man, who ordered you to his story-bed because of man-issues, we the new Sharyars are of all genders: men, women, and variations thereof. Your bed is a huge stage now, with franchises in all our houses. You have so many embassies, most of us don't even know that their stories come from you. When we become angry at a story, we threaten the screens, unaware that we are only threatening a void, the space in front of you through which you speak. You are thus protected from our ignorant anger by a faux-you, an e-Sheherezade, a facade, an electronic mask behind which you labor to keep the weave going so that the world's fabric won't unravel. Should you fail to entertain us angry mass-Sharyars, by having, for instance, an author break into the narrative (so you could nap), we will surely dismantle you in the morning. Happily, you'll be just out of reach. As always.

Generally, and I hope that I speak for all of us here, we cannot afford to let you discontinue the narrative; we must know what happens next. All of us believe that our power over your life entitles us to know what happens next. Our desire is not for storage and reproduction, dear Shezz, but for the real stuff, your stories of transformation and wonder organized by your insistence on the suspense of sunrise (or what little passes for it now). Still, when you pause, it is a new day. And when it is day, and we must go back to the prose of the world, our survival depends on breaking your spell, or detoxing, something we are less and less capable of doing, preferring instead to lie in bed and watch you. We are between a hard Roc, so to speak, and an equally dense obsidian horse. We lie in our Sharyar beds so-o-o hungry, our appetites growing like genies, because we are terrified when you are silent.

I took this opportunity to address Sheherezade directly, because one of the (not unpleasant) consequences of her continuing presence is precisely this opportunity. I also want to note, apropos of our terror at her possible silence, that if she'd had those babies the anthologists produced in order to seal their objects, she'd have been out of storytelling commission for a number of predawns, and Sharyar would have freaked so badly he might have annihilated the entire human race.

This book I have written is the prayer of an addict who tried, in his addictive way, to ease Sheherezade's burden. I asked myself if taking another look at storytelling might not accomplish just that. My flesh body lives now among fantastic creatures: robots, cyborgs, virtual beings, hybrid processors, mechanical and cloned animals. In this menagerie my human body maintains a certain beauty of form that remains attentive to the recumbent Storyteller. If I hold on to this form and detach it from the inevitable metamorphoses caused by stories, it is because I am holding myself in suspense for the arrival of dawn, when I might free myself from Sheherezade's web. A dawn that, as I've said, no longer comes. It's an idealistic dream of innocence, I know, but the beauty of being told a suspenseful story is great indeed, and Sheherezade is the Great Suspender. I know that she is threatened nightly with extinction (by me and my human brothers), but I, her faithful junkie-spectator, am too. I fear each passing night that I will not receive my maintenance dose of suspense, and then I will cease to exist. I will also cease to exist if I don't get my required dose of continuity. In this fold, continuity is relentless, and suspense difficult to come by, so each night that I overcome my terror I feel that I've gained something, but what it is I can't honestly say. If I thought that it was a matter of reenchanting the world, I'd tell you, but as it is, our world is fully and automatically enchanted. Maybe what we need is to break the spell. Science, technology, politics, and philosophy don't alter the enchantment; indeed, they have added their own narratives to many of the *Nights*. Within the confines of language itself, our attention has focused mainly on Sheherezade's lips, which has led to the abbreviations of some of her greatest stories to the point that some have become adaptations, simplifications, haikus, tweets. Every time her stories achieve what appears to be an acceptable brevity, we experience a renewed appetite for the continuity and suspense only she can provide. For all activities other than longing for her sequels we have long ago created substitutes to do the work: these substitutes are the new people made in pots that were spoken of with such awe in the early days. These pot-brewed creatures don't have ears; they are earless Mamelukes, genetically soundproofed genies. But they sure do the dirty jobs.[101]

And now here is a story that is also a consequence: in the second decade of the 21st century, a polyglot human of indistinct gender who called hermself Sheherezade.5 became known for singing the stories of the 1001 Nights in the 1001 remaining languages on earth in 1001 seconds. This Sheherezade.5 was known by many names, such as P.C. (the Perfect Creole), because herm was the child of many tribes, or E.M. (Every Media), because herm spun off the tales into all media, stage, films, video games, clothes, light projections, gene design, weather patterning. Herm was sometimes also called "The Simultaneous Translator," the name by which herm made the cover of Time.com. The Simultaneous Translator notwithstanding, many of us knew herm was fake. Herm did not console me. I know that Sheherezade still dangles over the precipice of extinction, holding on for dear life to the stone crag of Story, and we hang on equally despondent owing to our infantile need to know what happened next. And because of this interdependence, we go on, willing to do anything except be silent or uncurious.

---

[101] Each technical device wants to be a frame, like the "frame" said to surround the *Nights*, but the *Nights* have no frame: they arise like hatchlings from one egg; they are Russian egg-dolls that always keep the first egg in whatever comes next. A frame dissolves, it is just a pre-text, a technology to get the story-universe started, but the *Nights* are not "framed"—they are generative; they are life.

bibliography

Anthony, David W. *The Horse, the Wheel and Language.* Princeton University Press, 2007.

Arberry, A. J. *Aspects of Islamic Civilization as Depicted in the Original Texts.* University of Michigan Press, 1967.

Baker, Meguey. *A Thousand and One Nights: A Game of Enticing Stories.* Night Sky Games, 2009.

Blanchot, Maurice. *The Gaze of Orpheus, and Other Literary Essays.* Station Hill Press, 1981.

Blank, Hanne. *Virgin: The Untouched History.* Bloomsbury, 2007.

Borges, Jorge Luis. *Ficciones.* Edited with an introduction by Anthony Kerrigan. Grove Press, 1962.

Burton, Richard F., trans. *The Book of the Thousand Nights and a Night.* The complete Burton translation with the Burton notes, the terminal essay, a complete index, and 1,001 decorations by Valenti Angelo. 6 vols. 1885; Heritage Press, 1934.

Candlelight Stories. *The Arabian Nights.* http://www.candlelightstories. com/Stories/ArabianPage.php.

Corbin, Alain, Jean-Jacques Courtine, and Georges Vigarello, eds. *Histoire du corps.* Vol. 1, *De la Renaissance aux Lumières.* Seuil, 2005.

Cousineau, Phil. *The Art of Pilgrimage: The Seeker's Guide to Making Travel Sacred.* Conari Press, 1998.

Deleuze, Gilles, and Félix Guattari. *Nomadology: The War Machine.* Translated by Brian Massumi. Semiotext(e), 1986.

Djerassi, Carl. *Sex in an Age of Technological Reproduction: ICSI and Taboos.* University of Wisconsin Press, 2008.

Gardener, Alva. *Stockholm Syndrome or the Persistence of Humanity: Sheherezade, the First Feminist Prisoner.* Prothea Press, 1998.

Haddawy, Husain, trans. *The Arabian Nights.* Based on the text of the 14th-century Syrian manuscript edited by Muhsin Mahdi. W. W. Norton, 1990.

Irwin, Robert. *The Arabian Nights: A Companion.* Tauris Parke Paperbacks, 2004.

Lang, Andrew, ed. *The Arabian Nights Entertainments: Aladdin, Sindbad, and 24 Other Favorite Stories.* With 67 illustrations by H. J. Ford. Longmans, Green, and Co., 1898. Reprint, Dover, 1969.

Lewis, Bernard. *The Arabs in History.* Oxford University Press, 1958.

Lied, L. R. *Advice to Young Women Based on Literary Themes.* Scholastic Guides, 1899.

Luca, Ghérasim. *The Passive Vampire.* Translated by Krzysztof Fijalkowski. Twisted Spoon Press, 2008.

Lunde, Paul, and Justin Wintle. *A Dictionary of Arabic and Islamic Proverbs.* Routledge & Kegan Paul, 1984.

Macfie, Alexander Lyon, ed. *Orientalism: A Reader.* New York University Press, 2000.

Madhouf, Ali H. *Books I Will Never Write.* Four Beats Press, 2003.

Marzolph, Ulrich. *The Arabian Nights in Transnational Perspective.* Wayne State University Press, 2007.

———, ed. *The Arabian Nights Reader.* Wayne State University Press, 2006.

Miller, J. Hillis. *Ariadne's Thread: Story Lines.* Yale University Press, 1992.

Rice, Edward. *Captain Sir Richard Francis Burton: The Secret Agent Who Made the Pilgrimage to Mecca, Discovered the* Kama Sutra, *and Brought the* Arabian Nights *to the West.* Scribner's, 1990.

Ricoeur, Paul. *Time and Narrative.* University of Chicago Press, 1984.

Senner, Wayne M., ed. *The Origins of Writing.* University of Nebraska Press, 1989.

The Travels of Marco Polo. Marsden's English edition, 1818.

Warner, Marine. *Fantastic Metamorphoses, Other Worlds.* Oxford University Press, 2002.

Wilensky-Lanford, Brook. "Why I Love Lucy." http://killingthebuddha .com/mag/exegesis/why-i-love-lucy/

Wilson, Peter Lamborn. *Sacred Drift: Essays on the Margins of Islam.* City Lights Publishers, 1993.

———. *Scandal: Essays in Islamic Heresy.* Autonomedia, 1988.

Womack, Craig S. *Art as Performance, Story as Criticism: Reflections on Native Literary Aesthetics.* University of Oklahoma Press, 2009.

Wright, J. W., and Everett K. Rowson, eds. *Homoeroticism in Classical Arabic Literature.* Columbia University Press, 1997.